CINDY VILLANUEVA

SOMETHING Will Sing to YOUR HEART

Book Two
BLOOMING
The Series

ISBN: 978-1-7365956-9-5 (paperback)
ISBN: 979-8-9929057-0-0 (ebook)

This novel is entirely a work of fiction. The names, characters and incidents portrayed in it are the work of the author's imagination. Any resemblance to actual persons, living or dead, events or localities is entirely coincidental.

Cover design by Samantha Sanderson-Marshall, www.smashdesigns.co.uk

Also by Cindy Villanueva

Nonfiction

Don't Fight Mad :
A Black Belt's Quest to Reclaim Joy

Fiction

Bread Pudding in Barcelona,
book one of the Blooming series

To my Crow sisters and Cevennes friends.
Thank you for believing.

AUTHOR'S NOTE

While each book in the *Blooming* series is a love story, each addresses serious themes and none may be as difficult as Sara's in Something Will Sing to Your Heart.

In this novel, we'll explore themes of teen pregnancy, emotional abuse, adoption, miscarriage, and post-partum depression. It is my sincere desire that I have handled this story tenderly and with great care.

I believe in the power of faith, love, and friendship to help us transcend trauma, and I hope, dear reader, that Sara's story will uplift and inspire you.

Que estés bien, querida.

Cindy Villanueva
New Smyrna Beach, Florida
April 2025

1

Sara walked into the tidy house she rented with her best friend Lauren. Just walking to the mailbox felt like melting in a sauna and she fanned her face to cool off. Even for a native Floridian, July in Daytona Beach could be brutal, and she felt the sweat sliding down her back.

She lowered the air conditioning to 75 degrees and then flopped down on the sofa, looking through the mail, setting aside anything addressed to Lauren. She skimmed the bills and junk mail quickly, then stopped when she got to an envelope from Daytona Springs Middle School. She smiled and tore it open. It was a welcome letter from her new principal, thanking her for taking on the role in the mathematics department. After fifteen years teaching kindergarten, Sara looked forward to the new challenge.

She looked at her phone. *Should I?* She shook her head. *Of course not.* She picked it up to text her mother anyway.

I got a new job she typed. *I start teaching middle school math this year.*

She stared at the screen and was surprised to see a response.

Let me know when you get a real job and stop wasting those degrees.

And…that was it. Short, definitely not sweet, and absolutely to the point.

What did I expect? When will I stop hoping? She set her phone down and clamped down on the familiar ache.

She looked through the rest of the mail and picked up a letter. The return address was from a Natalie Allard, the handwriting crisp and her own name all in capital letters: SARA MASTERSON. She opened it and began to read:

Dear Sara,

> *I have wanted to write to you for some time but was worried that I would interrupt your life. I guess I'm still worried, but I just couldn't wait any more.*
>
> *After some research, I believe that you are my biological mother. I was born 23 years ago and placed for adoption with a wonderful family. Let me start by thanking you for giving me parents who have loved me and supported me my entire life! They weren't able to have their own children, so they've poured their lives into me and I'm very grateful.*
>
> *The reason I finally decided to seek you out is a hard one. My mom Jocelyn is in remission from breast cancer. She's only 58 years old. Her mother died from breast cancer when she was 70, so it looks like it's hereditary. The obvious good news is that I don't have their genes but it started me thinking about what genes I actually do have. Believe it or not, my parents encouraged me to find you.*
>
> *I really hope this letter doesn't upset you and that you might be open to meeting me in person. If not, maybe just a phone call? Like I mentioned, I don't want to disrupt your life and I don't want you to feel guilty for the decision you made so long ago. I have a wonderful life and I'd just like to know more about you and where I came from.*

Would you be open to it?

I look forward to hearing from you,
Natalie

Sara stared at the letter, her hands shaking. Emotions tore through her, faster than she could process. Shock and disbelief warred with guilt and sadness. Was it possible? Could this Natalie Allard be the infant her parents took from her so long ago?

Her daughter.

Carlos' daughter.

Tears pricked her eyes and her stomach clenched as she read the letter again and again, until the tears dripped onto the stationery, smudging the ink and the neat handwriting.

He had neat handwriting. She remembered the notes he passed her in class, the drawings in the margins. Carlos had been an artist. *I wonder what he does now.* She thrust the question from her mind. Over two decades ago she locked all thoughts of Carlos and their baby into a mental strongbox and tucked it far, far away. So far it couldn't hurt her.

Am I ready to open the box?

Lauren flung open the front door with a groan. "Ah! Air conditioning!" She tossed her purse on the coffee table and sat heavily on the sofa. "It is so hot out there."

"Mmhmm," mumbled Sara.

"Damn AC went out on the way to work," snapped her friend. "I have the car for, what? A month before it goes out?"

Sara stared out the front window, the offending car the last thing on her mind.

"…so yeah, the warranty is good but it still means taking time off work to get it fixed—" her friend stopped abruptly. "Are you even listening to me? You're off in space."

Sara's eyes refocused, looking down at the letter, then back at her friend. "I'm sorry. What did you say?"

Lauren frowned. "Forget about that. What's wrong?"

Sara looked at Lauren, measuring her words. "So, we're best friends, right?"

"Yeah…for like, almost twenty years." Lauren frowned, then leaned forward, glancing at the tattered letter in Sara's lap. "What's that?"

"There's something I never told you. I've never told anyone, actually." Sara paused. "When I was in high school, I had a boyfriend."

Lauren gaped at her. "That's your big secret?"

"No, no…. I—I got pregnant my junior year."

Lauren sat up straighter on the sofa and gazed at Sara. "Oh, damn. What did your parents say?"

"You know my parents so you can imagine. They were beyond furious. They pulled me out of school and made me do independent study during the pregnancy so no one would see me. Apart from taking me to the doctor every month, they just ignored my belly."

Sara watched as Lauren processed the revelation. Her friend's anger was barely held in check as she said, "I'm guessing Cecilia didn't throw a baby shower."

"It's not exactly the sort of thing you rent out the country club for," answered Sara. "We moved to Tampa and as soon as she was born, they made me place her for adoption. I never saw my boyfriend or the baby again." She looked up at Lauren and drew comfort from the compassion she saw on her friend's face.

"Damn," repeated Lauren. "You've been keeping that inside for all these years?"

"At first I was kinda numb," admitted Sara. "And then it got easier to pretend it never happened." She frowned. "That's how things are managed in the Masterson family."

"And you never tried to contact your boyfriend?"

Sara scowled. "C'mon, you know my parents." A single tear rolled down her cheek. "They were horrible and I was a coward."

"Stop it. You were just a baby yourself! And you've never been a coward."

"It sure feels that way."

Lauren scowled. "That's your mother talking and it's bullshit." She sighed and then looked kindly at Sara. "So what made you tell me today?"

Sara lifted the note. "I got a letter from her. From my daughter."

Lauren's look was incredulous. "You're kidding."

Sara held out the tear-smudged letter. "Came today."

Lauren took it and began reading. When she finished, she looked up. "I don't even know where to start," she began, then shook her head fiercely. "No, that's not true—I know exactly where to start. But cussing out your parents probably isn't productive." She set the letter on the coffee table and held out her arms to Sara. "Are you okay? What can I do for you?"

The two women embraced for several moments before Sara pulled away. "I don't know how I feel," she confessed. "I've buried this for so long, I'm just kind of in shock. I feel like I *should* be happy, but I'm not. I'm not unhappy either, though. I'm glad she's had a good life and I'm curious to know about her." She sat back against the cushions and wiped her eyes with the back of her hand. "It brings up a whole lot of stuff besides having a baby. My parents have never been good, but this was them at their worst. Especially my mom."

Lauren pursed her lips in disgust. Sara hadn't told her friend about the baby, but she'd shared plenty about her mother. Cecilia Masterson was definitely not in the running for mother of the year.

"So what are you gonna do?"

"I don't know. I don't know what's right."

Lauren shook her head. "I don't think there is a right or wrong here, Sara. I think you have to decide what's best for you. Do you want to meet this girl? Do you want to reopen that part of your life? Or do you want to push all this back into the past and just move on? You know I'm there for you no matter what you decide. You're my ride or die girl, remember?"

Sara grinned through her tears. "I know, and I love you for it." She closed her eyes to collect her thoughts, then almost whispered, "I need more time before I decide." She took a deep breath and this time her voice was strong. "I'm not sixteen anymore and I don't have to be that scared little girl. I can make a decision without worrying about what my mom will do."

Sara read Natalie's letter every day for the next week. She started several letters in return, only to throw them away.

What do I want to say?

Throughout the week, Sara was surprised to notice pregnant women everywhere she went. "It's like when I decided to buy the Kia," she told Lauren. "After that, it was like every other car on the road was a Forte." But seeing her favored car everywhere didn't thrust her back into the most painful time of her life. Being hyperaware of pregnant women seemed to rub salt into a wound she didn't realize she still had, a wound she didn't know how to heal.

On Saturday, she and Lauren went to the local farmers' market. The sun was bright and the air warm even early in the morning, and Sara was determined to enjoy the day. The two friends wandered through the stalls, Sara picking out fruits and vegetables while Lauren filled her bag with cheese, bread, and pastries.

"Look at these gorgeous tomatoes," gushed Sara, then laughed as Lauren rolled her eyes. "And there are some beautiful strawberries over on that table, too. You could cut them up and put them on your ice cream." She pointed toward the back of the stall where baskets of bright red strawberries overflowed onto a table. One man filled a small green basket and handed it to the young woman behind him. She smiled and put it into a bag, then leaned back to stretch and run a hand over her large belly. He smiled, then stepped behind her to rub his hand on her lower back, then leaned down to kiss the top of her head. She looked up at him and smiled broadly, saying something Sara couldn't hear. The couple laughed and continued their casual stroll, stopping at the sweet potatoes.

Sara winced with a pang of regret. She never had the experience of being a couple while she was pregnant, never had the feel of a lover's hand on her aching back or a kiss on her forehead. She remembered the feeling of heaviness, the pressure of the baby against her belly—but no tenderness.

No grandparents eagerly awaiting the birth of a grandchild.

She tore her gaze from the couple, paid for her vegetables, and stalked away, surprised at the swirling emotions. *I've made it all this time without feeling…whatever this is.*

Lauren followed and reached for her arm. "Hey, are you okay?" Sara turned a tense face toward her friend and Lauren's eyes widened in surprise. "Whoa—you're not okay. What happened?"

Sara steeled her features and shook her head. "I'm fine. It's nothing."

"It's not nothing. You look seriously ticked off." She chuckled. "Did that kid overcharge you for your awesome tomatoes?"

Sara didn't laugh and Lauren grimaced. "Okay, sorry—lame joke." The women began walking again and Lauren asked again in a serious tone, "What happened?"

Sara glanced back. She saw the couple a few stalls behind them, the woman sniffing a candle. The man's hand lingered on her back, and they chatted amiably with the vendor. She looked again at Lauren, her friend's face still showing confusion. "That couple over there," she finally answered. "The super pregnant woman."

Lauren glanced back. "I didn't even notice her." She looked at Sara with concern. "A week ago you wouldn't have noticed her either. I've never seen you like this. You know you're gonna see pregnant women everywhere."

They've never bothered me before, Sara thought. "I know…it's like everything makes me think about Natalie. I didn't exactly have a great experience. Obviously I didn't have Carlos there to share it with and my parents pretty much pretended it wasn't happening until I went into labor." She shrugged, remembering. "And then it was just a matter of solving the problem and moving on."

Lauren scowled. "God, I hate your parents."

Sara frowned. "I need to decide what to do. I can't keep going through this everywhere I go. It's ridiculous."

Her friend shook her head. "It's not ridiculous but it's not healthy." She glanced back at the couple. "C'mon. Let's go get some ice cream."

Sara chuckled. "You do know that eating crap isn't the answer to every problem, right?"

The following week, the women talked daily about Sara's impending decision. But they also talked frequently about being bridesmaids for Azalea and Esteban's wedding. The couple had met in Spain in a whirlwind and "so freaking hot" way, as Lauren put it. But Azalea's past relationship had nearly killed their fledgling romance. Thankfully, their other friend, Susana, had intervened, and Azalea and Esteban were finally tying the knot the next weekend on Azalea's beloved beach. Sara and Lauren were thrilled to be a part of the nuptials—the four women had been close for several years, despite their age difference. They all still laughed about Sara and Azalea's random meeting in the dressing room at Macy's, where Sara was shopping for a date night outfit and Azalea was doing some retail therapy during her divorce. Such was the genesis of what became a deep and abiding friendship.

One afternoon, the two friends sat in their living room, discussing the wedding. "How are you gonna feel seeing Tomás and Emily?" asked Lauren. Azalea's eldest son and his wife were expecting their first child and would be at the ceremony.

"I was thinking about that," confessed Sara. "I don't know. I'm super happy for them."

"Azalea's over the moon," said Lauren. "Cracks me up that she's gonna be a grandmother."

"And that's part of the hurt," responded Sara. "I'm jealous." She stopped, her eyes wide. "That's it. I'm jealous. I never got that. No adoring husband, no happy grandparents. No baby showers, no weddings." Tears threatened as she spoke. "No nothing."

Lauren asked, "What can I do?"

"Nothing. It's over and done and I need to deal with it." She sat back and wiped her eyes. "And figure out what to do about Natalie."

Lauren looked down, seeming to consider her next words. "It feels like it's way more than Natalie that's bothering you. You've talked a few times about your boyfriend and not having him around." She tucked her long legs up under her, setting a pillow on her lap. "At the risk of me being even more disgusted with your parents, you wanna talk about him?"

Sara gazed at her friend, trying to decide. She recognized there was still pain there and wasn't eager to touch it, but she knew Lauren was right. Maybe it would help. She nodded and began.

"We were in high school together. He was a jock and an artist and it won't surprise you to know I was the math geek." She chuckled at Lauren's mock astonishment. "Not exactly the prom king and queen. He was struggling in math and I was tutoring athletes. I got assigned to work with him and we just hit it off." She looked away, her memories overtaking her. "His family was from Puerto Rico. His dad owned a landscaping business and I knew my stupid posh parents would hate it. But I was dazzled by being the top varsity pitcher's girlfriend and he loved being able to pass his math class." Sara's wry smile belied her tender feelings. "It was more than that, though. We were just kids, but we really did care about each other. We planned to go to the same college to get away from our parents and have our own life.

"And then I got pregnant." The weight of the statement hit her as if it were yesterday. "My mother was furious—like crazy furious. She accused me of getting pregnant by a Mexican just to embarrass her."

Lauren barked a scornful laugh. "Mexican? I thought you said he was Puerto Rican."

"Exactly. She thinks all brown people are the same."

"*Que idiota*," muttered her Cuban friend. "Have I told you how much I hate your mother?"

"You may have mentioned it a time or two."

"So they dragged you off to Tampa?

"Yeah. They bullied the Segovias into signing away their parental and grandparent rights and off we went." Tears glinted on Sara's lashes. "I remember the only time I wrote a letter to Carlos and tried to sneak it into the mailbox, but my mom caught me. She made me read it out loud to her and then light it on fire in the fireplace. I had to stand there and watch it burn while she told me what a failure and a liar I was."

"No fucking way," growled Lauren.

"Yeah. She found a way to humiliate me and hurt me even more than she already had." Sara looked away, the tears sliding down her face. "I never bothered to write again."

Lauren reached for Sara's hand. "I'm so sorry."

"I feel like if I open this box I'm gonna unravel," admitted Sara. "Like I'll start crying and never stop." She roughly brushed away her tears. "I should have stood up to them. I should have been stronger. You would never have just given in like I did."

"Sara." Lauren's voice was firm but kind. "You were so young. How could you have been any different? You had no experience standing up to them." She squeezed Sara's hand. "Look at the woman you've become. You're amazing—you're strong and successful and you've put them behind you. I hate that you have such a bitch for a mom, but you're the complete opposite of her. I know you're gonna make a decision that's right for you this time. Not them."

2

Saturday was picture perfect for a wedding.

Azalea's long hair and gown fluttered in the light breeze. The sun glinted off the sea, and Esteban's smile lit the beach. The small gathering radiated joy as everyone attending knew this union brought together two wonderful people who adored each other.

Sara dabbed at her eyes as she watched the ceremony. She'd been fighting tears all morning, and she wasn't eager to break down as she stood in front of the assembled friends and family bearing witness to the nuptials. Lauren glanced over her shoulder and smiled. Sara could sense her compassion and was grateful.

She looked at the young men alongside Esteban. His namesake and only son stood next to his father, grinning as he listened to the couple's vows. The taller men behind him, Tomás and Landon, regarded their mother, pride and love clear on their faces. She'd always liked Azalea's boys. *They were, what? Ten years younger than Lauren and me?* She knew it was hard on Azalea to be so far from them out in Colorado, and she was thankful to see them all together for this special day.

Sara stopped listening as she looked out at the guests, her gaze stopping at Tomás's wife, Emily. She hadn't seen Emily since their wedding a year ago. The couple had gone back to Colorado and last night was the first time they'd returned to Florida. Tomás had proudly shown off his lovely pregnant wife at the rehearsal dinner.

Sara had made all the expected comments, hugging Azalea's eldest son and congratulating the couple. She noticed Lauren hovering and quietly assured her friend she was all right, yet she made her way to the restroom as soon as she politely could. After making sure she was alone, she sat in a stall, silently weeping. When she emerged, Lauren was waiting, tissues in hand, her face filled with concern.

"I'm okay," said Sara. "I can't avoid pregnant women for the rest of my life."

"Yeah, but it's not the same thing as seeing someone you know," replied Lauren. "I know that had to be hard."

"I feel so stupid." Sara shook her head, then blew her nose. "I'm genuinely happy for them. I only met Emily a couple of times, but Tomás is a great guy. He's gonna be an awesome dad."

Lauren looked at her friend and pulled her in for a hug. "It's okay, Sara. It's gonna be okay."

As they pulled apart, the two friends shared a knowing look. It would be anything but okay for a long while.

After the ceremony, the happy couple and their attendants posed for photos. Azalea was stunning, her eyes gleaming as she stood beside her new husband. While Lauren went to say hello to friends, Sara stood and admired the bride in her elegant gown. The simple ballet neckline showed off her shoulders, the off-white fabric grazing her slim hips and trailing on the sand. Sara wasn't jealous of her friend but wondered how she could always be so effortlessly glamorous. She'd been that way since the first day they met. Sara idly wondered what kind of wedding gown she'd wear if she ever got married.

Of course, I'd actually have to date someone to get married. She shook off the annoying thought. Dating hadn't been a priority for a long time. And now with the new job looming in the fall, Sara was pretty certain she wouldn't be meeting anyone any time soon. She'd be heads down in lesson planning for teenagers.

After the photos, the bride and groom approached Sara, and Esteban held out his hands, pulling her in for a traditional *dos besos* greeting. "*Gracias*, Sara," he said in his richly accented voice. "I am thankful to have you share our special day."

She smiled, her heart filled with joy for her friend. "I'm thrilled for you both," she said. "Azalea deserves a wonderful man and I'm just glad you aren't taking her to Spain forever."

Azalea smiled. "You know I love you girls. I couldn't leave forever." The couple planned a honeymoon in Europe and then intended to split their year between Spain and Florida, keeping both homes. Azalea would rent her place out for the six months they were in Spain, and Esteban Jr. would take care of their home in Cadaqués while they summered in Florida. Esteban Obregon owned cafés in Cadaqués and Barcelona, and Junior had been ecstatic at the idea of being responsible for both of them.

Lauren and Susana approached the trio, and Susana wrapped her arms around the newlyweds. "Are we gonna stand out here on the beach all day or are we gonna go drink some champagne? And I have a really impressive speech to make," she added with a wicked grin. The matron of honor was Azalea's best friend and loved to tease.

The women all rolled their eyes while Azalea groaned. "Suze, please don't do anything crazy," she begged.

"'Crazy' is her middle name," commented Sara with a laugh.

"Yep," nodded Susana. "And I'm gonna deliver it in English *and* Spanish, so no one misses out."

Esteban laughed, then shook a finger at Susana. "*Cuidado, hermana*," he intoned. "You don't want to get this wild Latina fired up." He kissed his wife on the cheek. "You never know what she'll do." The four women burst out laughing, well acquainted with Azalea's reserved nature. The thought of her doing anything remotely "wild" was hilarious.

Azalea smiled at her husband, then announced it was time to leave for the reception. As they headed for their cars, Sara looked once more around at the gathering. Tomás was hovering over Emily as she gathered her purse and sweater and she looked up at him, shaking her head. "I'm not a china doll," she asserted, playfully swatting at this hand. "I'm pretty sure I can walk to the car all by myself."

Her husband grinned, a rueful look on his face. "I know, I know. I'm sorry, babe."

"Don't apologize," said Emily, her face beaming. "I love how you love me and little Amelia. We're the luckiest girls in the world."

Sara turned, brushing away sudden tears.

Of course. It had to be a girl.

Lauren's words rang in her thoughts: "There are pregnant women everywhere, Sara."

This has got to stop.

Sara busied herself around the house all week, but by Wednesday, she'd gone grocery shopping, done laundry, and dusted every crevice in the house. She was out of things to do and knew the busyness was simply a cover for the decision she needed to make. When Lauren walked in that evening from work, Sara was lying on the sofa, idly flicking the remote. She looked up at her friend and saw her disapproval.

"Seriously?" asked Lauren, a frown creasing her brow. "Sara, this isn't you. It's been over a week since you got the letter. The house is immaculate and now you're just moping around. You're either gonna say yes or no but none of this is doing you any good." She started to sit down but then stood. "I'm not trying to hurt you, but c'mon." She shook her head and Sara felt a spike of shame.

"You're right," she said softly. "This isn't getting me anywhere."

Lauren kicked off her high heels and sat down. "I'm not trying to be mean—"

"You're not being mean," responded Sara. "You're being a good friend and I'm being stupid." She sat up and straightened her shoulders. "I just don't know what to do."

"Let's talk it out," said Lauren, her voice assured. "We talked about Carlos but we haven't talked about Natalie. What do you always tell me? 'Life is like a math problem. Isolate the variable and solve for x.'" She swatted her friend with one of the sofa throw pillows. "So c'mon, math diva. Let's solve the problem. What's the downside of agreeing to meet Natalie?"

"Well, maybe this sounds selfish, but I like my life the way it is. I've spent twenty-three years trying not to think about her and now it's like there's nothing else on my mind. I mean, this could completely change everything." She sat up and wrapped herself around one of the throw pillows. "And what if I don't like her? What if she's spoiled or looks down on me or hates math?" She grinned crookedly. "Okay, so that's a dumb joke, but seriously— what if we just don't get along?"

Lauren pursed her lips, thinking. "I suppose then you just part ways? I mean, if you don't like her, she probably wouldn't like you either." She shrugged. "She sounds nice in the letter, but I guess it's possible she's a brat." She sat up straighter, a light in her eyes. "Hey! Have you looked for her online?" She reached for her bag and pulled out her laptop as Sara shook her head.

"No. I didn't want to see her until I made up my mind about meeting."

Lauren looked surprised. "Are you kidding me? I would have been stalking her two seconds after I got the letter." She opened her laptop and launched Instagram. "What's her last name again?"

Sara looked at her friend, undecided. "Why am I so scared?"

Lauren's eyebrows drew together, her voice subdued. "Because you're a good woman and you won't do this halfway." She closed the laptop and took her friend's hand. "I know you, Sara. You're in or you're out—and right now you know that if you're in, it will change your life forever. But now that you know she's out there and she was looking for you, you're always going to wonder and it's gonna affect you anyway." She patted Sara's hand. "Courage, *amiga*. You don't have to do this alone."

Sara stared at their hands, wrestling with her thoughts and emotions. At last she spoke, her voice hushed.

"I think about her all the time," she confided. "When I first started teaching, I used to wonder if somehow she'd end up in my classroom, that I'd turn around to see a beautiful kindergartner and I'd somehow know it was her. Then years went by and I wondered what her life was like, if her—" Sara swallowed hard, "parents were good people and if she had a life full of love." She looked up, her eyes sorrowful. "You never know what will happen. I didn't really know much about them. The agency gave us different profiles and my parents pretty much made the decisions. Especially about there being no contact." She frowned. "They definitely won't be happy if I contact her."

Lauren cocked her head, her eyes questioning. "And do you care what they think?"

Sara glanced back at the letter. "Honestly? No. They dictated everything about my life after she was born. I felt so guilty about getting pregnant that I let them—except when I changed my grad school major from engineering to education." She smiled grimly. "My mother accused me of throwing my life away just to be around children. It's the only time I ever talked back to her, I think."

"What did you say?" asked Lauren.

"I asked her if that's what she felt like when she had me."

Lauren's eyebrows shot up in surprise. "You didn't!"

"I did." Sara's eyes filled with tears. "And then she slapped my face and told me not to bother coming home at the end of the semester. She said I could 'damn well take care of myself' and to stay in Tallahassee." She shook her head at the painful memory. "I had an apartment by then and I never lived at home again. She didn't even come to my graduation.

"Kind of a terrible family for Natalie to come from." Then she smiled, a faraway look in her eyes. "Natalie. What a pretty name."

Lauren took Sara's hand again and squeezed, regaining her friend's attention. "So? What do you think? If you want to meet her, you know I'll come with you. Your family sucks, but I don't." She grinned. "I may not be blood, but you know you're *la hermana de mi corazon.*"

"What would I do without you?" Sara asked. "I always wanted a sister, but I didn't know how much I needed one until we met." She pondered her friend's words: *You're always going to wonder.*

"Okay," she said at last. "Her last name is Allard. Let's see what's out there."

The two friends scooted closer together and Lauren reopened her laptop and began typing.

"Damn," said Lauren. "She's gorgeous."

It hadn't taken long for the two friends to uncover Natalie's social media presence. There were photos of her with friends and with what appeared to be her family. She was olive-skinned and had shoulder length, wavy brown hair. Her bright green eyes and wide smile animated every photo, and Sara's chest grew tight as she took in every detail of her daughter's appearance.

"She looks like Carlos," she whispered.

"She looks like you," countered Lauren. "I don't know what he looks like, but other than her coloring, you guys could be sisters." She looked up and asked, "Wanna find him while we're at it?"

Sara's eyes grew wide—she'd put Carlos out of her mind even more than Natalie, she thought.

Does that make me a bad mother?

"Oh, man…I don't know.…"

"Courage, *chiquita*. We're in it now—might as well go all the way." She looked at Sara, her face expectant.

"I'm having a hard time breathing," admitted Sara. "This is really overwhelming." But now that Lauren had suggested it, she couldn't say no. "Okay. Let's do it. His name is Carlos Segovia."

Lauren's fingers flew across the keyboard but they were less successful than with Natalie. "Hmm," she said, scowling. "What's wrong with a guy who doesn't do social media?"

Sara laughed, almost relieved. Finding Natalie's photos had nearly overcome her. Having to see Carlos' face might have been too much.

But Lauren wasn't finished.

"Okay, he's not an Instagram or Facebook kinda guy. But let's check LinkedIn." She pulled up the page and searched for his name. A long list of names followed, many in Spanish. But as Lauren scrolled down, Sara gasped at one photo. *Carlos Segovia, Regional Sales Executive, Orlando Florida.*

It was him.

"That's him," she said, pointing at the thumbnail photo. Lauren immediately clicked on it and they were looking at a handsome man in a suit and tie. Sara leaned forward and stared, finding the boy she'd loved in the face of the man. His full head of hair was still black but with a smattering of gray. His eyes were dark brown, just as she remembered, but his smile seemed restrained.

"I see what you mean," said Lauren. "Natalie does look like him, but she definitely favors you." She turned to look at her friend. "Good looking man." She began reading the profile, but Sara remained transfixed on the photo.

I wonder if Natalie has found him, too.

3

Sara sealed the envelope and added the stamp. She still felt a measure of trepidation, but knew she was doing the right thing. She kept her response short but warm and included her phone number and email address. She wondered how soon she'd hear from her daughter.

Dear Natalie,

I confess I don't have the right words for how surprising your letter was but I'm happy you wrote. I'm sorry to hear about your mother but I'm very glad she's in remission. She sounds like a wonderful woman.

This will be a bit scary for both of us but I would like to meet you. It looks like we live about an hour apart—amazing!—so it would be easy to meet. Please give me a call, text, or email me and let's schedule something soon.

Thank you so much for writing. I'm eager to meet you!

Sara

After giving the letter two days to reach Natalie, Sara began checking her phone and email every hour, but nothing came.

She busied herself with reading and planning for the new school year. After years of teaching kindergarten, she'd completed the courses necessary for a middle school credential and was spending the summer preparing herself for her new job teaching math to seventh and eighth graders.

"It's a time when girls tend to lose interest in math and science," she told Lauren. "I want to make a difference in how they see numbers—how they can be beautiful and exciting." Sara had begun her master's degree in civil engineering when she decided she'd rather teach kindergarten. Civil engineers build the infrastructure that runs cities, she reasoned, but teachers build the humans who live in them. Moving up to the middle school seemed the next important step in her career, a place she could make a real difference in students' lives.

I wonder if Natalie likes math. Carlos had hated it. She had a sudden flash of memory, the two of them sitting in the library, his hopeless efforts at trigonometry. She'd laughed and patiently explained again and again until he got it. His notebook was covered with sketches—*He loved to draw*, she remembered. He passed the trig class, but just barely. She wondered for the millionth time what had happened to the boy she'd loved. His LinkedIn profile was all business. He'd graduated from the University of Florida and gone on to a career in sales. There were no personal details on his profile, no interesting posts that gave her a clue as to his life.

She was about to close her laptop when an email notification popped up.

It was Natalie.

Sara closed her eyes for a moment, hesitating. *I wish Lauren were here*, she thought, but then shrugged off the trepidation. *This is what I've been waiting for.*

She opened the email and read.

Hi Sara!

> *Thank you so much for your letter. I know it will be weird and maybe hard for both of us, but I'm really excited to meet you.*
>
> *I was thinking maybe it would be good to talk on the phone first—just to get out the jitters. I don't know if you're feeling them, but I sure am. Maybe it's easier if we start there first? Would you let me know a good time when we could talk? I'm home for the summer—just finishing up grad school—and trying to spend as much time with my parents as possible.*
>
> *BTW, they're happy for me that you and I connected. I think someday they'd like to see you again. I don't know if you remember them from when I was born, but they remember you.*
>
> *Anyway, I'll look forward to your answer. I'm nervous and excited!*

Talk soon,
Natalie

It only took a minute for Sara to respond to the email.

Hi, Natalie,

> *I'm a teacher, so I'm home for the summer, too. Any time is great for me. I'm eager to talk!*

Sara

She sat on the sofa, staring at her screen, willing a response. Now that she decided to connect with Natalie, she was keen for it to happen. Eagerness welled up inside her and she wondered again how it were possible for her own parents to be so uninterested in her—distant, cold, and frequently unkind. She was certain they never wanted children and the old pain surfaced as she remembered leaving the hospital after Natalie's birth. They expected her to be thankful they'd "solved a problem," as if a baby were a quadratic equation. There was no sympathy, no mother-daughter confidences and tears.

There was no baby and no Carlos.

Natalie's email popped up. *Awesome—I'll call you tomorrow at 1:00. Can't wait!*

The next afternoon, Sara sat on her bed, leaning back on the soft pink pillows, her fingers nervously twisting around each other as she gazed at her phone. She'd done everything possible to keep from watching the clock all day, but now that there were only seven minutes until Natalie's call, she was out of things to do.

That morning, Lauren asked if she wanted her to stay home, but Sara demurred. "I promise to call as soon as we're done." She paused. "Wish me luck?"

"You don't need luck. You just need to be you. It's gonna be all right, I'm sure of it."

The minutes ticked by slowly and Sara again ran through all the things she wanted to say. "Don't make excuses," Lauren had cautioned. "This isn't about you doing anything wrong. She has a great life and you did a wonderful thing to place her with that family. Just ask her questions and let her talk about herself." Sara had agreed, and tried to put her guilty feelings aside.

It's all about Natalie, she thought once again. *This isn't about me.*

The phone ticked over to the hour and she took a deep breath. Her heart thudded in her chest, and her hands shook. She straightened her ear buds yet again, ensuring they were snug, ready to hear her daughter's voice for the first time since the infant cry twenty-three years ago. She tried to keep from staring at her phone, but couldn't stop watching as the minutes went by. At fifteen minutes past their scheduled time, her shoulders slumped and she fought back tears. Her thoughts were a swirl of anguish.

She changed her mind. She doesn't want to talk to me. Why would she? I gave her away.

Sara stood and looked around her bedroom, her excitement and nervous energy gone. Instead, she felt hollow, unsure what to do. Should she call Natalie? Text her? Just let her be? There was no guidebook for handling these kinds of situations. If it had been a crying five-year-old afraid to come into her kindergarten classroom, Sara would have been prepared. She even felt competent to deal with the middle schoolers she'd face in the fall. But this? She had no idea.

An ugly thought punched her in the gut. *My parents don't want me and neither does my daughter.*

She curled around her pillow and gave in to the tears.

That evening, Lauren walked into Sara's bedroom, two pints of ice cream in her hands. Sara was sprawled on the bed, propped against pillows, her phone and several tissues next to her. "Anything?" asked Lauren.

Sara shook her head, the tears welling again. Her face was blotchy from crying and now she was just wrung out. Her friend handed her a pint of raspberry sorbet and a spoon. "I'm so sorry," she commiserated. "Can I do anything?"

Sara shook her head again. "This is probably the best thing you could do," she said, opening the small tub. "Do you think she changed her mind? Or maybe something came up? I hope I didn't freak her out by being too eager." Sara turned her anguished gaze at her friend. "I don't blame her. Why should she show up after I—"

Lauren interrupted her. "Stop it. Just stop. You didn't do anything wrong—not then, not now. Who knows what happened? It's not like there's any kind of guidebook for this."

Sara frowned. "I was thinking the exact same thing earlier," she confessed. "I wish someone could tell me what to expect and how to handle it. What to say." She closed her eyes. "What to feel," she finished in a hushed voice.

"You didn't do anything wrong," repeated Lauren. "Don't feel guilty about what you did in high school and don't get twisted about today." She took a big bite of her ice cream. "Eat your dessert and tell me about your new job."

Sara looked askance at her. "You know you're really terrible at subtly changing the subject."

Lauren grinned. "Nevertheless," she said, fixing a prim look on her face, "I want to hear about your class."

The soon-to-be middle school math teacher sighed. "All right," she responded. "Looks like they're giving me a couple of regular math classes plus the eighth grade advanced class. I'll get to teach algebra to the kids who are already smart enough for high school math. Jenna called a couple of hours ago to give me the new schedule." Sara had interviewed with Jenna Dobson, the principal at Daytona Springs Middle School, and the two had clicked immediately, with Sara receiving the job offer the next day. "I'm excited to have the gifted kids," she admitted. "I wasn't as eager to teach basic math to kids who don't like it."

"Do you think you'll miss the little ones?" asked Lauren.

"I'm sure I will. There's nothing like watching kindergartners grow over a school year. But I'm looking forward to seeing these kids, too. It's gonna be so different." She chuckled, thinking. "Decorating my classroom will be the first big change. I'm guessing they don't want posters of bunnies on the walls or 2+2 on their flash cards."

Lauren smiled at her. "The students will be different, but you'll be the same. You'll still be the best teacher they have all year."

Sara laughed. "You're my best friend. You have to say that."

"Doesn't mean it isn't true."

They finished their ice cream, chatting about math classes and speculating about the drama she'd surely face with early teen students. After an hour, Sara crawled into bed. She hoped Natalie was all right, and she drifted off into a fitful sleep.

4

A week went by with no communication from Natalie. Sara checked email throughout the day and picked up her phone every few minutes to check for messages.

Nothing. It was as if they'd never corresponded, as if her daughter had never sought her out.

I was fine before that letter, she told herself. *I'll be fine again.*

But she wasn't fine. Corresponding with Natalie brought up memories she'd carefully packaged and locked away, memories that threatened to undo her. She had never let herself forget she was a mother—that memory was safely tucked into her heart. Other images, however, had been too painful to keep.

Like her parents' fury.

"You have shamed your family by whoring around," snarled her mother. "You have no say in what will happen now."

Sara's father stood impassively next to his wife. She knew she'd disappointed him, too, but he wouldn't berate her. He wouldn't contradict his wife, though.

"You are not to see that boy again and you are not keeping this…this *half-breed* bastard. It's getting adopted. Your father and I have already seen to the arrangements."

"That's not fair!" she'd retorted—in her head. In reality, she'd looked down and done exactly as her mother demanded. She hadn't seen Carlos again.

She knew her parents' beliefs would never sanction an abortion. In fact, she was pretty sure that's the only reason she'd been born. And so they moved to Tampa, leaving behind her boyfriend and the life they'd dreamed of. She relinquished her baby, finished high school, and left for college.

But now she couldn't stop the memories from flooding her mind. The carefully curated life she'd built for two decades began to fray.

That weekend, she and Lauren drove to Azalea's house to water the plants and bring the mail inside. The newlyweds were due back home in a few days and the two friends looked forward to their last weekend at the coast. They chatted amiably, Lauren regaling her with the latest in a long line of ridiculous moves by her boss.

"When are you gonna leave that place?" asked Sara. "You've been miserable there this entire year. Life's too short."

Lauren nodded. "You're right. I guess it's just the 'devil you know.'"

"I can't stand the way he takes advantage of you," said Sara. "You're so good at what you do. Why don't you go back to MPG? You know they'd be thrilled to have you and Susana would help." A year earlier, Lauren had left Miles Porter Gelbarr, the marketing agency where Susana was a vice president. She'd been recruited by a start up, offering her a fancy title and loads of cash, but had quickly come to regret the decision. Her boss, Hunter Linsom, was a twenty-eight year old prodigy—or so she thought at first. What she'd learned over the past year was that Hunter, while bright and capable, was actually best at taking credit for others' work. He'd milk her for ideas, get her to produce plans, and then present them to the C-suite as his own. Sara had listened to Lauren's complaints for months and pretty much hated the guy.

"I know…I should probably call Susana this week," agreed Lauren. "Thanks for the push."

"What are friends for?" asked Sara as the two pulled into Azalea's driveway. She stopped for the mail as Lauren opened the front door and they entered the charming cottage. Sara dropped the mail on the coffee table and they went to their respective bedrooms to drop off their bags.

Returning to the living room, Lauren called out, "Beach time? Or coffee in the lanai?" She poked her head into the guest room where Sara sat on the bed, staring at her phone. "Oh, damn. You okay?"

Sara looked up, a pained expression on her face. "It's Natalie," she said, her voice thick with emotion. "She's apologizing for missing our call. Evidently she had second thoughts." She looked down at the screen, reading Natalie's words aloud.

Hi Sara, I'm really sorry for missing our call. I hope I didn't hurt your feelings. I just got a little spooked at finally hearing your voice. If it's ok I still want to communicate, but I don't think I'm ready for a phone call. I hope that's ok with you and you're willing to just email or text. Please let me know and thanks.

Sara looked at her best friend and sighed. "I don't know what I expected," she said. "It can't be easy for her." She lay back on the bed and closed her eyes. "Part of me wishes she'd never written. But part of me is dying to meet her and put that piece of my life back together." Tears ran down into her hair and she roughly brushed them away. "The worst part of this is I'm hating my mother all over again." She looked long at Lauren.

"And when I hate her, I hate me even more for not fighting back."

That afternoon, Sara took advantage of a quick walk to the beach while Lauren caught up on a work project. After a few minutes reading a book, she fell asleep but the music and laughter of nearby vacationers woke her. She gazed out at the waves and watched as a young boy, probably the same age as her kindergartners, rode his boogie board onto the sand. His father pulled the child back out several yards and let him ride in again, and Sara was transfixed by the little boy's delight. He grinned and laughed as the swells lifted and pushed him again and again to the sand. After several trips, she heard his father tell him it was time for lunch, but the boy begged for "Just one more, Dad. Please?"

His father laughed and relented. His pride in the youngster was evident, and Sara wondered what her life would have been like if she'd had parents who took pride in her achievements. She'd hoped graduating high school as valedictorian and getting accepted to the engineering program at Florida State might— *Might what?* she wondered. *Make them love me?* But they'd only used her success as bragging opportunities with their friends.

Shaking off her maudlin reverie, Sara decided to go for a swim. She waded out and bobbed along the swells, letting the sun and warm water calm her. Small fish darted around her legs and she gave in to the rhythm of the waves, diving under the larger ones and floating on her back when they passed. When she at last calmed her mind, she swam back to shore to dry off.

Music and laughter rang out as families covered every open spot on the sand. She looked down the beach to see the boy and his father sitting with a woman and two older children. An infant lay asleep in a carrier next to the blanket. She marveled that the baby could sleep with all the noise and once again felt a pang of regret. She and Carlos were only children themselves when Natalie was born, but she wondered what they might have become if they'd been allowed to stay together—to raise their child. *Would we be a family now?*

Her peace once again in tatters, Sara decided she'd had enough sun and walked back to the cottage.

Sara and Lauren enjoyed the weekend, although Sara's heart wasn't in it to go out Saturday night. She apologized and promised she would snap out of her funk soon. "I just need a little time."

"*Paciencia, chica.* Take all the time you need," Lauren answered. "This isn't something you can script—it's gonna come at you differently every day. And don't worry about me. You know I'm here for you."

"I count on it," she replied.

After they straightened up the house on Sunday evening, the two drove back home. "I've gotten so used to weekends down here it's gonna suck when Azalea and Esteban come back," lamented Lauren. The women lived a close drive to the beach themselves, but they'd been spoiled by the two minute walk from Azalea's cottage to the sand. Sara nodded in agreement, but remained silent for the remainder of the drive.

They arrived home and Sara went straight to her room. "I'm beat," she told Lauren. "I'll see you tomorrow."

She unpacked her overnight bag and got ready for bed. She was determined to overcome the melancholy that shrouded her heart but couldn't muster the energy to do anything. *I just need a good night's sleep*, she assured herself. *Things will look different in the morning.*

But she couldn't sleep and after an hour grabbed her phone. She contemplated a quick answer to Natalie, but decided to wait until she'd slept, not trusting herself to say the right thing in her fatigued and sad state. She began scrolling through the photos she and Lauren had found of her daughter. She condemned herself as voyeuristic, but she was so hungry for information, she didn't care. She looked through image after image of the smiling young woman. There were dozens with friends—she looked so happy.

There were also photos with her parents. Sara looked hard at the woman who had raised Natalie. She looked kind and clearly loved her daughter.

Not my daughter. Jocelyn's daughter.

And then she wondered: *What makes a woman a real mother?* It was obvious that Natalie's adoptive mother loved her and cared for her. What made her so different from Sara's mother, a woman who'd never displayed affection? *Did something happen to my mom to make her so cold?* It was hard to imagine Cecilia as a daughter herself, a child who needed love. Sara had never met her grandparents—they both died when she was a baby. Were they good parents who loved their daughter? Or were they responsible for her mom's inability to care for her, to be there for her throughout her life? Too many questions and too few answers.

And what kind of mother am I?

Sara's stomach clenched and she put down her phone. She lay awake for a long, long time.

The next morning, Sara determined to regain her composure— she'd had enough of the angst and was ready to return to her typical, placid self. Over the years she'd worked hard to overcome her past and build a pleasant, if unexciting life. She wanted that peace back. And so she was up before Lauren and made a vegan protein shake, concentrating on how she wanted to structure her new middle school classes. *I have plenty to keep me busy,* she thought. *A new year, new school, new students.* She had only two more weeks of summer before she could get in and set up her classroom and Sara wanted to get a head start on her lesson plans. After teaching five-year-olds for so long, she was certain she was in for a challenging few weeks as she adjusted to the new school and classes.

She wandered out to the backyard. It was early enough in the morning that the August heat wasn't unbearable. She wished she were still at Azalea's place enjoying the easy walk to the beach and the lanai where the ocean breezes blew through nearly all day. *First world problems,* she laughed at herself. She thought about Azalea and wondered what she would think about all this. Her friend wasn't just a great mother, she was a steady influence on all their friends, always ready with a kind word or wise counsel, especially when the fiery Lauren or Susana started to spin over the smallest problems. *I could use her counsel right now,* she thought. But Azalea was on her way back from Spain and Sara didn't want to bombard her with problems and questions so soon after the honeymoon.

She opened her laptop and sipped at her drink. Browsing quickly through her new middle school email, she read the welcome notes from her principal and department chair. As she set up her calendar for the first two weeks of school, Sara began to relax. She'd loved teaching the little ones, but math was her gift. She found herself grinning as she began planning the first day for each of her classes. She especially wanted to challenge the advanced students right away and was completely engrossed in Fibonacci numbers when Lauren stepped out to say goodbye.

"Oh, hey!" she said, pulling herself away from her screen. "Sorry—I got a little lost there. Heading to the office?"

Lauren grinned. "It's nice to see you happy. Let me guess: Some famous Italian mathematician?"

Sara groaned. "Am I that predictable?"

"I've known you for a long time, my friend. I don't know anything else that would put that goofy smile on your face."

Lauren shouldered her laptop bag and waved. "Wish me luck. I'm gonna talk to Susana today about MPG. It's gonna suck admitting I messed up."

Sara nodded. "Take your own advice: You don't need luck. Just tell her the truth and let her know you've learned a lot. You know Susana. She'll be happy to help."

"And give me a big ration of crap while she's at it." The friends laughed and Lauren headed out.

Two hours later, Sara was ready for a break. She rinsed her cup and poured herself some coffee. The last weeks of summer were always difficult. She loved the time off, but especially this year she was eager to get back into the classroom.

New job. New challenge.

But first I have to respond to Natalie.

Sara began typing.

Hi, Natalie. Thanks for letting me know. I won't pretend I wasn't disappointed, but I do understand. This is really new for both of us and I respect your decision. I'm happy to keep chatting like this until you're ready.

She looked at the words on the screen. *Is that too cold?* She didn't know how Natalie would take her admission of disappointment, but she figured it was important to be honest. *Especially from the start*, she thought. *No sense in pretending I don't feel what I feel.*

Sara waited before she pressed Send. Her mother never minced words—she was direct and never cared what damage she might inflict. For years, she watched her father simply take his wife's bluntness and wondered how he managed not to react. Sara learned early on that her sensitive nature did her no favors—her mother despised her daughter's tears and sent her to her room whenever they threatened. Over time, she mastered the skill of masking her hurt, stilling her features and refusing to let a single tear fall. She only cried when she was alone.

I wonder if my mom ever cries.

After reading the text a few more times, Sara sent it on its way, hoping her daughter would see it as a relief, an opportunity to continue connecting without overwhelming her. She wondered if Celia Masterson had ever agonized over anything she said to anyone—especially her daughter.

Probably not.

A week went by and each day got easier. Sara immersed herself in her work and felt a degree of excitement she hadn't felt in a long time. She couldn't wait to tackle this new challenge and was eager to see how she would get along with the teens in her classes. She thought about meeting new colleagues—she didn't know anyone at the school other than the principal and department chair. *Maybe I'll make some new friends.*

At last, a text arrived.

Hi Sara, thanks for being so cool about the other day. Sorry for the delayed response. I go back to school in a week and I'm trying to see friends before I go. Anyway, I hope you're well and I'd love to hear from you. You said you're a teacher? What do you teach?

Sara laughed. *So I'm cool—that's nothing I'd ever have said to my mom.* She thought a moment before answering. *This feels like a casual conversation—I can do this.*

Hey, Natalie, she wrote, *great to hear from you. It's nice that you have some time with your friends. I've been a teacher for the past 15 years, teaching kindergarten. But this year I've moved up to middle school where I'll teach math. I'm super excited for the change!*

Natalie's response came quickly. *Wow, that sounds awesome! Big change from kindergarten to middle school. Are you ready for all the bratty teenagers? LOL*

Sara smiled as she typed. *It will be different for sure. The kindergartners are adorable…most of the time. So what are you studying in grad school?*

I'm working on an MFA but I'm also working on illustration. Funny you taught kindergarten—that's the age group I'd love to write for. Someday!

Sara stared at the phone. Her daughter—Carlos' daughter—was an artist. She hesitated before answering, unsure what to say. Should she tell Natalie that she got her talent from her father?

Then Natalie texted again. *Sorry, gotta run but it was nice to talk to you. Have a great day and let's catch up again soon!*

Sounds great. Take care!

Sara set her phone down, glad not to have to make the decision today.

One step at a time.

5

Sara walked into her classroom and set down her bag. She looked around at the walls—she'd hung up posters of famous mathematicians, taking care to position her hero Hypatia in a prominent position. She was certain none of her students would recognize the woman as the first known female math teacher in history, born in Egypt nearly two thousand years before Sara.

They'll get to know her now, she thought with a smile. She was excited to share her passion not only for numbers, but for the brilliant mathematical minds throughout history.

The bell rang and Sara stood in front of her desk. *Here we go.*

The day flew by, and Sara was in her element. The kids were friendly and seemed excited to start the new year. By 4:00, she was tired but happy with the day's accomplishments. As she packed her bag, Principal Jenna Dobson popped her head in the door. "How'd the first day go?" she asked.

"Really well," enthused Sara.

"I'm glad to hear it," said Jenna. "Let me know if you have any kids who either act up or seem to fall behind early. We try to nip that at the very beginning of the school year."

"Makes sense," said Sara. "Does that happen often?"

"Not a lot, but sometimes a student will be dealing with stuff outside school that we're unaware of. Or they have a hard time getting back into the swing of things and get behind on homework or do poorly on tests. We want to makes sure our students are supported and given every opportunity to succeed."

Sara smiled. "I guess I never really had to deal with those issues in kindergarten."

Looks like the teacher has things to learn, too.

"So how did it go?" asked Lauren. "I've been thinking about you all day!" She flung her backpack on the sofa and walked to the kitchen where Sara stood rinsing vegetables at the sink.

"It was great—the kids were wonderful, and the day went so fast." Sara smiled at her friend. "But I want to hear about your day first. Did you talk to Susana?"

Lauren opened the refrigerator and pulled out leftover pizza. "I did and it was just what we expected. She's thrilled I want to come back *and* she bitched at me for ten minutes about what a moron I was to leave." She laughed. "I'm sure I deserved it. And honestly, I'd rather have Susana on my ass than one more day dealing with that *pendejo*."

"So what's next? Did you give your notice?"

"Ha!" snorted Lauren. "I did. And you should have seen Hunter's face. I was gonna just drop the letter off on his desk, but then I figured I'd tell him in person. He wanted to know where I was going, so I told him I'm going back to MPG. He's actually gonna have to work on his own now and I'm pretty sure he's freaked out." She started laughing, then began mimicking her former boss. "You know, Lauren, the grass always seems greener and all that. I mean, look at what I've given you here and think about everything you'd be leaving to go back to a junior level role in a corporate environment." She rolled her eyes and shook her head. "I swear he turned white under that fake tan of his. He's so smarmy."

Sara began chopping vegetables and dropped them into a saucepan to sauté. "Smarmy? Is that even a word?"

Lauren laughed. "Is Fibonacci even a word?"

Sara grinned. "Okay, okay. Anyway, I'm proud of you. I can't stand that jerk. How does somebody even move up like that?"

"He probably bought all his university papers off the internet," groused Lauren. "I can't imagine him doing anything on his own." She began eating the pizza cold and talked around a mouthful. "Anyway, he came by my office a couple of hours later and offered me a forty thousand dollar raise and a promotion."

Sara gaped at her friend. Her own teaching salary was barely more than that—the money that was tossed around in the corporate world staggered her. "And you turned it down?"

Lauren's eyebrows came together in a severe line. "My soul isn't worth forty grand. And besides, MPG is giving me plenty of money plus I can work from home. It's gonna be great."

The friends continued chatting while Sara cooked her vegetables and stirred in some vegan sausage. When she was finished, she asked, "So that's your dinner? Leftover pizza standing by the stove watching me cook?" She shook her head at her lithe friend. "It's crazy how you can eat like that and stay so fit. You know I hate you, right?"

Lauren laughed and threw away a piece of cold crust. "Yeah, but I'll probably die by the time I'm fifty and you and Mr. Fibonacci will still be teaching math to kids going through puberty, dealing with all their drama."

The two sat at the dining room table and talked, Lauren sipping a glass of wine while Sara ate her dinner and drank a glass of sparkling water. When they finished, Lauren headed for the sofa to watch Netflix while Sara pulled out her laptop to prepare for the next day. She'd just begun when a text popped up on her phone.

Hi, Sara! Just checking in—how was the first day of school?

Sara grinned. The now nearly daily texts with Natalie always made her smile, and she was delighted that her daughter had remembered the importance of today. She pushed her laptop back and typed. *It was great—the kids are nice and I had a blast. Thanks for thinking of me!*

She wondered if this would be the sum total of her interaction with Natalie—texts that scratched the surface, yet maintained a connection. It had become comfortable and easy to chat informally with the girl. *The young woman*, she corrected herself. She wished she had the courage to push for more, but wasn't certain she was ready for it herself.

I'm juggling like crazy right now with the creative writing program and the illustration course. That probably sounds like first world problems! I'm lucky to be able to just worry about school and not have to work, too.

Sara refocused on Natalie's message. *Plenty of time to think about more*, she mused. Then she typed, *What are you working on?*

I really want to write and illustrate children's books. I'm thinking kindergarten to second grade, but I'm not sure.

She took a moment before replying. While she loved messaging with Natalie, she worried that she'd say the wrong thing and the girl would bolt like a feral animal. Was this the time to nudge for a deeper connection? She wanted to offer her help— who knew kindergartners better than she? But she hesitated and, in the end, settled for safety.

That sounds great. I'd love to see your work one day.

There. That was enough. Sara waited for Natalie's reply.

Well, gotta run. Talk soon!

She sighed. *Talk soon.*

At the end of the next day, Sara walked out of her classroom to head for home. It had been another good day and she felt positive about the progress she was making. *Don't get too excited*, she cautioned herself. *It's only the second day of classes.* But the way the students were responding left her content and eager for more.

There were a few she'd keep her eye on, though. A couple of the students in her fifth period class seemed like they wanted to test her, sneaking looks at their mobile phones while she wrote on the white board. One girl strolled in late to class and feigned getting lost as her excuse. Sara didn't intend to be hard-nosed, but she wasn't going to let any of her students behave disrespectfully or disrupt the class. She knew she had to set the standards early so they could all enjoy the year.

And there was one young girl in her fourth period advanced class who seemed—just *off*. Sara reminded herself, again, that it was only the second day, far too early to make any judgments. But the girl, Marisa Segovia, radiated sadness. She hadn't said anything or participated in class, but maybe she was just shy? Sara mused that the girl had the same last name as Carlos—*Small world*, she thought. But it wasn't an unusual name in Florida, and she'd had other Segovias in previous years.

She locked her classroom door and turned to see another teacher leaving his room across the hallway. Tall and tanned, he had chin-length curls, brown but with a touch of blonde. *Typical Florida beach boy*, she thought. *Handsome.*

The man caught her eye and smiled. *Very handsome*, she corrected herself at the sight of his dimples and strong jaw.

"Hi," he said, striding towards her, his hand extended. "I'm—"

"Mr. Billings!" A pair of beaming middle schoolers approached him. One of the girls nudged the other, clearly unwilling to speak.

"Um…I didn't write down the chapter we're supposed to read tonight. What is it?" The speaker was flustered and blushing. "I want to be sure I stay on top of all your assignments." Her friend stifled a giggle and again nudged her friend.

Mr. Billings looked askance at the students. "It's only the second day of school, girls. I'd like you to read the first chapter by Friday."

"Ohhh…right! Thank you, Mr. Billings!" The girls turned and ran down the hallway, giggling and whispering to each other.

Sara tried not to but couldn't help laughing.

He smiled and shook his head. "Don't start. You're new and beautiful—they're gonna act the same way around you." He seemed to recollect himself and held out his hand abruptly. "Sorry—I'm Terrence Billings. I teach language arts."

Did he just call me beautiful?

She shook his hand, adopting his more formal tone. "I'm Sara Masterson. I teach math."

"Very nice to meet you, Sara Masterson. So how's your first week going?"

"It's great so far. I'm enjoying the kids and learning a lot. Seems teaching middle school isn't quite the same as kindergarten," she laughed.

"Oh, wow—kindergarten. How long did you teach that?"

"Fifteen years," she replied, shaking her head. "I can't believe it was that long."

"So why the change to middle school?" He stopped abruptly. "I'm sorry—you were trying to get out of here and I just start bombarding you with questions."

"It's okay," she answered, realizing she was enjoying the conversation. "I felt like it was time to stretch myself and try something new. Plus," she added, "I'm eager to see if I can keep the girls interested in math past elementary school. Too many of them abandon it once they become teenagers." She shrugged. "It's not exactly cool to like math."

Terrence grinned. "You seem pretty cool to me."

Sara felt her cheeks grow hot. *Is this guy really flirting with me?* "Well, that's debatable, but thanks."

"I'm heading out, too," he said, nodding toward the front of the school. They walked together to the parking lot and Terrence said, "Have a nice evening, Sara. See you in the morning."

She found herself looking forward to it.

"So how was your second day?" asked Lauren. She flopped onto Sara's bed where her friend lay reading. Before Sara could answer, Lauren picked up a pillow and smacked her friend's leg. "Are you ever gonna get rid of this godawful pink?"

Sara shook her head. "Nope. It's my favorite color and it has the added benefit of annoying you."

Lauren laughed, then lay her head on the offending pillow, an expectant grin on her face. "So, are you still happy you switched to the big kids?"

"I am," she answered. "It's nice to be teaching just one subject, especially something I love."

Lauren furrowed her brows and propped herself up on one elbow. "Something's up. You look like you're holding back."

Sara put down her book and sighed. "Well, there may actually be kind of a hot guy who teaches Language Arts across the hall from me." She smiled at the memory. "And he thinks I'm beautiful."

Lauren burst out laughing. "That was fast."

Sara sat up, grinning. "I think it might be a really great year."

6

The next afternoon, Sara prepared to leave her classroom, very ready to get home and relax. It had been her first challenging day teaching, with three students strolling into class late for third period, then nearly taunting her to discipline them.

"What's the big deal, Miss Masterson?" asked one. "It's not like I'm gonna be a math teacher or something." His friends smirked and several other students chuckled, clearly enjoying her discomfort.

Sara schooled her features and at last she responded. "You're right," she said. "Certainly not with that attitude. But even if you decide to spend your life flipping burgers, you'll need skills like, oh, I don't know—time management? Respect for coworkers?" She filled out the tardy slips as she talked, keeping her voice even while her hand shook. "Corinne?" She motioned to a girl in the front row. "Would you mind running these up to the office for me? Thanks so much." As the girl left, Sara stood at the front of the class and smiled. "Not to say there's anything wrong with flipping burgers. I hear managers at fast food restaurants can make a lot of money." She waited a heartbeat before continuing. "But even they need to understand math."

After lunch, her fifth period class was likewise disrupted by two students texting in the back row. At first, she was inclined to ignore them, but when they became unruly, whispering and showing their screens to each other, she told them to stop.

"Miss Masterson," said one haughty eighth grader, "I'm a straight A student. I don't see how checking my phone is gonna make me bomb this class." She tossed back her hair and tapped her pencil on her desk. "I mean, it's not like it's hard or anything."

In the previous fifteen years, Sara had never experienced a five year old being so disrespectful and it took her aback. *And so it begins*, she thought. She was certain whatever she said would affect the entire room—and likely be spread amongst the student body before morning. "It sounds like you're in the wrong class, Danielle. Let me speak to Ms. Dobson about changing your schedule so you can move into my fourth period advanced class." She smiled sweetly at the girl. "I know how straight A students love to be challenged."

The remainder of the week went by and Sara felt she was making progress with all the students. She'd dealt with the sassy Danielle, but Marisa still didn't participate in class and she hadn't turned in her homework. Sara wondered how long she should let it go before talking to the principal. She hated to think of the girl failing her class. She was putting her things away when Terrence walked in.

"So how was your first week?" he asked. "Big change from kindergarten."

Wow, haven't heard that from anyone all week, she thought, then stifled a grin. *But not from anyone this handsome.* "It's different, but it's great." She gathered a stack of papers and slid them into her bag, then locked her desk. "Really looking forward to the weekend."

"Any big plans?" Terrence didn't look like he was in a hurry to leave and she sighed inwardly. *I just want to go home*, she thought. She longed to put on her sweats and curl up on the sofa with a book. Lauren had offered to cook, which meant she'd probably end up making a salad or warming up a mug of soup, but still…it was Friday and that meant a chance to relax.

But Terrence Billings was undeniably worth a few extra minutes before leaving. *And he did call me beautiful,* she remembered.

"Nope. Just hoping to kick back with a good book after a pretty challenging week."

"What are you reading?" he asked.

Not the sexiest opener, but okay….

Sara glanced up as she finished packing her bag and realized that Terrence was genuinely interested. "I'm reading a fantasy series called *The Wheel of Time*," she began.

"Robert Jordan!" he exclaimed. "Which book are you on? Are you at the Brandon Sanderson ones yet? You know Jordan died, right? And his widow had to find a replacement author for the last three books."

Sara was pleasantly surprised at his knowledge and enthusiasm. She'd been disheartened to learn of the author's death, but had read Sanderson's work and deemed him worthy of continuing the Jordan series. "I'm on the twelfth book," she answered. "And I love Brandon Sanderson! He's done a fantastic job picking up right where Jordan left off."

"I know! I'm halfway through book thirteen and I don't want to finish. But now that I know Sanderson is a legit fantasy author, I'm gonna dive into his stuff next."

"You have to read *Elantris* or *Warbreaker*," she said, warming to the topic. "They're brilliant—he's a master of world-building."

Sara and Terrence walked out her door, talking about fantasy literature and tripping over each other's sentences as they debated the merits of their favorite authors. She felt her spirits lift. While she'd loved it, the week had drained her and she now found herself grateful for the unexpected and animated conversation. Before she knew it, they were in the parking lot and standing next to her car.

"Well, this is me," she said, opening the back door to toss in her bag. "It's nice to meet another fantasy buff."

He looked down, then back at her with a shy smile. "Any chance you'd like to get together this weekend?"

Her eyebrows shot up in surprise. "Oh. Wow." *Didn't see that coming.*

He looked away, abashed. "It's okay—I just thought maybe...."

"No, I'd...I'd like that," she replied, her voice tentative. *I really would like that*, she thought in surprise. "That sounds nice," she finished, her voice growing stronger.

He took a deep breath, clearly relieved. "How about brunch tomorrow?" he asked. "Then maybe a drive to the beach?"

She realized it was just what she needed. A nice man and a nice outing. Between Natalie and the new job, she'd been keyed up all week long.

"Yes," she answered. "That would be lovely."

"So where are you guys going?" asked Lauren the next morning.

"Dancing Avocado Kitchen," replied Sara. "I can get veggie stuff and he can eat meat."

"Ooh, I like him already," joked her friend. "I mean, how do you get any hotter than a guy who loves dragons *and* bacon?"

"You know, you can be so narrow minded," scolded Sara, a mock frown on her face. "The fantasy books we read don't have dragons—"

"Oh, you mean *that* kind of fantasy...."

Sara swatted her friend with a towel before stuffing it into her beach bag. Her enthusiasm for the date had dimmed a bit. It had been months since she'd gone out with anyone, and she was a bit leery of a date with a colleague—*Especially one right across the hall from me, no matter how gorgeous he is.*

"What if we don't get on?" she asked. "What if he eats with his mouth open or has some gross naked woman tattoo on his chest? How am I supposed to work with someone like that?"

Lauren stared at her. "Why do you go straight for the negative? What if he uses the right fork and has a six pack like Wolverine? How are you gonna work with someone like that? You'll never be able to concentrate knowing he's right across the hall." She laughed, shaking her head in disbelief. "What does Azalea always say? *Don't be daft.*"

Sara knew her friend was right. Terrence seemed like a nice guy and this was just brunch, not a marriage proposal. She slipped a cotton sundress over her swimsuit and looked in the mirror. Never one for heavy makeup, she opted for a tinted sunscreen, some mascara, and a rosy lip gloss. She wore her sun-kissed hair in a loose braid that fell over her shoulder, her blue eyes bright.

"You're the prettiest nerd I know," said Lauren, hugging her at the door. "Smartest girl in the room *and* a Florida beauty." She stood back and looked at her friend. "Now please go and have some fun. You've been off for months and it's getting pretty damned annoying to watch you be so sad all the time."

It was true. Since she'd received the first letter from Natalie, she'd been variously confused, sad, worried, and excited. It was time to have some fun. She blew Lauren a kiss and headed for her car.

"So you're vegan?" asked Terrence as they perused the menu. "I think my best friend is, too—but he eats fish, so maybe that's something else?"

"Pescatarian," responded Sara. "I've thought about that, too. It's hard not to eat seafood living at the beach."

"Yeah, my buddy lives on the other coast. He's out in California teaching high school and he gave up meat a few years ago. What made you decide to try it?"

"It won't shock you to know I read a book about it." Sara grinned. The waitress came and took their order, and the two teachers returned to their conversation. "Anyway, the health argument was compelling enough for me to give it try." She sipped her water and asked, "So how long have you been teaching?"

"It's been twelve years," he replied. "Middle school language arts the whole time. But I'm really interested to hear about kindergarten. I love my students, but I'm thinking about moving into elementary school next year."

"Elementary school is really different," she began.

"I know!" Terrence broke in. "I have a niece and a nephew that age and they are nothing like our students." He stopped, chagrined. "Oh, crap…I just totally cut you off. I'm sorry."

Feigning shock, she said, "What? A man who interrupts and then apologizes?" She leaned forward and adopted a David

Attenborough whisper: "Here we are in the wild, following this extremely rare and endangered species, the well-mannered and considerate human male…."

The two laughed as their food arrived, and Sara marveled at how comfortable she felt with him. *We're only an hour into the first date*, she cautioned herself. But she couldn't help it. It was more than Terrence's good looks.

I like this guy.

Sara set her beach bag down on the sand and took a deep breath. She hadn't been sure if Terrence intended to stop at the beach or just go for a drive when he'd asked her out, but she wore a swimsuit under her clothes just in case. She was proud of the work she'd done on her always curvy body—she'd never be lean like Lauren or Azalea, but she was pleased with the results of her yearlong experiment with new eating habits. Her mother had always pushed her to be thin but now she concentrated on being healthy. She thought back to the time after Natalie was born. She gained weight with her pregnancy—a fact her mother never let her forget.

"Do you really need another serving?" Cecilia Masterson had asked her sixteen-year-old daughter just months after the birth. "Don't get used to that extra weight, dear." Sara set down her fork and looked at her mother with tears on her lashes. "And stop blubbering any time someone corrects you. You are excused from the table." Her mother turned to her father, who refused to look at his daughter. Sara took her dish to the sink where she scooped the offending second helping into the trash, then rinsed her plate and put it into the dishwasher. She walked in silence to her room to practice not crying.

I'm not sixteen anymore, she reminded herself.

She slipped out of her sundress and resolved to put her mother out of her mind. She glanced at Terrence, who was taking off his shirt. *Oh, Lauren,* she thought with a grin, *you're missing out.*

He spread out a towel and turned to her. "Wow," he said, his smile wide and appreciative. "Um…nice swimsuit."

She laughed and spread out her own towel, lying on her stomach and looking up at him. "Thanks. Do you get to the beach a lot?"

"I bring my niece and nephew down here every couple of weeks. Gives my sister a break—she and my brother-in-law go do something alone." He flopped down on the sand next to her, a puff of grains hitting her face. "Oh, Sara! I'm sorry...." He reached over to wipe the sand off her nose.

"It's okay," she laughed. "We're at the beach. I didn't expect to be sand-free." She was acutely aware of his gaze and his fingers that lingered on her cheek. He dropped his hand, looking away and resettling himself on his towel. *He's as nervous as I am*, she realized. "So you bring the kids here?"

"Yeah, they love the beach as much as I do. Mackenzie is five and Oliver is six. We build sand castles and run in the waves and I just get to be the goofy uncle." He quirked a smile. "It's almost as good as being a dad for the day."

The words were out of her mouth before she could stop them. "And is that something you want? To be a dad?" *It's only the first date—are you crazy?*

"Oh, yeah," he said, a wistful look on his face. "I'd have a dozen if I could. But I guess I'm a little old for that." He brushed another grain of sand from her cheek. "I'd settle for two or three."

"He's really nice," said Sara that evening. "I had a nice time."

"*Nice?*" groused Lauren. "So much for brunch and a drive to the beach. That's a two hour date. You've been gone for hours! " She flopped down on the bed. "Tell me *everything*. Does he have Wolverine abs?"

Sara laughed. "Okay, yeah," she replied. "He has Wolverine abs. And no weird tattoos. And he used the right fork. And he's super smart."

Lauren flipped over onto her back. "So what did you talk about?" A sassy grin covered her face. "I mean, when you weren't fantasizing about his abs."

Sara rolled her eyes, but blushed. "Well, we talked about books we've read and authors we follow."

Her friend groaned. "So not sexy. What else?"

"We talked about school and teaching. He actually had a lot of questions about me teaching kindergarten. He has a niece and a nephew around that age and he loves them." She stopped, a tentative smile on her face. "He wants kids of his own."

"Hmm. Still not sexy." Lauren pulled on Sara's braid. "So will you see him again?"

"Well, yeah. Like Monday morning."

"Very funny, goofball. You know what I mean."

"I hope so." Sara smiled at her friend. "He's really nice."

"Nice? Not sexy?" Lauren buried her face in her hands. "What am I gonna do with you?"

7

Terrence was waiting outside Sara's door when she arrived on Monday morning. His smile was contagious, and her step quickened as she approached. "Good morning," he called when she was halfway down the hall. "Happy Monday!"

"You're awfully perky for a Monday," she said, smiling. "What's got you so excited?"

He raised his eyebrows and cocked his head, and Sara noticed a slight flush on his tanned cheeks.

Is he that shy? she wondered. *That's adorable.*

"I guess I'm just happy to see you again," he confessed. "Did you have a nice day yesterday?"

Sara thought briefly about how flirtatious she should be. *It was only one date*, she cautioned herself. But his reticence somehow bolstered her confidence. "Not as nice as Saturday," she answered with a coy grin.

His face lit up. "I had a great time Saturday. I'd—would you—" He fumbled a bit but then continued. "I'd like to see you again."

She struggled to keep from laughing, not wanting to embarrass him. *How is someone this gorgeous so awkward?* she wondered. "I'd really like that." She watched as his shoulders relaxed and he took a step forward.

"That's great, Sara. How's this weekend?"

She agreed and then looked at her watch. "Oh, geez—we need to get in our classrooms," she said. "Bell's gonna ring in a minute."

Terrence nodded, then walked back to his door. She was just about to turn when he caught her eye and winked.

So cute.

The morning passed quickly and Sara didn't have much time to think about Terrence and their next date. Before she knew it, it was fourth period. As she took attendance for the eighth grade algebra class, she had one student collect the homework. Marisa sat at the back of the classroom, seeming to fold in on herself in the chair, and Sara noticed that she didn't turn in anything. Sara tried to catch her eye, but Marisa steadfastly looked away.

The girl had dark hair and eyes, and was dressed in jeans and a white t-shirt, her hair pulled back into a loose ponytail. Even from the front of the classroom Sara could see the girl's sorrow.

I need to talk to Jenna. Something's wrong.

At the end of class, she moved to the back of the room as Marisa put her book into her backpack.

"Hello, Marisa," she said softly. "Could you stay a minute?" Now that they were close, Sara could see the dark circles under the girl's eyes. She was loathe to say more, not knowing how skittish the girl might be.

Marisa stood and lifted her backpack. "Sure."

Sara waited until the other students had left. "So, I noticed you haven't turned in any of the homework yet. This is the advanced class, so I have to assume you're good at math or you wouldn't be here. If you're struggling with any of the lessons, I'm happy to help. I just don't want you to get behind."

The girl shoved her hands into her pockets and looked away. "Nah. I'm fine. I'll catch up this week." She glanced at Sara, a flicker of annoyance on her face. "It's not hard."

Startled at the teen's reaction, Sara stepped back. "Great. I'll look forward to seeing your work." She began walking back to her desk, then turned. "I'll make you a deal: If you get all caught up this week, I won't deduct any points for late work."

Marisa nodded blankly and stepped past Sara as she headed for the door. "Yeah."

Sara was grateful for the lunch break and she left her classroom, planning to walk around the campus while she drank a protein shake. Instead, she ran into Terrence.

"Hey, Sara," he called as he walked across the hall. "How's week two shaping up?"

She dismissed her need for fresh air and solitude and smiled. "Great. How's your week going?"

"It's good so far. This is the first week I really teach—I always spend the first week just getting these kids to remember they're back in school. We started reading *Fahrenheit 451* on Thursday, so I'm trying to get them excited about the book."

Sara grinned at his enthusiasm. It was wonderful to meet someone who shared her love of reading. She'd dated a few men over the years, but hadn't found anyone with her same literary passion. "Ten bucks says a lot of them saw the movie," she cautioned. "You'll need to convince them to actually read Bradbury instead of assuming they know and understand the point of the novel. They won't remember Guy Montag but they sure know Michael B. Jordan."

Terrence grinned. "Oh, Miss Math Goddess, are you telling me how to teach my class?"

Sara colored, embarrassed. "I'm so sorry! That was incredibly presumptuous."

He was laughing as she spoke, then dropped his voice to copy her David Attenborough imitation. "And here we are in the wilds of Daytona Beach, sneaking up on that ever so hard to find creature, the human female who apologizes for—"

Her laugh rang out and she swatted his shoulder. "Okay, okay. I'm sure you'll find a way to persuade these kids to read the book and be inspired."

"Oh, you'll be astonished at how persuasive and inspiring I can be, Sara," he said, his eyes twinkling.

She was surprised to find she was eager to learn.

By the end of September, life had settled into a smooth rhythm. Sara loved her new job—even the students who didn't like math enjoyed her classes, as she scoured the internet for creative ways to engage teens. "I want them to see the relevance," she told Terrence one Saturday afternoon as they bobbed in the shallow surf at their favorite beach. The Florida autumn was gorgeous, the water still warm as it caressed their skin. "When they can see how math affects so much in life, I hope they'll appreciate it. It may not become fun for all of them, but maybe they won't dread it."

Terrence gazed long at her until she became uncomfortable. "What? Do you disagree?"

He laughed quietly and leaned over to kiss her. "I'm just so impressed with you. It's a beautiful day, you're at the beach with your hot man, and all you're thinking about is how to be a better teacher."

Sara blushed and took his hand. They'd been dating for six weeks but it was the first time he'd referred to himself as hers. "So is that what you are?" she asked quietly. "My man?"

He gently pushed a stray hair from her brow. "I'm kind of offended that you omitted the 'hot' before 'man,' but yeah…I hope so." His eyes grew soft as his continued. "I've never met anyone like you, Sara. You're smart and beautiful and compassionate. I hope it doesn't scare you off, but I'm falling for you."

Sara's heart began to pound. *I'm falling for you, too*, she thought. "So can I ask you a serious question?"

"You *may*," he answered with a grin.

She rolled her eyes. "Okay, Grammar King." She steadied herself, suddenly nervous. "Does this mean you aren't seeing anyone else?"

Terrence's surprise caught her off guard. "Are you serious? I haven't had a thought for anyone else since I met you, Sara." He grimaced. "Clearly I don't play the romantic lead character very well." He paused. "And you? Are you seeing anyone else?"

She shook her head. "You're the first person I've dated in a year. And the truth is," she continued softly, "I don't want to date anyone else either."

As they held hands and walked back to their spot on the beach, Sara again admired his body—the sunlight making the water drops on his tanned muscles sparkle. He glanced at her, a knowing smile on his face. "Are you checking out your guy?"

She blushed and batted her head against his shoulder. "Maybe," she replied. "He is pretty hot."

"That's okay," he said, pulling her in for a kiss. "I check you out constantly." His voice grew quieter. "I've had enough beach for the day."

She smiled at their pet phrase for heading to his apartment—and his bed. "Me, too."

His grin was electric and she squeezed his hand, smiling back at him.

They were quiet as they packed up and drove to Terrence's place. Sara sneaked quick glances at him, her stomach fluttering at the thought of making love with this wonderful man. It had been three weeks already but every time felt new. She looked out the window and smiled. Before she knew it, they were at his front door.

When they entered, she smiled and asked, "*May* I use your shower first? Get all this sand off me?"

He lightly stroked her cheek. "How about we do it together?" he asked.

"I'd like that."

Terrence took her hand and led her to his bedroom. The bed was covered with a dark green comforter and pillows, a large photograph of the ocean hanging over the headboard. One wall was lined with bookshelves, but Sara didn't take the time to look over the titles. He reached for her and pulled her close. "I've been wanting this all day," he murmured.

She leaned back to better see his face. Reaching up, she touched his jaw, then ran her thumb across his lips. "All day?" she asked with a playful tone.

"Since I woke up," he answered as he began to undo her long braid. "I dream about you almost every night. There's something incredibly special about you, Sara." He buried his face in her hair, then leaned back to look at her.

Sara sighed as he slipped off her sundress, sliding the straps off her shoulders. She stood in the sunlight in her bikini and he gazed at her. "You are so beautiful," he murmured as he reached behind her to untie her top. It fell to the floor and he leaned forward, his hands sliding down her shoulders to cup her breasts. "Oh, Sara," he whispered, his lips against her collarbone. He untied the bottoms and she shivered as they slid down her thighs. She began to slide her arms around him, but he stepped back. "I just want to look at you."

Suddenly shy, she bit her lip. "And I want to look at you," she answered.

He nodded, then pulled his t-shirt over his head. His muscles rippled as he lifted his arms and tossed his shirt to the floor. He quickly took off his board shorts and the two stood, mesmerized.

He broke the spell by sweeping her up and carrying her to the shower.

Their lovemaking had been feverish, passionate, and urgent as they barely made it out of the shower, but now they lay quietly, Sara's head resting on Terrence's shoulder, his arm around her. She stroked his chest and marveled at how comfortable she felt. It was as if this spot were made for her, their bodies molding perfectly. She had nearly fallen asleep when she heard Terrence opening his nightstand drawer and then the crinkle of another package. She smiled at his tentative kiss.

"Are you awake?"

She reached over to help him slide on the condom, then pulled him to her. "Oh, yes…I'm awake," she whispered as they once again melded, this time slowly, their coupling slow and tender as they explored each other's bodies.

"I—I can't—" Terrence breathed heavily into her hair.

"It's okay," she responded, gripping him tightly. "Don't wait."

She wrapped her legs around his hips, pulling him into her as he groaned her name.

"Sara—Sara—"

I am completely falling for you, she thought.

Terrence lay propped up on one arm, his other hand stroking Sara's hair as he gazed at her.

"I need to tell you something," he began, his voice husky.

She nodded, unsure how to respond.

"I know we haven't been together very long." His smile was tender. "But Sara, I can't stop thinking about you. Is it crazy to think that this could be a forever thing?"

A forever thing. Her heart leapt.

"I don't think it's crazy." Sara's voice was soft.

"Sara." He looked long at her before taking a deep breath. "I love you. I'm sure of it. I'm more sure of it than anything." He stroked her cheek then whispered again, "I love you."

Sara put her arms around him and pulled him close. "I love you, too, Terrence."

They held hands as Terrence drove her home. "I wish you'd have stayed," he murmured as he walked her to the door.

"I didn't bring anything with me," she replied.

"I have a spare toothbrush." He grinned, pulling her close.

"And I have a ton of work to do tomorrow—"

He sighed. "I know. I do, too. All those fascinating *Fahrenheit 451* papers to grade." He grimaced. "Can't wait for that."

Sara laughed and kissed him. "Thank you for a wonderful day, Terrence."

"I love you so much. I'm not going to sleep at all tonight, my beautiful math goddess." He kissed her gently and walked back to the car.

Nor I, she thought, as she waved goodbye.

The next morning, she was up early and sitting at the kitchen table with her laptop and a pile of math tests.

Good morning! Terrence's text appeared on her phone. *Did you sleep well?*

Good morning! she responded. *Not much, but I was awake for a good reason.*

I couldn't stop thinking about you.

Same. I'm having a hard time concentrating on quadratic equations =)

I'm just about to start grading papers. I hope you have a great day.

You too!

She sipped her coffee and was startled by Lauren's cough.

"Well, well, well," began her friend with mock severity. "Somebody didn't get home until the wee hours this morning."

Sara laughed. "Sorry, *Mom*…I should have called."

Lauren pulled out a chair and plopped down. "Tell me. *Everything.*"

"Uh, no. Not everything."

They laughed and Lauren sat back and looked fondly at her dearest friend. "You look happy."

"I am." Sara gazed out the window, remembering Terrence's declaration of love. "I'm so happy. He's really great. So sweet, so attentive, so smart."

"So hot?"

"Well, yeah, there's that." She looked back at Lauren, her face soft. "I know it doesn't sound super sexy or exciting, but he's just so…so kind. He's romantic and sweet." She trailed off. "He told me he loves me."

Lauren's eyes widened. "Damn. And you? How do you feel about him?"

Sara smiled, her eyes bright. "I think I've fallen in love with a middle school language arts teacher," she laughed. She shook her head in wonderment. "I love him."

Lauren reached for Sara's hand and squeezed. "I'm happy for you. It's about time for something wonderful to happen in your life. You deserve to be happy and I'm thrilled." She sat back grinning. "I still wanna hear details."

8

The semester flew by and before Sara knew it, the holidays were upon them. Her classes progressed well and she found she loved teaching middle schoolers. Marisa still lagged behind, seeming unwilling to participate in class. When she did engage, the girl clearly excelled in math and Sara wondered at her student's inconsistent behavior.

She straightened her desk, getting ready to leave for the Thanksgiving holiday, when Marisa walked into her classroom.

"Miss Masterson? Do you have a minute?" The girl's tentative voice signaled concern.

Sara was eager to leave; Terrence had invited her to his parents' home for Thanksgiving and they were heading for Ft. Lauderdale that afternoon. *But this is why I became a teacher*, she thought, and set down her bag. "Sure, Marisa. What's up?"

The teen's lip quivered as she fought tears. "I'm sorry—you probably want to get out of here and start your Thanksgiving…."

"I'm sure you do, too. What's bothering you?" Sara walked around her desk and pointed to the front row. "Here. Let's sit."

Marisa took a seat and breathed heavily. "I don't really want to go home." Her eyes brimmed with tears. "It's the first Thanksgiving without my mom."

Without her mom?

Sara's eyes widened. "Oh, Marisa—I'm so sorry." She longed to take the girl in her arms. "I had no idea."

Marisa wiped her eyes and spoke quietly. "Nobody really does. I told my dad not to tell my teachers anything. He wanted to tell everyone at the beginning of the year so they'd watch out for me. Make sure I was okay or whatever."

"You don't seem okay." Sara's voice was gentle. *How could you be?* "How can I help?"

"I dunno," confessed the girl. "I wasn't really thinking about anything you could do. I just don't want to go home. My dad's gonna pretend like everything is fine and my grandparents will be cringe AF and no one will say a word about my mom." Her words spilled out in a rush.

Sara took a moment to respond, schooling her features not to react to the teen's language. *I need to get this right*, she thought. "I think everyone grieves in their own way," she began. "Maybe it's too painful for them to talk about her yet. Can you find a way to remember her privately? Have your own little Thanksgiving celebration just the two of you?"

"Why should I have to?" The teen grew angry. "Why can't they do something special for *me*?"

Sara didn't know what to say, but knew she couldn't miss this moment to be there for her student. "I'm so sorry, Marisa. You're right—no kid should ever have to go through this." She thought a moment. Terrence would be ready to leave any minute. But could she leave Marisa without trying to help?

Marisa's face was tight with grief. "Anyway—I just needed a minute before I go home." She sat back, shaking her head. "I don't want any drama. I just want a break."

Sara sat quietly, hoping her presence alone would provide some comfort. At last she said, "I'm sorry, Marisa. I really am. You can stay as long as you need to."

The teen slumped in her seat, looking down at her hands. When she looked up, her eyes were glassy with tears. "Thanks, Miss Masterson." She rose, shouldered her backpack, and left the classroom without another word.

Sara was still sitting, wondering what she could have done differently when Terrence walked in.

"Almost ready?" he asked.

She stood and walked to her desk to put the last book in her bag. "All set," she said, her tone solemn.

Terrence frowned and came around her desk. "Is everything all right? You didn't change your mind, did you?"

"No, no—I'm sorry. I'm a little distracted." She reached for him and he wrapped her in a hug. "Marisa Segovia was just here. Did you know she lost her mother?"

He nodded as he squeezed her. "Yeah. I heard the other day. I guess she died in a car accident this summer. Poor kid."

"She said she didn't want to go home because no one wants to talk about her mom." She looked up at Terrence. "I don't want to interfere, but should someone talk to her dad? Let him know what she's feeling? She aces tests but she's still behind with homework and she barely engages in class." She rested her cheek against his chest. "Maybe he's hurting so much he doesn't see her pain."

"I doubt it. He's a great dad. I met him last year when Marisa was in my seventh grade class. He and her mom were super engaged parents." He kissed the top of Sara's head. "I like the guy."

"Anyway, maybe Stacy should reach out to him." Sara had met the kindly guidance counselor the week before school started. It would make sense for her to help the family. She pushed away and finished packing her bag. "I hope Marisa is okay this weekend," she said, and then she smiled. "I'm very ready for a nice holiday with you, but I'm still a bit nervous to meet your entire family." For several years she celebrated Thanksgiving weekend in Miami, but she knew the Ochoa clan—especially Lauren's grandmother, *Abuela* Lupe—would be thrilled that she "finally had a *novio!*" and wouldn't join them this year. Instead, she and Terrence would drive south where she'd meet not only his parents, but his youngest sister Savannah and her husband DJ who lived nearby. *If they're anything like the ones up here*, she thought, *they'll be wonderful.* She already met his sister Talia and brother-in-law Darren on a couple of occasions and they got on like old friends. The previous weekend she and Terrence took his niece and nephew Mackenzie and Oliver to the beach and she thoroughly enjoyed the day.

"Don't worry," he told her. "They're gonna adore you." He looked as if he wanted to say more, but held back. He nodded toward the door and the two walked to the parking lot and got into their cars. "See you at your place," he called out the window.

After dropping her car off at her house and saying goodbye to Lauren, Sara put her bag into Terrence's car and they set off for the three and a half hour drive. The two chatted companionably for a few minutes but then grew quiet. She sensed there was something he wanted to say so she waited, hoping everything was all right. *It's only been a few months,* she worried. *But he wouldn't be taking me to meet his parents if he were unhappy with our relationship.* She willed herself to wait until he was ready.

At last he spoke. "I need to tell you something before we get to my parents' house," he said. "It's no big deal, but I want you to know."

She nodded. "Okay."

"I've never brought anyone home for a holiday before."

That's it? The big reveal? Sara stifled a laugh. "Seriously?"

"It's kind of a big deal that I'm bringing you and I guess I want to warn you that Savannah especially will be super annoying about it."

Sara's heart caught in her throat. His nervousness was palpable and she took his hand and kissed it. "Thank you," she murmured. "I'm flattered and honored and—"

"Are you kidding?" he interjected. "I'm taking the most wonderful woman I've ever known to meet my family for Thanksgiving." He glanced at her and smiled. "I know what I'm thankful for this year."

Is this guy for real? She marveled at her good fortune and squeezed his hand. "So tell me more about your family," she prompted.

"Well, they're pretty amazing," he began. "I know that sounds lame, but it's true. My parents have been married for forty years and still act like newlyweds." He chuckled. "It's a little bit disgusting, actually. Be prepared for them hugging and kissing and my dad swooping her up in his arms in the kitchen. And my sisters are incredibly annoying, especially Savannah, but I love them to pieces."

"I already like Talia," said Sara. "She and Darren are a lot of fun, and the kids are precious."

"You'll like Savannah and DJ," he replied. "I tease about her a lot 'cause she's the spoiled baby of the family, but I love her. And her husband is a terrific guy—especially putting up with her."

Sara looked out the window, keenly aware of how different her family was. There had never been any spoiling in her home. "Do they want kids, too?"

"Oh, yeah—they've only been married a couple of years, but I wouldn't be surprised if they start soon." He glanced at Sara and grinned. "Just gotta hope they're more like their dad than their mom."

"It sounds like family means everything to you guys."

He looked at her with a warm smile. "It does. We've been close our entire lives and have stayed that way even as adults. I know how fortunate I am—lots of families don't love each other like that." He frowned. "You don't talk much about your family. Not at all, really. What are they like?"

Sara looked away. How to describe the Mastersons? A wealthy, successful couple, they had provided well for her: a beautiful home, a great education.

But no love.

She gazed out her window at the green landscape lining the highway. "Nothing like your family," she said, her voice soft and hesitant. "I'm an only child and I'm pretty sure they didn't even want one. 'Love' wasn't a word we used in our home."

His smile was tender as he stroked her hand. "How could anyone not love you?" He lifted her hand to his lips and kissed her softly. "It's impossible."

If only that were true. "Well, they seemed to have found a way," she said ruefully. "I never wanted for anything material— they made sure of that. They didn't want me to get my master's in education, but they still paid for it. When I got out of school and all my friends had debt, I was free and clear." She shook her head. "I suppose that's something."

Terrence glanced at her, his face thoughtful. "My parents paid for most of my tuition, too. I had a part-time job in the library during undergrad and then worked as a teacher's aide during grad school. The girls did the same thing, but neither of them went back after they got their bachelor's degrees. They were pretty eager to get to work."

"Does Talia have a job or does she stay home with the kids?"

"She stayed home until they went to kindergarten," he answered. "Now she's working part-time doing the books for Savannah's design business." He laughed. "How they manage to work together is beyond me. One second they're the best of friends and the next one they're arguing over every detail. Savannah has no concept of money and Talia is a CPA. It's kinda funny, actually."

Sara imagined what it would be like to have sisters and brothers to love and to argue with. Over the years, she had built a sisterhood of sorts with Lauren, Azalea, and Susana, but nothing like what the Billings siblings had. "It sounds kinda wonderful," she said, her voice quiet.

9

"Sara!" boomed Donovan, enveloping her in a hug. Terrence's father was a large man, but his personality exceeded even his physical size. "It's so great to meet you."

"Let the poor girl in the door," chided Alicia. "She's barely set foot on the porch!" The diminutive woman reached past her husband and took Sara's hand. "Come in, come in. There's hot cider on the stove and something stronger if you'd like." She pushed her hip against her husband and looked sideways at him with a fond smile. "Move aside, big boy," she said as she and Sara walked into the house.

Donovan leaned down to kiss his wife's cheek. "Get on with you, woman. I've a son to hug," he teased and then reached for Terrence.

"It's good to see you, Dad." The two men embraced in the doorway, but Alicia bustled Sara through the entry and into the living area. The great room was large, featuring a kitchen, dining room, and family room, and the spicy smell of cider wafted across open space.

"Oh, that smells fantastic," said Sara. "Thank you so much for having me. I love the holidays and spiced cider is one of my favorite things."

Terrence's mother nodded. "Mine, too. My mother made it every year and it's always been a part of our celebration. We do love our family traditions." She looked up and smiled as her husband and son entered. "And now might you have a moment for your poor old mother?" she teased.

Terrence crossed the room quickly and swept her up in a hug, spinning her around and kissing her cheek. "It's good to see you, Mom," he said. "Happy Thanksgiving." He set her down and she reached for his arm to steady herself after the spin. He grinned and reached out to Sara, his eyes alight. "And I brought someone very, very special."

Sara took in the scene with alternating emotions. Her smile wavered and she felt suddenly awkward, tugging at her long braid and looking from mother to son, unsure how to respond.

Alicia swatted at him, moving to Sara's side and then mock glaring at her son. "You've only just arrived and you're already as bad as your father. Don't embarrass the girl—go get settled and then come back down for some cider and snacks." She surprised Sara with a quick side hug, then patted her back. "The evening before Thanksgiving we just have a bunch of appetizers." She smiled at father and son. "I'll be sure they mind their manners. I promise you, he wasn't raised in a barn."

Sara laughed—in only a few moments, this woman had found a way to put her at ease. She glanced up at Terrence, who gazed at the two women fondly. "Thank you, Alicia," she said.

She followed Terrence up the stairs to a small bedroom. "Your mom is so sweet," she whispered as they entered the room. He set their bags on the bed and pulled her in for a hearty kiss. "I didn't realize I was so nervous," she confessed, pulling slightly away. "But they've made me feel comfortable already." She pressed her cheek to his chest and held him tightly.

The tender moment ended abruptly as a young woman burst into the room. "Big brother!" she shouted as she jumped onto Terrence's back, pulling him away from Sara. He laughed and spun, flinging her onto the bed. She shrieked as she landed, but was soon on her feet again. "What took you so long?" She eyed Sara. "And this must be the *ahmayyyyzing* girlfriend we keep hearing about over and over and over...."

Her brother shot a hand over her mouth, playfully stifling her teasing. "Okay, okay," he said. "That's enough." He pulled his hand away and looked at Sara, shaking his head. "This is Savannah Billings-Walker, perhaps the single most annoying little sister on the planet." He turned to his sister, affection plain on his face. "Sis, this is Sara."

Savannah startled her by hugging her. "You might have noticed," said Terrence's sister, "we're kind of a huggy family. Hope that's not a problem."

Sara shook her head. "No, no. It's…fine. Just a little different from mine," she admitted with a wry look.

"And if you can tolerate this guy," Savannah backhanded her brother on the chest, "then you're gonna be our favorite person."

"Speaking of tolerating, where's DJ?" Terrence winked at Sara. "I don't know how he tolerates this crazy woman."

As if on cue, a tall man poked his head around the corner. "Did I hear my name?" He walked into the room and the two men embraced. "Good to see you, Terrence." He glanced at his wife. "This one has missed you, no matter what she says. And you," he looked at Sara, "must the amazing girlfriend we keep hearing about."

Sara blushed and Savannah burst out laughing. "See? He never shuts up about you. We have these family video calls and it's always 'Sara this, Sara that.'" She giggled, shaking her head. "No pressure, Sara. It's not like we expect you to be perfect or anything."

No chance of that, thought Sara. Then she wondered, *family video calls?*

Donovan's voice called up the stairs. "Get down here and help your mother." Terrence and Savannah turned immediately to the door, with DJ close behind. "And give Sara a moment's peace to settle in," he added.

Terrence reached back for Sara's hand. "I know we can be a little overwhelming," he said, a bit abashed. "But we're really a great group once you get to know us."

She smiled and squeezed his hand. "You're all *ahmayyyyzing*," she teased.

He laughed and kissed her. "Go ahead and take however long you need to get settled. Come down when you're ready." He followed his sister and brother-in-law downstairs.

Sara was grateful for the respite. The Billings family was boisterous, loving, and, she agreed, a little overwhelming. She sat on the bed and looked around Terrence's room. It wasn't like a TV show where the parents never changed a thing after a child left home. It was tastefully decorated in soothing gray and white with navy accents. She hadn't been sure what the sleeping arrangements would be—she and Terrence didn't discuss it before they'd come—but she was thankful they'd be together. No way would they have sex in his parents' house, she thought, but she looked forward to snuggling in his arms at night after family time. She closed her eyes and took a deep breath, letting the hum of the downstairs conversation flow over her. She reached for her phone to text Lauren, knowing her best friend was waiting to hear how the first meeting had gone.

Everything is great, she wrote. *Everyone is super nice.*

And you're not being an awkward dork? Lauren added a hysterically laughing emoji.

Very funny. I'm being my normal self.

Oh, well. It was good while it lasted, I guess, teased Lauren.

You're the worst best friend on the planet. Go say hi to everyone and hug your abuela for me.

I will—go have fun! I miss you but I'm so glad you're there. Love you!

Love you too

She hesitated before going downstairs to text Natalie.

Hi Natalie

She watched the screen, unsure if her daughter would respond. They'd gotten into a comfortable cadence, texting each other a couple of times a week, and Sara didn't want to upset their routine. *When will this get easier?* she wondered.

Hi Sara, came the response. *Happy Thanksgiving!*

Happy Thanksgiving! How are you?

I'm OK. My mom's not feeling so great so I'm trying to do some cooking. Just want it to be as normal as possible.

I'm so sorry, responded Sara. *I can't imagine how difficult this must be for you both.*

The doctor says she's fine but it's just gonna take some time for her to get her strength back

I'm glad to hear that. I wish there were something I could do to make it better.

It's just nice to know you're there

Sara's heart caught in her throat. *I am here, Natalie. However and whenever you want me.*

Thanks, Sara. Gotta go now. I'll write soon.

Sara stared at the screen a long time. She thought about loving families—about Natalie and her parents, about Lauren and all the Ochoas, about Terrence and the extended Billings clan.

She thought about Marisa and her father, now missing one essential piece.

She wondered what her parents were doing. She knew she wouldn't hear from them. *Will it ever stop hurting?*

Before heading downstairs, she took a tissue from her purse and dabbed at her eyes, not wanting anyone to see her tears. Determined to have a happy Thanksgiving, she straightened her shoulders and went to join the festivities. It wasn't her family, but she could pretend.

The room was abuzz with activity, every member of the family seeming to move in choreographed steps from refrigerator to counter to table. The occasional bump was clearly premeditated: Savannah leaning in to catch DJ's hip and then turning her face up for a kiss, then Terrence pushing her aside to make way for his plate of hors d'oeuvres. Sara stood transfixed at the foot of the stairs, watching the family as they bantered and set up for the Thanksgiving eve meal.

At last she ventured into the room. "Can I help?" she offered.

"Don't be silly," chided Alicia. "You're the honored guest!" She beckoned Sara to a chair. "Come, come, sit down. We're ready to—" She stopped abruptly to slap Terrence's hand away from a bowl of olives. "Seriously? Do you want your young lady to think you were raised by wolves?" She shook her head, affection for her son plain on her face.

Terrence grinned and pulled out Sara's chair. *He looks like a little boy when he smiles at his mother*, she thought. She looked around the table and marveled at the easygoing camaraderie. *One day I'll have a family like this*, she thought fiercely.

The evening progressed, with the Billings family's lively conversation filling every moment. The siblings' good-natured ribbing kept them all laughing, and Sara found herself relaxing and enjoying herself. She felt a flicker of guilt knowing that Natalie's holiday was stressful, but resolved to think about her daughter later.

"Do you like to play games?" asked Alicia. Terrence had told Sara about his family's love of after dinner card and board games.

"It can get a bit vicious," he'd warned her. "We're all very competitive." Sara had no experience with family game night, but she'd been willing to try.

"I don't play much," she answered Terrence's mother. "I'll probably be terrible, but I'd love to join you."

Savannah laughed. "Let's play something easy. You've played Monopoly before, haven't you?"

Sara groaned inwardly. There wasn't a game she hated more than Monopoly, but she was determined to fit in. "I have," she answered, smiling.

"Great! You're the guest, so you pick first. Which piece do you want?

Sara looked over the pieces as Savannah and Terrence set up the board. He looked up at her and winked, a gentle encouragement. The game was old, with the original silver metal pieces. She wondered which were their favorites and hesitated before choosing the race car.

"Ha!" barked Savannah, backhanding her brother's shoulder. "She picked your favorite."

Terrence scowled at her before selecting the Scotty dog. "Guess I'll just have to take yours," he joked.

"Brat," mumbled Savannah as she reached for the racehorse.

"Good grief," sighed their mother. "You'd think you two were still children." She scooped up the thimble while Donovan took the battleship, and DJ the top hat. "Are we all happy now?"

The family nodded, and the game commenced.

Two hours later, Sara sat back, flushed and smiling. She'd never won a Monopoly game in her life, and tonight was no different. Yet here she sat with a stack of properties and thousands of play dollars. She hadn't gone bankrupt, and that counted for a win in her mind. "Well done, Sara," said Donovan, grinning at his children. "I haven't beat them in ages. You actually got them to stop bickering and work together for a change."

Savannah grimaced, then leaned over to hug her brother. "Don't get used to it, big brother. You're still my nemesis in every game."

Terrence tousled her hair, eliciting a push from Savannah while DJ laughed. "Didn't think that would last long," he muttered.

The siblings put the game away as Alicia brought out plates for dessert. Just then, the front door opened and Talia, Darren, and their children streamed in. Sara stood back as the family all swarmed together, hugging and chattering all at once. While Donovan scooped up both his grandchildren, Talia looked over their heads to smile at Sara. "It's so nice to see you again," she shouted over the din.

Sara smiled. "It's great to see you, too!" she called, marveling at the noise such a small gathering could create.

Oliver and Mackenzie squirmed out of their grandfather's arms and ran to their grandmother. Their little voices trilled as they wrapped their arms around her and hugged. "Happy Thanksgiving, Nana!" they squealed. Alicia bent to nuzzle the two of them and then introduced them to Sara. "This is Sara, Uncle Terrence's girlfriend."

The children looked at her and smiled. "We already know her," said Oliver proudly. "She went to the beach with us and Uncle Terrence."

"Happy Thanksgiving," she said. "It's nice to see you again."

"Happy Thanksgiving," they replied in chorus and then Mackenzie ran over and threw her little arms around Sara. She looked up and said, "You're pretty."

Terrence put his arm around Sara and squeezed, then looked down at his five-year-old niece. "Yes, she is pretty." Then he scooped up Mackenzie and held her upside down. "Pretty funny, just like you!" The little girl screeched and giggled in her uncle's grasp.

The family laughed and Talia shook her head. "Just don't drop her."

Terrence released his grip on the child's ankles and Sara gasped—just as he caught the little one in his arms and spun her around. Everyone laughed at Sara's horrified look, and she realized this was a familiar game. She smiled, listening to Oliver's "My turn, my turn!"

I could get used to this, she realized.

10

It was 1:00 in the morning before the adults called it a night.

"Your family is wonderful," said Sara, sliding in to bed. Terrence wrapped her in his arms and she snuggled against his chest. "I'm having a great time."

"Well, everyone likes you—except Savannah," he replied. He kissed the top of her head as she stiffened and looked up in alarm. "Relax," he said, smiling. "I think she wants to adopt you."

Sara closed her eyes. *Calm down*, she urged herself. *He's joking. It's all right.* "I like her a lot. She kinda reminds me of Lauren, she's so sassy and funny. And it's nice to see how DJ adores her."

"Mmhmm," mumbled Terrence. "I love them all, but they wear me out." He kissed her lightly and within moments was breathing deeply and rhythmically.

She rolled to her side, careful not to wake him. She was far from sleep, still buoyed by the warmth and love the family displayed and the way they'd accepted her into their holiday festivities. *Not just accepted*, she thought. *They welcomed me.* She was still surprised that Terrence had never brought anyone home for a holiday before.

But then, she hadn't either.

She looked at the sleeping man beside her, his face calm and handsome. One dark curl had slipped across his forehead, and she reached up to gently slide it into place. They'd been together for just over three months, but it seemed like forever. She felt cherished in a way she'd never experienced. She realized she never wanted this to end.

Omigod, she thought. *I really do love him.*

Sleep evaded her for a long time as she pondered her emotions. She'd never been in love before, not as an adult. She rolled to her other side and Terrence followed, his arm draping across her waist as he snored lightly. Sara's heart swelled as she realized there was nowhere else in the world she'd rather be than curled up here, safe and warm next to this wonderful man.

The next morning saw the same activity in the kitchen as the Billings family gathered for breakfast. Alicia was up early and directing traffic, with her offspring and their spouses laying out the scones, bacon, and fruit while she scrambled eggs. Sara stood by, wanting to help but unsure how to insert herself into the well-oiled machinery that was the family.

Alicia noticed her and smiled. "Be a love, Sara, and grab the salsa from the fridge. And some ketchup, too." Sara responded quickly, eager to be of help. "And don't get disgusted when you see Donovan put ketchup on his eggs. It's a weird thing his family did and he hasn't broken the habit."

Sara put the condiments on the table, taking care to put the ketchup near Donovan's place. She longed to have her own family history, even one with quirks like ketchup on scrambled eggs. "I'll be right back," she said to Alicia. She went upstairs and took out her phone. There was a text from Lauren, complete with a photo of the entire Ochoa clan.

We miss you, said Lauren's text. *But my abuelita is thrilled you're with Terrence and his family this year.* Sara grinned—her best friend's grandmother had been asking "When are you gonna get married, *mija?*" for years. Lupe Ochoa had given up on Lauren. Her granddaughter had made it clear her career was the most important thing to her, not a husband or children, so Lupe decided Sara's marriage was the next best thing.

I miss you, too, answered Sara. *Say hi to everyone for me and happy Thanksgiving. Having a wonderful time here—T's family is as loving as yours!*

Lauren responded with turkey emoji and a heart, and Sara returned to her messages.

She began to type. *You're on my heart today, Natalie. I hope your day is happy and you have some fun cooking for your family.* She took a deep breath as she decided what to write next. Cautious? Or vulnerable?

She took the plunge.

My own family wasn't a loving one. I'm so glad yours is. I'm thankful for you today and every day.

Seconds ticked by slowly as she awaited a response.

Happy Thanksgiving, Sara. I hope your day is great. I really am thankful you gave me such a good family.

As she gazed at her phone, she was startled by Alicia's voice "Breakfast is ready. Come join us, Sara!"

Mackenzie poked her head into the bedroom. "Boo!" she cried, than laughed. "Nana says come down now." She walked toward Sara, reaching out a small hand. "Will you sit by me?"

Sara glanced once more at her phone and then took the tiny hand. "Of course I will!"

The Thanksgiving breakfast was as boisterous as the evening before, with the added commotion of two young children. Yet even the interruptions felt comfortable and warm rather than harsh or unkind. Sara spoke little, content to watch and enjoy the interactions.

After everyone finished eating and teasing Donovan about his ketchup, the family cleared the table. "Time for either football or a nap," announced their father. "I prefer football."

"Only if I Q," declared Savannah. "And no cheap shots, Terrence."

Her brother laughed. "Then make sure your offensive line doesn't leave you wide open, Sis." He looked at Sara, who gazed back and forth at the siblings.

Talia stepped between them. "It's an annual thing, Sara. Just ignore these two. Savannah insists on being quarterback for her team but then complains when Terrence stops her." She looked at her sister with fondness. "Maybe throw the ball sooner, you big baby."

"Maybe get open sooner, slowpoke," retorted Savannah.

The family continued their good-natured ribbing as Alicia came alongside Sara and nudged her back to the table. "Do you play football?" she asked.

"I never have," admitted Sara.

"Good," answered Alicia. "You and I can sit and have another cup of coffee while these wild ones go burn off some energy." She looked up at her husband and smiled. "Take your heathens and go outside."

Donovan just grinned and leaned down to kiss his wife. "I'll be back in an hour, all sweaty and grimy, just like you like me," he teased.

Alicia shook her head and shooed him away, a twinkle in her eye as she watched him walk out the front door. Terrence stopped to kiss Sara as she sat at the kitchen table.

"Sure you don't want to join us?" he asked. "I know it sounds violent and extreme, but it's really good fun."

Sara smiled and shook her head. "No, I'll stay here and visit with your mom." She looked up at Savannah's retreating back. "And don't hurt your sister."

He burst out laughing. "She's the toughest one on the field. We're supposed to be playing two-hand touch, but I end up with Savannah-shaped bruises every year." He kissed her again and followed everyone outside.

Alicia looked at her grandchildren and asked, "Do you want to watch the parade on TV?" but the children were shaking their heads before she finished. She grinned. "All right, get on out there but stay far back from the game. Your aunt and uncle get a little crazy sometimes."

The two youngsters bolted after the adults with a quick, "Thanks, Nana!"

The two women sighed at the same time, then laughed. "It can get a bit nuts here when they're all home," said Alicia.

Sara smiled, her heart full. "It's wonderful," she said. "I love it."

"Where is your family?" asked Alicia as she poured their coffee. "You don't celebrate with them?"

Sara's smile vanished. "They're in Tampa. We don't get together." She looked away, suddenly embarrassed. "They aren't… big on celebrations."

Alicia frowned. "I'm sorry, honey. I didn't mean to pry. I'm glad you're here with us. We've heard so much about you and we've been looking forward to meeting you in person." She took a sip of her coffee, then continued. "So Terrence says you were a kindergarten teacher?"

Sara brightened. "Yes. I just started at the middle school this year but I love it."

"I was studying to be a teacher but I got pregnant early in our marriage. Donovan and I decided I would stay home and raise this brood." She sipped her coffee, then continued. "I've never regretted the decision, but I do wonder sometimes how life would have been different."

"What would you have taught?" asked Sara.

Alicia grinned, a sparkle in her eyes. "I would have done just what my boy is doing. He comes by his love of literature naturally." She chuckled. "Donovan seems like a big goofball, but he's an avid reader, too. We read to these kids every night when they were little and then we'd have what we called the Billings Book Club when they were older. They'd read a book and basically do an oral report for the family at dinner time, but they never saw it as work. Terrence loved the chance to read and then show off what he learned in front of all of us."

Sara marveled at the thought of Terrence as a young boy, sharing a beloved book with his parents and sisters. There was more to him than she knew, of course, but this thread in the tapestry of his early years seemed important. It was beautiful.

Alicia sat back and Sara was amazed at the kindness in her eyes. "My son is a wonderful man," she began. "I've been longing for him to find a special woman. His sisters married so young, but Terrence is a bit of a late bloomer." She patted Sara's hand. "Maybe he was just waiting for you."

Tears pricked her eyes—*Why am I crying?* she thought. "We've only been together a little over three months," she answered. "I don't know if he's thinking that way yet."

Alicia tilted her head and smiled gently. "And you? Are you thinking that way yet?"

Sara sat still, surprised at how comfortable she felt. It was strange but captivating. This woman had the uncanny ability to disarm her, to make her feel seen, wanted, and accepted. To feel loved.

Isn't that what mothers do?

"I guess I am," she whispered. As Alicia's smile broadened, she added, "But there's something I'm worried about."

The older woman shrugged. "I can't imagine there's anything so terrible, honey. Do you want to talk about it?"

The gentleness of Alicia's question nearly overpowered Sara. She had kept her secret for twenty-three years—other than her parents, only Lauren knew about Natalie. She hadn't even told Azalea and Susana, her other closest friends. How could she open up to this woman she'd known for two short days?

Yet Sara realized she wanted nothing more than to unburden herself, to share the secret she'd held for years. Her longing to be cared for overcame her reticence and the tears threatened again. She took a shuddering breath and began. "I—I had a baby when I was sixteen. My parents made me place her for adoption and blocked me from any contact." She looked away as the tears spilled from her eyes. "She found me a few months ago and we've been communicating by text and email. Her adoptive mother got breast cancer earlier this year and I guess she wants to know more about where she came from. We haven't met yet, but I really want to. It's like I found this hole in my life that I didn't even know was there."

Alicia gazed at her with sympathy. "Sara…I'm so sorry. That must have been awful for you."

"It was," she replied simply. "My parents made all the decisions for where she was placed. We moved to Tampa and I never saw my boyfriend or my baby again." She looked up, her face hardening. "I didn't abandon my daughter. I never got the chance to be her mom."

Alicia looked confused. "Of course you didn't abandon her. Who says you did?"

Sara looked at her hands. "No one. But what if Terrence thinks that? He doesn't have any experience with people like my parents. You all have this amazing, loving family. What if he doesn't understand and he thinks I was a terrible mom?" The tears fell and Sara finished in a whisper. "What if I've finally fallen in love and he leaves?"

11

By Saturday night, Sara was exhausted.

The Billings family was everything she'd dreamed of. Yet her inexperience with such togetherness wore her out and she found she was ready to go home. As she and Terrence packed their suitcases and prepared for the last night under his parents' roof, she thought back over her time with the family—especially her time alone with Alicia.

"Terrence does have some strong opinions," Alicia had told her. "He and Donovan especially are all about family. I know my son longs to have his own." Sara had struggled to stop crying as Terrence's mother consoled her. "He's my boy and I know his heart. He'll understand and he'll be supportive."

Sara told her about Natalie—how the girl first reached out and then pulled back. She shared the most recent Thanksgiving Day text exchange, and Alicia assured her that she was doing the right thing by continuing the conversation and giving Natalie space. By the time the rowdy Billings football players returned, Sara was calm and dry eyed.

The remainder of the day was a Thanksgiving to remember, with food and laughter and love. Sara mused over the similarities between the Billingses and the Ochoas. The Ochoas wove a distinctly Latin flair throughout their celebration but the tenor of the families was the same. Lauren's parents welcomed her with open arms to every holiday, calling her *chiquita linda*—pretty girl. She marveled at the generosity of the two clans, the way their hearts seemed to stretch effortlessly to include her.

Still, she was ready for a quiet day at home to prepare for the week ahead.

Terrence interrupted her reverie. "Ready to get home?" asked Terrence. "I hope four days of us wasn't too much for the first time."

Sara smiled and reached for his hand. She sat on the bed and pulled him to her, then leaned her head on his shoulder. "I loved every minute of it," she said, her voice thick with emotion. "They're wonderful—every single one of them." She looked up and their eyes met. "You are so lucky."

He put his arm around her and squeezed. "They are pretty great," he said, leaning down to kiss her. His lips were soft and gentle. "But the luckiest thing about me is that I found you." They lay back and he stroked her hair, his thumb grazing her cheek. "I know it hasn't been that long for us, but it feels like forever. I love you, Sara."

She lay still, her eyes closed as she absorbed his words, his touch. His lips met hers again and he murmured, "I'm so glad you're here."

"So am I."

The couple lay quietly in bed, arms around each other. Terrence cradled Sara's head against his shoulder and he stroked her hip. "You make it pretty hard not to make love to you," he whispered. "I want you so bad right now."

Sara sighed and snuggled closer. She stroked his chest, feeling his heart beat beneath her hand. "I want you, too, but not here…not in your parents' house." She looked up at him, his dark eyes barely visible. "Am I being weird? I know four days is a long time for us—"

"Shh…." He held his finger to her lips. "It's okay, babe. I get it." He pulled her close, his desire nearly causing her to give in. He kissed her deeply, his hands in her hair, and then rolled away from her. "Just cuddle up to me," he said, reaching behind his back to stroke her thigh. He laughed quietly. "I'll get through this somehow. But all bets are off when we get back to Daytona Beach."

Sara molded her body to his, her arm draped across his waist. She kissed his back and whispered, "Thank you, love. Thank you for understanding." She kissed him again. "Thank you for bringing me here."

The next morning was a bustle of activity as the Billings children and grandchildren all prepared to depart. Talia hugged Sara and told her they'd see her soon. Savannah pushed her sister away with a scowl. "When are you coming back down here?" she asked. "You don't even have to bring my dumb brother. You and Talia just come hang out for a girls' weekend." Sara hugged her and thanked her for a lovely time.

Despite her exhaustion, Sara found she didn't want to leave after all. *They're so warm and loving,* she thought. *Last night I was ready to go and today I just want to move in.*

Donovan stood slightly apart, watching his family. His eyes met Sara's and he opened his arms wide. Without a thought, she moved across the room to his enormous hug. "You come back here any time, young lady," he said. "You're part of the family now." He looked up and winked at Terrence. "You hear that, boy? She's welcome here any time."

Terrence smiled as Sara extricated herself from the large man. "I hear you, Dad." He was next to receive his father's embrace, and the two men held each other for a long time. Sara could tell Donovan was whispering into his son's ear, but couldn't hear the words. He clapped his son on the shoulder and then nodded at the door. "Get on with you," he said gruffly. "You have a long drive."

Alicia finished saying good bye to her daughters, sons-in-law, and grandchildren and approached Sara. She reached both hands out to clasp Sara's and leaned in to kiss her on the cheek. "I'm so glad you came, honey," she said. She looked up at Terrence, her face solemn. "She's special, Son. Very, very special." She looked back at Sara and squeezed her hands, then let go of one of them. Reaching for Terrence, she pulled them both close to her. "Be good to one another," she said.

Sara and Terrence gazed at each other. "We will," they answered in unison.

The couple drove home, their comfortable chatting punctuated by long moments of peaceful silence. Sara mulled her Thanksgiving conversation with Alicia and the woman's parting comments to the two of them. She still felt hesitant to share her story with Terrence, yet his mother's confidence that he would understand and accept her began to sway her. At last, when they were an hour away from home, she found the courage to speak.

"I had a really great talk with your mom on Thanksgiving morning," she began.

Terrence smiled at her. "She's pretty special. She likes you a lot."

"I feel the same way about her. She made me feel like part of the family. Before I knew it, I was spilling my guts to her."

"She has that way," he agreed. "Even when we were kids and all three of us trying to get her attention, she'd always make me feel like I was the only one in the room when she talked to me. Like every thing out of my mouth was the most important thing she could think about." He glanced at her. "I think I compare every other mother in the world to her. Pretty high bar, I know.

"So you spilled your guts. What was your big reveal?" he asked, a teasing note in his voice.

Sara looked out the window and breathed deeply. Alicia's words sounded in her mind: *He's my boy and I know his heart.*

"We talked about family and I explained how strained mine is." Her heart pounded and she let out a slow breath. "My parents weren't great my whole life, but they were awful when I was in high school. I told your mom I…I had a baby when I was sixteen. She was adopted by a family in Orlando and she's recently contacted me." Her words were soft and Terrence was quiet. Long moments passed.

Did I make a mistake telling him? Was Alicia wrong?

After a moment, he glanced at her, then looked forward. "So you gave your baby up for adoption? That must have been a difficult thing to do." His voice was low and taut.

"I wasn't given the choice. My parents made me relinquish her and then they blocked me from any contact. We moved and I never saw her or the family."

"And you never tried to find her?'

Sara closed her eyes. *His voice is so cold.* She looked out the window again. "I told you. My parents blocked all contact. I didn't know the family's name or any details." Sara's voice was monotone and her breathing shallow.

This was a mistake.

"So what did my mom say?"

Sara's voice was somber. "She was lovely—kind and understanding. She asked questions and—"

"Your parents sound awful. Why do people like that even have a family?" he interrupted. He looked sidelong at her. "So what are you doing about it now?"

Why do people like that even have a family?

Do you mean why did they have me*?*

Sara's eyes welled with tears as she realized she wasn't getting the tender response she hoped for, that Alicia anticipated. Her voice flat, she answered, "She apparently was able to do some searching and she found me a few months ago. We've been communicating by text and email. She's not ready to talk on the phone or meet in person yet and I'm trying to give her whatever space she needs. Her adoptive mother was diagnosed with breast cancer earlier this year, so she's worried and confused."

Terrence's response was short and disdainful. "I can imagine it must be hard for the kid to have one family give her away and then have her mom maybe die."

Stunned at his vehemence, Sara couldn't stop her tears. "I didn't give her away. She was taken from me." She shook her head, anger displacing her sorrow. "Terrence, I was barely older than the kids in our classes. It's not like this happened last year. I didn't do something wrong—*it was done to me*. I'm sorry that I don't have a perfect mother like yours," she finished, her voice heavy with sarcasm.

His jaw tightened and he didn't respond.

Realization formed a knot in her stomach: *It's over. Alicia, you were wrong. You don't know your boy.*

They drove in tense silence until they arrived at Sara's house. Terrence started to get out of the car, but Sara stopped him. "Don't bother." She got out, retrieved her suitcase from the back seat, and walked to the front door, never turning back.

As she walked in the house, she heard his car leaving while Lauren jumped off the couch to greet her. "You're home! I want to hear everything!"

"No," she sighed. "You probably don't."

"I hate that guy," muttered Lauren.

"I don't hate him," said Sara, wiping her tears. "His only experience is with a great family."

Lauren scowled. "You're seriously gonna make excuses for him? C'mon, Sara…he's a jerk. He's what, 36 years old? So he has a great family. You have a shitty mother and *you* don't treat people that way." She looked hard at her friend and repeated, "I hate that guy."

The women were sitting on the sofa, Sara curled around one of the pillows and clutching a tissue. Lauren sat crosslegged, then abruptly stretched. "I know you're hurt, but you have to admit: It's better to find out early that he's so immature. If he's got issues, he should take care of them. Go to therapy or something."

Sara nodded. Her friend was right. Terrence had completely overreacted. She didn't know how she'd deal with having him across the hall at school every day, but she knew she had to find a way to put her feelings aside. By tomorrow morning, she'd have to face him.

"That's it," decided Lauren. "Time for the big guns." She took Sara's hand and pulled her off the sofa. "We're going out for ice cream."

Sara laughed and followed her friend to the car. "Only if it's non-dairy," she reminded her.

Lauren threw back her head. "Gah! Can't you even be brokenhearted like a normal person?"

12

Sara made it to her classroom the next morning without seeing Terrence. Ordinarily, he would pop his head in to say good morning and sneak a kiss before the other teachers or students arrived. *No more of that*, she thought firmly. She finished organizing her desk and the first bell rang. She knew once classes started, it would get easier—she hoped her students would distract her.

The day wore on, each class grumbling at their return after the holiday, no matter how much they loved the subject or their teacher. Sara did her best to engage them, getting them up to the board to solve equations or moving their desks around to work on group problems. By the time her fourth period class arrived, she hadn't thought about Terrence in hours.

Marisa was one of the last students to enter. Sadness radiated from her like a beacon—Sara felt it as the girl passed her desk. She tried to make eye contact, but the teen's eyes remained downcast and she was quiet for the entire hour. When the bell rang, the students raced to the door for their lunch period, but Marisa lingered in the back.

Sara's heart went out to the girl. She busied herself at her desk, glancing up but giving Marisa time and space. At last, the teen approached.

"Miss Masterson," she began, her voice soft and quavering, "Do you have a minute?"

Sara walked around her desk and leaned against it. "Of course, Marisa. What do you need?"

The girl's lips quivered and she looked at the ground. "I—I—" A single tear slid down her cheek and Sara longed to pull her in for a hug. There were firm district rules against initiating physical contact with students and those rules warred with her heart as Marisa continued to look away. The girl, no longer a proud teenager determined to be strong, was simply a grieving child, and Sara's heart nearly broke.

"You want to talk about it?"

After a moment, Marisa began, her voice dull. "Thanksgiving was horrible. It was exactly what I expected. We went to my grandparents' house and they wouldn't even talk about my mom. When I tried to bring her up they just kept saying how she's in a better place and isn't it nice we're all together for the holidays." She blew her nose roughly. "But we weren't *all* together, were we? My stupid father didn't say a word. He just sat there and when we got home that night I screamed at him." She looked up at Sara, her eyes red and filled with tears. "He told me it's been almost six months and it's time for me to get on with my life." She shook her head in disbelief. "I hate him."

She reached for Sara, clutching her teacher and sobbing. After a moment, Sara smoothed her hair and let the girl cry. When her tears finally subsided, Marisa pulled away and reached for another tissue. "Would you talk to him?" she asked, her voice quavering.

Sara tensed, unsure she should get in the middle of such a fraught situation.

"What about the school counselor?" she asked. "I'm not sure your dad would listen to me—we've never met and he might not appreciate me getting involved."

"Please? I really need your help." Marisa grasped Sara's hand. "I feel like he didn't even love her. How can he just forget her like that and expect me to?" She shook her head fiercely. "I can't. I won't forget my mom."

Sara looked at the child before her and her heart swung from compassion to anxiety and back again. *Isn't this why I became a teacher?*

"Let me talk to Ms. Dobson," she hedged. "If she agrees, then I'll talk to him. Do you mind if he knows that we spoke? I'm sure he doesn't know what he's doing. He would never want you to hurt like this. I know he's the adult, but don't forget that he's hurting, too. Neither of us can imagine what it must be like for him to have lost his wife."

Marisa grimaced and nodded. "I know. It's why I couldn't believe how he acted at my grandparents' house. He could have stood up to them. They're so old fashioned—they don't like it when I cry and I bet they'd freak out if my dad did." She blew her nose and tossed the tissue into the wastebasket. "I've never seen him cry about anything. Not even at the funeral."

Sara nodded. "I'll talk to Ms. Dobson before I leave this afternoon."

Marisa stood. "Thanks, Miss Masterson. You can tell him I talked to you." She squared her shoulders and offered a weak smile as she left the room.

After school, Sara went to the principal's office.

"Yes," nodded Jenna Dobson. "I think your instincts are correct and Marisa's behavior warrants it. For something this serious, I'll want to be included."

"I was just about to ask if you would," admitted Sara. "It'll be my first parent-teacher conference in middle school, and this is a pretty serious topic." She frowned. "I can only imagine how hard it is for him having just lost his wife. I don't want to misstep."

"All right. I'll send a note to see if he can meet after school tomorrow. Once we meet with dad, we can decide if we need to get the school counselor involved."

The two women left the building, each heading to her car. Sara was surprised at the relief she felt. *Wasn't ready to do this on my own*, she realized.

The next afternoon, Sara stood at the front row of desks in her classroom. She turned as Jenna walked through the door, followed by Marisa's father. The principal turned to introduce Sara.

"Carlos, this is Sara Masterson, Marisa's math teacher," she said.

Sara's face froze, her fingertips suddenly numb. Even without having seen his LinkedIn profile, she knew that face.

Marisa Segovia's father.

Carlos *Segovia.*

A sudden dizziness nearly overtook her. "H-h-how do you do?" she stammered. She couldn't seem to control her body enough to shake his hand. Her thoughts were inarticulate, a jumble of words pulsing through her.

Carlos stood ramrod straight, staring at her then back at Jenna, who motioned them to chairs. "I can't tell you how sorry we are to hear about your wife," she said. "It's understandable that Marisa is struggling."

Carlos nodded, then cleared his throat. "Thank you. You said she's not completing her work?"

Jenna looked questioningly at Sara, who sat mute.

I can't do this. Her voice couldn't seem to escape her lips as she stammered, "She—she's a great kid—"

The principal frowned at her, then interjected. "Marisa is two weeks behind on turning in her homework. She doesn't participate in class, even though we all know math is her favorite." She smiled encouragingly at Carlos. "I remember her winning that seventh grade contest last year. We thought it would help for the three of us to collaborate on a plan for her to get back on track with school. Maybe that will give you one less thing to worry about while your family navigates this terrible loss."

Carlos nodded without speaking, his face taut.

Sara thought her chest would explode. Jenna glanced at her, a puzzled look on her face. Sara knew she was disappointing her principal by not contributing to the conversation, but she felt paralyzed with—what? Fear? Shock?

Sara took a deep breath to speak when Jenna's phone buzzed and the principal looked at the screen. "I'm terribly sorry," she said, shaking her head. "I need to take this call." She smiled at Sara and Carlos. "I'm sure the two of you can come up with a plan for Marisa, but please don't hesitate to bring me in if you need help." She looked pointedly at Sara, then reached out to shake Carlos' hand again. The principal left the room, leaving Sara and Carlos to look anywhere but at each other.

It was the first time they'd been alone in twenty-three years.

Carlos looked around and Sara noted his agitation—the mirror image of hers.

What do I say?

At last she found her voice. "Carlos, I didn't have any idea that you were Marisa's father." Her stomach knotted as she searched his face for a glimmer of emotion, but there was nothing. "I've had a few students with your last name in the past, but—" Sara trailed off, then continued, her voice trembling. "I'm as shocked as you are."

He sat very still, looking at his hands, his jaw clenching. At last, he answered, "What's going on with Marisa?"

She flexed her hands in her laps, the feeling slowly returning. *Don't your extremities go numb when you're in shock?* she wondered idly, then gripped her hands together. *Calm down. Breathe. Think about Marisa.*

She felt guilty that all she wanted to do was shout that they had a daughter, that they hadn't lost her after all.

She forced her thoughts into some semblance of clarity. "Marisa is struggling with homework," she said softly. "She's behind and losing ground."

Carlos glanced at her, then back to his hands. "I can get her a tutor."

Sara frowned. "She doesn't need a tutor. She's the smartest student in the class—probably the school. She understands the concepts. She's just not doing her homework and she hardly gets involved in class at all."

"That's it? She's quiet in class and missing a few assignments?" He scowled. "She lost her mother this summer. I think it's to be expected."

"Of course—you're right." Sara considered ending the conversation. No one would expect her to continue, yet she thought about Marisa's tearful plea. *This isn't about me or Carlos or Natalie,* she told herself. *I said I would help a child in need.*

"Carlos, I don't mean to pry or interfere, but Marisa asked me to talk to you."

He glanced up then, frowning. "Why?" he asked. "Why would my daughter talk to you?"

Sara blanched. *Was that a dig? Or am I just reading into it?*

She folded her hands and gazed at him. She saw the same boy she loved two decades ago, now slightly heavier, his suit and tie replacing the gym shorts and baseball jerseys he favored as a youth. He was still handsome and she wondered what he thought when he looked at her. Did he see the girl he'd loved? Or did he see a woman who'd abandoned him and their child so long ago?

After the shock of seeing me, I'm just Marisa's teacher, she reminded herself. *That's what he's here for.*

Clearing her throat, she began, "Marisa is struggling to get her work done on time because she can't focus at home. She confided in me that she was upset about Thanksgiving. She felt like you didn't listen to her and she thought maybe you would listen to me." Carlos' face was impassive. "Obviously she doesn't know anything about our past and I hope we can set that aside for her sake."

He nodded. "I'll do anything for my daughter."

Sara's throat constricted and she wished for a bottle of water. "Carlos, may I just be blunt?" When he nodded again, she continued. "Marisa thinks you're forgetting about her mother too quickly. She feels like you're expecting her to do the same thing and it hurts. She can't just pretend everything is fine. She wants to talk about her mom, to keep her memory alive."

His jaw clenched and he flexed his hands. Sara saw his knee bouncing up and down under the desk. "You're right," he said at last. "You shouldn't interfere."

His coldness unnerved her and Sara's stomach clenched. Guilt and embarrassment warred with frustration as she debated her response.

But then Carlos's face fell and he continued, his voice grim.

"It's not that easy. Hanging on just makes the pain worse. She needs to remember without wallowing in the misery." He stopped bouncing and when at last he looked at her, his pain was bleak and raw, his voice a whisper. "Or did you find some other way?"

My God, she thought. *He's not just talking about his wife.*

She stood and walked to her desk, busying herself with her attendance book—anything to avoid looking at him, to keep from seeing his anguish. At last, she looked up, hoping her own face didn't betray her. "Carlos," she began, "I didn't find another way. I wish I could have." She closed her eyes briefly, then opened them, tears on her lashes.

He stood abruptly, running his hand across his face as if to wipe away his thoughts. "What do we need to do to for Marisa?"

Sara walked back around the desk and stood in front of him. Now that she was close, she noted the circles under his eyes and how he seemed to want to run from the room. Her voice was gentle as she began. "Please. Let me say this first. I know it's the wrong time but I may never get another chance to tell you. I'm sorry, Carlos. I'm so very sorry. About your wife. About us. About…our baby." He put up a hand to forestall her, but she continued, her words pouring forth. "I truly felt I had no choice—you know my parents. They took her from me just as much as they took her from you." She took a deep breath and noted how still he'd become. "We may not have our daughter, but I promise I will do everything I can to help yours."

Carlos' squeezed his eyes shut and he pinched the bridge of his nose. Then he spun and strode to the door. "I can't do this, Sara. I can't." Looking over his shoulder as he opened the door, he said, "Just be there for Marisa." He closed his eyes and leaned his head against the door. "I'll do my best."

13

By the time she got home, Sara was drained. She was thankful she'd been able to avoid running into Terrence—that would have made a hard day nearly unbearable. She pulled up to the house and stopped for the mail before entering. Lauren was still at work, busy rebuilding her reputation at MPG after her stint at the start up, so Sara stretched out on the sofa, setting her bag down next to her. She had assignments to grade, but couldn't muster the energy to start. Her thoughts whirled everywhere but on math.

Two hours later, she still hadn't begun and was surprised to see Lauren coming in the door.

"You aren't working?" asked her friend. "You're never out here when I get home. Are you okay?"

Sara frowned. "What time is it?"

Lauren laughed. "It's seven o'clock. Seriously. Are you okay?"

"I'm fine. It was just a long, hard day and I've just been sitting here feeling sorry for myself."

Her friend dropped her bag and sat next to her on the couch. "Wanna talk about it?"

Sara yawned, then frowned. "You know the kid I told you about who lost her mom this summer?"

Lauren nodded.

"Her name is Marisa Segovia. Her father is Carlos Segovia."

Lauren looked confused, then her eyes widened. "Carlos? As in your Carlos?"

"Yes."

"Holy shit."

Sara grimaced. "Yeah."

Lauren sat down on the other end of the sofa, pulling her legs beneath her. "Are you okay?"

"Not really. We met today after school." Sara went on to describe the meeting, and soon was in tears.

Lauren squeezed her hand. "So what's he like?"

Sara thought a moment before responding. "Sad. He just seems so sad. I'm sure he must have had some goodness in his life since I knew him. He did get married and have a beautiful daughter." She cocked her head, her face contemplative. "But right now, all I see is sadness.

"And I feel like a complete jerk. I know he was there to talk about Marisa but all I wanted to do was tell him about Natalie. I know how I've dealt with it all these years, but I have no idea what happened to him. And it's the worst possible time to reconnect with him—I have no right to drop this in his lap when he's dealing with his wife's death and a brokenhearted teenager." She shook her head, her eyes downcast. "I know it's selfish but I just wish we could talk about what happened to us. We shared something life changing and we've never had the chance to talk about it or cry about it or scream at each other—nothing. Nothing for all these years. I know we were just kids, but there was something there, Lauren. My parents never cared about me and they treated me even worse than usual once I got pregnant. Carlos was my rock but after we moved away, I was completely adrift." Sudden sobs rolled through her body. "I was so lost. They took everything from me. Everything."

Lauren wrapped her arms around Sara's shaking shoulders and rocked her friend in silence. After a moment, the friends broke apart.

"I probably shouldn't be hugging you," said Lauren, frowning. "There's some stomach bug going around in the office and I actually don't feel that great tonight. I think I'm just gonna shower and go to bed early—see if I can get rid of it quickly." She squeezed Sara's hand. "Hang in there. I know it's hard right now and I wish I had some brilliant thing to say. But listen: It's okay to be self-centered once in a while, you know." She made a face and rubbed her stomach. "Ugh. I feel like crap."

"Can I get you anything?"

"Nah. Just take care of yourself." She stood and smiled. "See you tomorrow."

The next two weeks passed without incident. Sara saw Terrence every day, but the two assiduously avoided eye contact, even when they passed each other in the hall between their classrooms. It was uncomfortable, but as the days passed, she found she didn't dread running into him. Sara and Marisa began meeting at lunchtime every other day, ostensibly to work on math. Usually, Sara just listened as her student talked. Sometimes it was about music, clothes, or boys. Often it was about her mother. Occasionally, it was about Carlos.

"I can't believe you didn't tell me," accused Marisa one day.

"Tell you what?"

"That you and my dad knew each other in high school."

Sara eyes widened in surprise. She and Carlos hadn't discussed telling Marisa and she wasn't sure how she felt about him making the decision without her input. *She's his daughter,* she thought. *It's his call.* But she felt a glimmer of annoyance regardless.

"I tutored him in math," hedged Sara. "He was a big superstar jock and had to pass his classes to stay on the baseball team."

"Yeah, that's what he told me. Weird how I ended up being so good in math and now you're my teacher, too."

Weird doesn't begin to describe it.

"Anyway," continued Marisa, "why does he have to be so strict? It's like he thinks everyone is sketch. I can't go out with friends if there's no parent around, and he always has to meet everyone I want to hang out with." She took a bite of her sandwich and talked around the turkey. "It's annoying."

Sara smiled. After the trouble they'd gotten into, she wasn't surprised he kept a close watch on his daughter. "He just loves you," she said.

"What was he like in high school? Was he so uptight?"

Sara's stomach clenched. She didn't want to talk about her high school love, the father of her daughter. But Marisa was finally coming out of her shell and seemed to relish these lunchtime meetings. So she dodged the question. "He was really into baseball. Made varsity his freshman year, if I remember correctly." Carlos had in fact not only made varsity, but had been an all-league pitcher as a freshman. Many people expected him to be drafted to the pros when he graduated and the young couple had fantasized about the future glamorous lifestyle of a major leaguer and his engineer wife.

"He doesn't even work out anymore," said Marisa. "He and my mom used to go to the gym all the time but now he just sits in front of his computer or the TV."

Sara frowned. That didn't sound like the Carlos she remembered. He was always training and spent hours at the gym or on the field when he wasn't with Sara. "Maybe ask him to take you? That might motivate him."

"I tried that. He said he had a hard day at work and was too tired. I asked a couple more times, but then just gave up." Marisa wadded up her trash and tossed it into the garbage can ten feet away. "Swish!" she grinned.

"Do you play basketball?" asked Sara.

"Yeah, usually. But this year was kinda hard for me." She made a face. "I had a little trauma before the season started, you know."

Sara's eyebrows shot up. Was Marisa making a joke? "I—I'm sorry," she started, but her student laughed.

"It's OK, Miss Masterson. I was just messing around." She stood and pulled on her backpack. "Anyway, gotta go to Mr. Billings' class now. Thanks for talking to me." She added, "Maybe I'll see if he wants to play catch. I'd rather shoot HORSE in the driveway, but right now I just want my dad. Maybe baseball will do the trick." Sighing, she exited the classroom and headed across the hallway.

Sara watched her go, her mind full of memories of Carlos. He was the superstar of their high school—the entire district, really. He was a phenom with a blazing fastball and a dazzling smile. She'd been the envy of all the girls as she sat in the stands watching him pitch—and seeing him wink at her as he entered the dugout between innings.

She was startled out of her reverie by a text on her phone. It was Savannah.

Hey, Sara! Wazzup girl? I don't know if you guys are coming down for Christmas (I hope so!) but I need some help getting a gift for my dumb brother. Any ideas? And puhleeeeze don't say a book!

She sat back heavily. *So he hasn't told them*, she thought. She looked at the clock—only five minutes until classes resumed. She texted back quickly.

Hi Savannah, wish I could help. I guess Terrence didn't tell you, but we broke up. I'm really gonna miss you and your family. Happy holidays and hello to everyone. Gotta run—next class is starting.

Before she could slide her phone into her purse, Savannah replied.

That dumbass. I know it couldn't have been you.

"So he hasn't told them? What a coward," declared Lauren. "I guess I don't dislike him anymore. Now I have no brain space for him at all." She pantomimed flicking dust off her shoulder. "Terrence who?" she asked.

Sara laughed at her friend's antics. "I'm a little surprised, but maybe it makes sense. His family did kind of embrace me over Thanksgiving. He probably feels awkward."

"*Who* feels awkward?" Lauren's eyes were wide with sarcasm.

Sara smacked her on the arm. "Don't be petty. You didn't see his family. They can be a little intimidating."

"Whatever. I'm over it." Lauren dismissed the conversation with a wave of her hand. "So what are you gonna do for Christmas? I hope you're coming to my parents' house with me now that you're single again."

The Ochoa family had welcomed Sara to every holiday for years. Sara had long ago given up any hope that her parents would ask her to come home for any reason. Now she almost dreaded the notion that they might one day turn into real parents.

"I'd love to," she answered. "You know I adore your family. What's the gift giving plan this year?" With such a big family, the Ochoas either drew names or only bought presents for the grandchildren. Some years they skipped gifts altogether in favor of a special activity the entire family could enjoy.

"Mom's decided we're not doing gifts and we're all delivering Christmas baskets with the church in the morning. Then we'll come home for *tamales* and Christmas cookies."

Sara laughed. She'd been diligently following a plant-based diet for a year, but Mrs. Ochoa's *tamales* were worth breaking the rules. "I'm guessing she hasn't found a vegan tamale recipe."

Lauren grinned. "You know my mother. If there isn't a pound of lard in the *masa*, they aren't traditional. Which means they are…"

The two friends shouted together, "*No bueno!*" They laughed, well acquainted with Señora Ochoa's penchant for traditional Cuban recipes that never considered heart health.

Oh, well, thought Sara. *It's only once a year.*

"Hey, did you grab the mail?" asked Lauren.

"Oops," answered Sara. "I got yesterday's and just tossed it on the table. Didn't even look today." She moved her bag to look for the mail and stopped when she saw her phone light up with a text. She looked at Lauren. "It's Natalie. I haven't heard from her since Thanksgiving."

"You want some privacy?" asked Lauren.

Sara shook her head. "You know everything I do by now." She opened the message and began to read aloud.

Hi Sara I'm really sorry for the long gaps. I don't want to keep starting and stopping. TBH I'm just confused and scared. But then I remind myself that I'm the one who looked for you!

Lauren was nodding. "She's right. She started the whole thing." Her voice was dismissive. "Boss up and meet your mother, *chiquita*."

Sara smiled. Her dearest friend had very little filter and even less tolerance for anyone who might hurt Sara. She looked back down at her phone and continued reading.

So here it is. I'm ready to meet you. It's sorta last minute, but could we meet for coffee this weekend? I'm happy to come wherever you want.

Sara's chest tightened as she read to the end.

I can't pretend this doesn't terrify me, and I'll probably be weird and awkward and I might cry. I hope I don't embarrass you.

LMK and thanks

Sara sat back on the sofa and the phone dropped into her lap.

Lauren reached out and took her hand, a look of deep concern on her face. "Hey…are you okay?"

Sara bit her lip. "I can't breathe," she whispered.

Her friend enveloped her in a hug as sobs wracked her body. Lauren held her and murmured soothing sounds as Sara released her pent up emotions. At last, she sat back and stared at her friend in disbelief.

"She finally wants to meet me," she said, her voice tinged with wonder. "My baby—my baby. She must be so nervous." She paused. "So am I! But another part of me is excited." Her smile beamed through her tears. "Is this really happening? I'm going to meet my daughter?"

"Text her back," said Lauren. "Do it now before you think too much."

Sara nodded and began to type.

I'd love to meet you, Natalie. I don't care if you're weird, awkward, or cry. I probably will, too. And there's no possible way you could ever embarrass me. How about Saturday morning at the beach? It's about an hour from Orlando and half an hour for me from Daytona—Surf Java on Flagler Avenue? If you'd rather I come to Orlando, I'm absolutely fine with that.

Sara held back from typing *Love, Mom*. She knew it was far too soon—in fact, she might never be anything other than Sara. But her heart swelled at the idea that one day Natalie might think of her as *Mom*. She bit her lip as she waited for an answer.

She watched the ellipsis appear and then disappear, only to reappear again. What would her daughter say? Might she have changed her mind already? It wouldn't be the first time. *Don't get too excited*, she warned herself. *It could all unravel again.*

The text was short.

Surf Java is great. I love that place! See you there at 10 on Saturday?

Sara's smile burst forth. *Yes! Perfect!*

Lauren's patience finally gave out. "So? What did she say?"

Sara turned the phone screen to face her best friend. "We're meeting on Saturday morning!"

Lauren's smile darkened. "Uh…you have another text."

Sara's heart sank. It was too good to be true. Her daughter was having second thoughts. She turned the phone around and was surprised to see no new message from Natalie. She turned a quizzical look at her friend.

"A text from Terrence popped up."

Sara moved back to the incoming messages screen and saw Terrence's name on top. She glanced at Lauren, whose face was a disapproving scowl.

Hi, Sara. I was hoping maybe we could talk. I think I might owe you an apology.

"So what does the *cabrón* have to say?" Snapped Lauren.

Sara frowned and showed Lauren the screen.

"Might?" Lauren's voice rose. "Might?" She grabbed the phone and shouted at the screen. "There's no 'might,' *pinche cabrón*! You can never apologize enough. You're a jackass and she's so done with you." She handed Sara's phone back. "I need to give this to you before I throw it across the room. Who does he think he is? What a jerk." Glaring at no one, she finished, "I hate that guy."

Sara sat back on the sofa, her mind awhirl. There were too many emotions to process at once. *I'm meeting my daughter*, she reminded herself. *I don't have the emotional space to deal with him right now.*

She began to type and Lauren broke in angrily. "What are you doing? You should block him. He has no right to just show up like that."

Sara cocked her head and raised her eyebrows. Lauren sighed as she flopped back into the sofa pillows. "Okay, okay. You're my best friend, not my little sister. You're perfectly capable of figuring this out on your own and there's no 'should' involved. I need to just sit here and be supportive." She stuck out her lower lip in frustration and Sara stifled a laugh at her friend's tantrum. "What does Azalea always say?" Lauren sat up straight and mimicked their older friend. "*How can I be the best friend to you right now?*"

Sara grinned and patted Lauren's arm. "That was very good. You owned your mistake and you reframed your response."

Lauren rolled her eyes and muttered, "What are you, my fucking therapist?"

"Some days, yup." Sara looked back at her phone and resumed typing. *Now isn't a good time. I have a lot going on. Perhaps next week?*

Immediately he responded. *Sure, whenever is good for you. Just let me know.*

14

Sara walked through the rest of the week in a daze. She taught her classes but couldn't have said what she did in each period. The students were restless as the winter break approached, and she tried to keep them engaged as much as possible. On Friday, she was exhausted and keyed up—an unusual combination as she finished the week and prepared to meet Natalie in the morning.

She locked her door and turned to leave when she saw Terrence leaving his classroom. Other than seeing him across the hall and their brief text, she'd successfully avoided conversation or meeting for three weeks since their breakup. Sara groaned inwardly as she saw no way to evade him. *He looks awkward*, she thought, then decided it wasn't her problem.

"Hey," he said.

"Hey," she responded, her voice guarded.

He looked around, seeming to search for a place to rest his gaze.

Anywhere but on me.

"Busy weekend?"

If you only knew, she thought. *Three weeks ago, I thought this was something wonderful I could share with you.*

"Nothing special. You?"

"Nah—might do some Christmas shopping."

Sara was tired and eager to get home and she had her fill of small talk. "Well, have a good weekend," she said, walking past him with purpose. She didn't turn back as he responded.

"You, too, Sara. Still good to talk next week?"

"Yeah, that works," she said over her shoulder. *Whatever.*

Sara sat fidgeting in front of Surf Java. She arrived early, but the chairs on the deck near the front door were already filled with an assortment of coffee drinkers—locals sat alongside tourists, each enjoying the Saturday morning fresh air. She looked at every woman who walked by, longing to see Natalie approach, certain she would recognize her immediately. She'd memorized every feature of her daughter's face from the online photos. Her heartbeat quickened—what if she changed her mind at the last minute? Sara didn't know how she'd manage her emotions if Natalie backed out again. The back and forth was harder than not knowing her at all.

And then she saw her.

Olive skinned with brown hair, Natalie was beautiful. She looked to be about Sara's height, but with Carlos' coloring. She was wearing a white cotton sundress with sandals and stylish sunglasses, a yellow and green pashmina wrapped loosely around her shoulders. The girl approached the coffee shop with a confident stride, then appeared to slow as she got closer. Sara's chest constricted and the tears threatened.

My daughter.

She wasn't sure she could stand, but she forced herself up and waved. She saw Natalie hesitate, then bite her lip as if considering her next move. *Don't stop,* Sara whispered. *Please don't stop.* She walked toward the steps leading from the café deck to the sidewalk and suddenly they were facing each other. Sara's arms longed to reach for her daughter but instead she stood rigid, not knowing what to do.

This time, I'm going to fight, she remembered.

"I'd recognize you anywhere," she said simply.

Natalie looked at her, then removed her sunglasses. Bright green eyes—unlike Sara's blue or Carlos' brown—looked out, shiny with unshed tears. She seemed caught in the moment, likewise unsure of her next move.

Fight, thought Sara. *Fight for what I love.*

"Could I—would it be okay—" she stammered.

"Yes," whispered Natalie.

And Sara threw her arms around her daughter, holding on as Natalie's arms came around her. Oblivious to the world, they embraced on the sidewalk and cried.

Two hours later, they were still in the café. Sara longed to know everything and soaked up each detail Natalie shared. She'd grown up in Orlando, a typical suburban kid with slightly older but doting parents. She'd done all the typical Florida things: season passes to the theme parks, participation in sports and dance. But her passion was creative writing and painting and she was working on her MFA at Florida State when her mother received her cancer diagnosis.

Natalie grew somber when she talked about the treatment Jocelyn received, then smiled as she related the recent good news of her remission. Sara sat quiet, listening to her daughter share details of the woman who had loved and raised her.

"I hope this doesn't make you feel weird," said Natalie. "I didn't mean to come here and just talk about her."

Sara shook her head. "She's part of you. I want to know everything about you—everything you want to share, that is," she hastened to add. "Do I wish I had been able to raise you? Of course. But the fact that you have a lovely, wonderful mother makes me very happy."

Natalie's eyes filled yet again, but the tears didn't fall. "Thank you, Sara. She *is* wonderful. Not perfect, but wonderful. You picked really great parents for me."

Sara sat back and frowned. "I wish I could take credit for that. My parents managed the whole thing—I wasn't allowed any say in the matter. They worked with the agency to review different candidates and they picked your parents." Her throat tightened.

"And then they locked the whole thing down so I could have no contact with any of you." The words tumbled out in a rush. "They made your father and his parents sign away all their rights. I never saw him or you again."

Natalie's eyes widened. "That's horrible," she said quietly. "I'm so sorry." She looked thoughtful, then added, "I haven't been able to find him yet, but I hope to."

Sara looked at her beautiful daughter, so like the boy she'd loved, yet so much like her. She took just a moment to decide.

"I might be able to help you with that."

Mother and daughter finally got hungry and Sara went to the counter to order them sandwiches. When she returned to the table, Natalie was texting and had a bright smile on her face.

"Everything good?" she asked.

Natalie looked up. "Everything's great. Just telling my parents about our morning. They're really happy for me." She finished her text and set her phone down. Looking at Sara expectantly, she said, "I do want to hear about my father, but I want to hear about you first. I totally just rambled for two hours and didn't ask you anything. So what do you do? Are you married? Who are your friends? What did you study in college? What's your favorite color?" She laughed, her questions tripping over each other as they sprung from her lips. Then she grew somber. "Do you have any other kids?"

Sara sat and marveled at the young woman. She was charming, warm, and well spoken. Their hours together had flown by and Natalie had seemed to grow more comfortable every moment. Her smile and bright eyes were all Sara, but her coloring and some of her mannerisms were more reminiscent of Carlos. When Natalie tilted her head and rolled her eyes at some story she was telling, Sara could see the boy in his daughter's mien.

"Well," she began, "I'm not terribly interesting. I think I told you already I'm a middle school math teacher—"

"That totally made me laugh when you texted me that!" burst out Natalie. "I missed out on that gene. Math was my worst subject."

Sara laughed. "That you would have gotten from your father. He hated math."

"Sorry to interrupt—go on."

Sara answered all her daughter's questions, describing her career path and her friends. Natalie paid rapt attention, occasionally interjecting a nod or a question. When Sara talked about Lauren, her daughter grinned.

"She sounds great—I can't wait to meet her."

That means we'll get together again, noted Sara, tucking away the thought.

"You'll love her. She's super smart and very sassy. We're polar opposites but she's like a sister to me."

The two finished their lunches and Sara went to the counter for lemonade while Natalie went to the restroom. She returned to their table, in awe that the day had finally come and she was face to face with the child she'd lost. She was still marveling when Natalie sat down.

"So now let me answer the really important questions," she said, her face serious.

Natalie's brows furrowed and she sat very still.

"You should know that—" Sara stopped. *I'm getting as silly as Lauren,* she thought. She took a breath and continued. "My favorite color is pink."

Natalie burst out laughing. "You scared me! I thought you were gonna say something horrible." She shook her head. "Although having pink as your favorite color when you're a 39-year-old woman might be considered a little bit horrible."

"Lauren completely agrees. She hates pink and makes fun of me constantly." Then she sat back and looked directly at Natalie.

"No other kids," she said quietly. "Just you. Just my one, perfect daughter." A tear slid down her cheek. She began to brush it away but Natalie caught her hand.

"I'm so sorry, but I'm not ready to call you Mom," she confessed, almost in a whisper. "I hope that doesn't hurt you."

Sara shook her head. "I didn't expect that you would." *I don't deserve it,* she thought.

"I want to honor my adoptive mom without hurting you."

Sara squeezed Natalie's hand. "Honey, the simple fact that you met me today has made me happier than I could have imagined. You could call me anything and it wouldn't matter. I've seen you, talked to you, touched you…." She trailed off, shaking her head. "I don't have words for how I feel."

Natalie's smile was warm. "I feel the same way." She took a steadying breath. "Now will you tell me about my father?"

Sara sat quietly for a moment, then began. "We met our freshman year in high school. We were just babies. He was a jock and I was a math geek—didn't seem like a great match, but he needed to pass math to stay on the baseball team and I was a peer tutor." She looked at her daughter's face, alight with curiosity. "He was so funny and he made me laugh.

"I didn't laugh a lot in those days."

Natalie reached for her hand. "If this is painful, you don't have to tell me," she said.

Sara smiled sadly. "No, it's okay. This is your history, too. You deserve to know it." She sighed. "You look like him."

Natalie's eyes widened. "Really?" Her eagerness was palpable and Sara smiled.

"I wish I could just download all these memories into your head at once," she said. "But I suppose that would be pretty overwhelming." She patted her daughter's hand. "Anyway, we were just friends that first year—my parents wouldn't let me date until I turned sixteen, and they wouldn't have liked him anyway."

"Why?"

Sara cleared her throat—*Well, time to start the embarrassing part*, she thought. "They're pretty bigoted. It's just one of their many awful personality traits."

"So they won't accept me?" asked Natalie timidly.

Sara frowned. She hadn't seriously considered telling her parents about Natalie. *No kid needs grandparents like that*, she reasoned. "I don't know. I don't spend any time with them. It breaks my heart to say it, but they just aren't good people. They don't even accept me."

Natalie's eyes took on a faraway look as she considered the new information. "Okay, I'll stop interrupting you. Tell me the rest."

"Well, we started dating our sophomore year. I say 'dating' loosely, because it was mostly meeting places like the movies or a school dance. My parents would never have allowed him to pick me up at our house." She swallowed some lemonade and continued. "By our junior year, though, we were inseparable. I went to all his baseball games and everyone knew we were a couple. We were sure we were in love and we had all these plans about how we'd go to the same university so we could be together all the time."

Natalie sat quietly, leaning forward as if to capture every word. "And then?"

"And then we went to the beach one night after homecoming." Sara blushed but continued. "We were so in love, Natalie. I want you to know that. We may have only been teenagers, but you were conceived in love." Sudden tears pricked her eyes, and she wiped them away with her napkin. "As you can imagine, everyone was pretty freaked out when I found out I was pregnant. I was terrified to tell my parents."

"And my father?" Natalie's words were nearly a whisper.

"He was great," said Sara. "Scared to death, but great. From the very start, he was thinking about how we were gonna have a baby. He was the first one to talk about names."

Natalie's eyes widened. "Really? What did he want to name me?"

Sara saw the girl's eagerness and angst warring in her face. She longed to protect and comfort her as the story grew more difficult. "He liked Angel or Angela," she said simply. "He was convinced you would be an angel, whether you were a boy or a girl."

It was too much. Natalie's tears flowed down her face and Sara couldn't bear another moment. She stood and moved to the other side of the table and enveloped her daughter in her arms. "Oh, baby…" she soothed, her own tears sliding into Natalie's hair. "Shh…It's okay…." She didn't know what she was saying, only that every motherly instinct in her body exploded in love and concern for this precious girl. She cradled her daughter's head, stroking her hair and murmuring quietly. At last, Natalie sat back, her eyes red and her cheeks splotchy.

"I don't even know what to say or how to feel," she began in a choking voice.

"It's okay," soothed Sara. "This is new for us both—there's no right or wrong way to feel."

Natalie nodded and squeezed Sara's hand. Her mother recognized it as a sign to move back to her own chair.

"Do you want to take a break? Or stop talking?"

The girl shook her head fiercely. "No, no! Please keep going."

Sara wiped her own eyes and gazed at her daughter. "You know the next part. I was so intimidated by my parents, I just went along." She sat back, remembering. "I think I was in shock, mostly. I was in love but I was also terrified.

"When you were born, they didn't even let me keep you for a day. They delivered you and then whisked you off." She began to cry, soundless sobs that became harder. "They took you away from me," she finished in an anguished whisper. "I never saw you again."

Now it was Natalie's turn to come around the table. Sara sat dejected with her face in her hands, startled to feel her daughter's arms around her. "I'm so sorry," she whispered.

Sara's heart nearly stopped beating at her daughter's words, at her touch.

15

The two sat quietly for several minutes, neither willing to break the silence. At last, Sara spoke.

"I do have something else to tell you," she said softly. "I don't have any other children, but your father does." Natalie's eyes widened and it seemed to Sara that she held her breath. "He has another daughter."

Natalie reached for her lemonade and Sara saw her hand shaking. "A sister," she said, as if trying out the word in her mouth. Then she looked up. "Wait. I thought you hadn't seen him since I was born."

"I hadn't. Until just recently." Sara took a sip to steady her voice. "In one of those 'how on earth did this happen' situations, his daughter ended up in my math class."

Natalie sat back, a stunned look on her face. "You're kidding," she said flatly.

"I'm very serious. I saw him the other day for the first time since before you were born."

Her daughter leaned forward, an eager gleam in her eyes. "Tell me about him. About her. What are they like?" Her excitement was palpable and Sara quelled a momentary flash of jealousy.

"Your father is very much as he was when we were in high school. A little heavier, but still handsome." She smiled at the memory, then frowned as she realized she was sharing too much. "I don't mean to just drop this on you and then stop. I don't feel comfortable talking about them without his permission." She looked away, then back at her daughter. "I'm so sorry—that was thoughtless of me."

Natalie's eyes showed a flash of disappointment, quickly quelled. "It's okay."

Sara sat uneasily in her chair. She knew she'd gone too far talking about Carlos and Marisa and wondered how she could salvage their conversation. She excused herself to use the restroom to hide her discomfort. As she washed her hands, she looked in the mirror. Her mother's blue eyes looked back at her, but the rest of her face was her father's. Natalie had her smile, but her nose was Carlos'. *She's such a combination of the two of us*, thought Sara. She dried her hands and went back to the table, determined to put her own needs aside for the remainder of the visit. *My daughter needs me*, she thought. *This is a lot to process and she needs me.*

She sat and folded her hands, gauging her daughter's reaction. She watched as emotions flitted across the young woman's face, yet Natalie remained silent. "I told you I could help and I will. I know you probably want to meet them, but it might be better to give them a bit of time. His daughter only knows her dad and I knew each other in high school and she has no idea she has a sister."

Natalie nodded slowly. "This is a lot to take in," she admitted. "I don't know if I'm ready to meet them anyway." She looked away, thoughtful. The two women sat quietly for a moment before Natalie said, "Thank you, Sara."

Then she looked at her watch and her eyebrows shot up. "Four o'clock! Oh, no—I'm supposed to have dinner with my parents." She looked up at Sara. "I'm so sorry but I need to go. We're supposed to meet at five and I need to get all the way back to Orlando." She stood and reached for her purse, then stopped as Sara rose from her chair. "This is awkward—I don't know how to end today."

"It's okay. It's not the last time we'll see each other." *At least I hope not.*

"Of course not! We still have a lot to talk about." Natalie grew somber—*Almost shy,* thought Sara. "I want to get to know you."

Sara reached for her daughter and hugged her tightly. Natalie rested her cheek on Sara's shoulder and the two embraced for a long time.

"I'll give you whatever you need," murmured Sara. "I'm just thrilled to be a part of your life."

"And then she left to go meet her parents," finished Sara. She and Lauren sat crosslegged on each end of the sofa, wine glasses in hand and a nearly empty bottle on the coffee table. "I'm happy and wrung out at the same time."

"It sounds fantastic," mused Lauren. "I can't wait to meet her. Did you guys talk about getting together again?"

"We did, but we didn't make any specific plans. I'd love to see her before Christmas—maybe have her over here for dinner?"

Lauren nodded. "Absolutely. That would be perfect and super low key." She looked around their living room. "We need to start decorating if she's coming over. When's the last time we got a Christmas tree?"

Sara laughed. "Um, never?" They spent every Christmas with Lauren's family in Miami, so they didn't bother to decorate their home. *Maybe this year should be the first,* she thought.

"Let's talk about this tomorrow," she told her friend. "Six hours sitting and talking, and I'm beat." She stood and held out the wine bottle. "Want the rest?"

"Nah, I'm good," answered Lauren. "I'm gonna go to bed, too." She stood and hugged Sara. "I'm really, really happy for you."

Monday morning came and Sara left for school. Before walking out the front door, she looked around and smiled. She and Lauren had spent Sunday shopping and decorating their small home for the holidays. *We went a little crazy,* she thought, smiling at the sparkling tree in the corner of the room. With no fireplace in their coastal home, they'd hung stockings off their bookcase, and Lauren had insisted they buy one for Natalie. There were spiced candles in reindeer holders and a large wreath on their front door. It changed the entire space and she wondered why they'd never bothered to decorate before. *It's beautiful*, she decided, and closed the door behind her.

Terrence was waiting outside her classroom door when she arrived. "Good morning," he said brightly. "Have a good weekend?"

Sara looked at her former lover for a long minute. He'd hurt her deeply with his rejection and she wasn't ready to bounce back as if nothing had happened. "It was nice," she said, her voice guarded. "How about you?"

He reached for the door as she opened it, holding it while she put her keys away. "I went Christmas shopping and then took Oliver and Mackenzie to the beach." He followed her into the classroom and stood awkwardly as she set her things down at her desk. "Mackenzie always asks about you."

Sara looked up at him, waiting for him to go on. *I'm not going to be hateful*, she thought, *but I'm not making this easy for him.*

"She's not the only one who misses you." Terrence took a deep breath. "Sara, I was a jerk. I—I have some baggage. I guess I didn't realize it still was there and I took it out on you." He stepped forward, shaking his head. "I treated you shamefully," he said, his voice soft. "I'm so sorry."

Sara waited before responding, considering his words. Especially during the holiday with his family, she'd realized her feelings for him were deeper than she'd known. And while she recognized his rejection was far more about him than about her, it had wounded her.

"You hurt me, Terrence," she said simply. "You don't know anything about my situation and you jumped to conclusions about me. You made me out to be a terrible person—someone I'm not."

He reached for her, then stopped. "You're right—you're completely right. I don't know your history, but I know *you*, Sara. I know the incredible woman you are. I should have known what I was feeling had nothing to do with you." He looked directly at her. "Can you forgive me?"

She hesitated, then replied, "Of course I can forgive you. But I'm not ready to just forget about what happened."

Terrence closed his eyes for a quick moment. "Sara—I need to say this. I didn't only realize what a jackass I'd been. I realized something else." He reached for her hand but she pulled away.

"Not now, Terrence." She shook her head as she stepped back. "Not now."

His face fell, but he rallied. "I understand. I—"

Sara interrupted him as the bell rang. "We'd better get ready for class," she said.

Terrence nodded and tried again. "How about lunch?"

She looked long at him before answering. Anger continued to mingle with hurt as she turned to her desk. "Not today," she answered, refusing to look back at him as she heard him leave.

"So I guess my dad totally listened to you," said Marisa, talking around her sandwich. "He's gotten a lot better. This weekend he wanted to hang out and he even talked about my mom while we cooked dinner. We made her favorite—*arroz con pollo*. It was really cool, but weird to have him back to almost normal." She smiled. "Thanks for talking to him."

Sara and her student sat in her classroom having lunch. While Marisa chattered away, Sara found it difficult to concentrate on the girl's conversation. She looked carefully at Marisa's face, noticing her similarities to Natalie. They both had high cheekbones and beautiful almond-shaped eyes, although Marisa's were espresso brown like Carlos'. Natalie's green eyes were different from anyone in either family—*I guess we both had a recessive gene*, she thought idly.

"Miss Masterson?" Marisa looked quizzically at her teacher. "You okay?"

Sara realized she'd been daydreaming. "I'm sorry—I…I didn't sleep well last night and I'm just a bit off today." She smiled at the girl. "I'm glad you had a good weekend with your dad. It sounds really positive."

What would Marisa think about having an older sister? The teen had been through so much already this year. Would the knowledge that she had a sibling be welcome or even more disruptive? And how would Carlos react to having Natalie in his life?

Sara knew her distraction stemmed from more than her thoughts of Natalie, Marisa, and Carlos. Terrence's behavior had unsettled her, though he seemed genuinely contrite. She was by nature a forgiving person, so offering him the forgiveness he asked for wasn't difficult.

But forgetting? That was another story.

"And then he asked me if I wanted to visit her gravesite once a month or something—just to take flowers and be together." Marisa looked pensive. "Is that sus? Or is that a thing?"

Sara chuckled at the eighth-grader's slang. Offering to visit her mother's grave wasn't suspicious, and she was pretty certain it could be considered "a thing" by teenagers. "I think it would be lovely for you and your dad to do that together," she answered. "I'm really glad you two are talking about it."

Marisa finished her lunch and aimed the wadded up bag at the trash can. As it did every time, her lunch bag sailed through the air and landed squarely in the middle of the receptacle. "Swoosh!" she declared, smiling widely.

"I hope you play basketball again," said Sara. "You obviously love it and if your court game is as strong as your trashcan game, you'll make varsity your freshman year." *Just like your dad.* The two laughed and Marisa gathered her things to leave.

"Thanks, Miss Masterson," she said, her face now serious. "Thanks for letting me come and just hang out with you." She looked around the classroom. "I hope it doesn't suck having to be home alone with my dad every day for vacation."

Sara looked at the teen fondly. "It sounds like things are really improving. Maybe getting along with your dad will become 'a thing'?"

Marisa laughed. "Stick to talking like a grown up, Miss Masterson. See you later!"

The last three classes of the day went by and Sara was at her desk finishing some paperwork when she heard her door open. She looked up and was surprised to see Carlos.

"Hey, Sara," he said, his voice quiet. "I hope I'm not interrupting anything. I sorta snuck past the front office so I could just come see you. Do you have a minute?"

She stood and came around the desk. "Of course. Here—sit down." She motioned to the students' desks in the front row, but Carlos shook his head.

"I'd rather stand—I'm a little too keyed up for sitting."

Sara leaned against her desk and looked questioningly at him. "Is something wrong? I talked to Marisa today and she said you had a wonderful weekend together. It sounded really positive."

His shoulders slumped and he nodded. "It was nice. We talked and laughed, we cooked together. We even reminisced about Lisa."

"Your wife?"

He nodded again. "Yeah, sorry—my wife." He began pacing in front of her, rubbing his hands together. "Sara, I can't stop thinking about you…about…our daughter." He stopped in front of her. "I don't know how you've managed all these years, but I've tried hard to forget both of you for so long. And now here you are." His eyes dropped and he shook his head.

Sara stood very still, gazing at the man before her. She felt the tension radiating from him and spoke quietly. "I crammed it as deep as I could. I concentrated on school and then on more school and then I started teaching school. I've spent all these years trying to forget you both, too. But, Carlos, I can't cram it anymore." She took a step toward him. "Her name is Natalie and I met her this weekend."

Carlos' head shot up, his eyes wide. "Oh, my God," he murmured. "How—how—"

"She found me a few months ago and we've been messaging each other. This is the first time we met in person."

He began pacing again, then stopped to look at her. "What's she like?"

"She's wonderful," began Sara. "She's beautiful and smart and kind. You'd be so proud of her." She hesitated, wondering how much to share. "She looks like both of us, but it's clear she and Marisa are sisters."

He flinched, then brought his hands to his face. He was quiet at first, but then began to shake as the sobs overtook him. He stood directly in front of her and Sara thought her heart would break.

Without hesitating, she reached for him and cradled his head on her shoulder as he cried. His arms went around her and she held him close. "She's wonderful," she repeated. "Our daughter is the angel you always knew she'd be." She stroked his hair, his anguish moving her to tears.

More than two decades of loss nearly consumed them as they held each other.

She heard the door to her classroom and saw Terrence walk in.

His smile froze and his eyes widened as he saw their embrace. His jaw tightened in an anguished expression and he spun around to leave.

Carlos turned slightly at the sound. He rubbed at his eyes and asked, "Who was that?"

"It was Terrence—Marisa's language arts teacher," she answered quietly. "Give me just a second."

They awkwardly released each other and Sara followed Terrence into the hallway. Her nerves were frayed, and she wasn't in the mood to coddle him. There was no one around, and so she called out.

"Terrence!"

He stopped, but didn't turn around.

Sara strode up to him, grabbed his arm, and spun him to face her. She knew it was obvious she'd been crying and she didn't try to hide her emotions. "If you're gonna jump to conclusions again, let me know now," she said roughly. "Don't assume you understand any of what you just saw."

"I promise, I'm not making assumptions about you ever again—" he began, his eyes pleading.

She interrupted him. "I was comforting an old friend who is grieving. A friend I have known for *over twenty years*."

His brows drew together in puzzlement. "Isn't that Marisa Segovia's dad?"

Sara released his arm. "Yes," she said quietly. "We went to high school together." *And that's all you need to know.*

Terrence stood quietly, his arms by his side. He started to speak, then stopped. Sara stood very still, waiting to see how he would respond, yet eager to return to Carlos.

At last his shoulders relaxed and he spoke softly. "I'm sorry for interrupting. Please, go take care of your friend. " His hands twitched, as if he were trying not to reach for her. He looked at her, his eyes hopeful. "Maybe tomorrow we can have lunch or go out for coffee after school? I really want to see you, Sara."

She looked into his face and saw the sincerity in his eyes. *I can't focus on you right now.* "We'll see," she hedged. "I need to go."

As she turned, he said, "Sara," his voice quiet and low.

She turned back and he took a step toward her. He reached up and gently wiped her cheek. "Little bit of mascara," he said, his fingers lingering on her face.

Sara reached up and pulled his hand away. "I'll see you tomorrow, Terrence."

He nodded and she returned to her classroom.

She nearly ran into Carlos leaving as she entered her door. "Oh, sorry—" she began.

"It's okay," he answered. "I—I need to go." His eyes were red and swollen, but he seemed to have regained his composure. "I'm sorry about that. I didn't plan on falling apart."

They walked back into her classroom and Sara closed the door. "Carlos, please don't apologize. I've had months to think about this and process everything. I'm still processing. You've only had a couple of days—and it's compounded by everything you've been through this year."

"Thank you," he said simply. "And thank you for everything you're doing for Marisa. She's so much better." He took a deep breath. "To be honest, I wasn't crazy about the idea of her leaning on you. It was just too much. But I want what's best for her and she loves spending time with you."

"She's a great kid, Carlos. You and Lisa have raised a wonderful daughter. She's bright and curious and funny."

She reminds me so much of you.

"Thank you," he repeated. He looked away, then back at her. "So what do we do now?"

"That's really up to you." She flushed as she remembered her heedless conversation with their daughter. "She said she hadn't found you yet and…." Sara looked away, embarrassed. "I told her a little about you and Marisa—no names, nothing about Lisa. I'm sorry. I know I should have asked you first but it just sort of tumbled out when she asked."

Carlos frowned. "I wish you'd talked to me first, but I get it." He ran a hand through his hair. "I'm a little concerned about telling Marisa. She's been through so much this year and having a sister suddenly appear might be too much." He looked long at Sara. "Not to mention finding out about us."

"I understand and I'm really sorry. I'll do whatever you want and I did make it clear to Natalie that I had overstepped. I didn't even give her your name," she added. Then she asked, "What do you think Marisa will say?"

"I honestly don't know. She always wanted siblings, but it just never happened. She could be happy or it could throw her into a tailspin. But about you and me? No idea. We'll have to pull her out of your class, I guess," he finished weakly. "It would be weird for her to stay here."

Sara was shaking her head before he finished. "No, no," she said emphatically. "This is the advanced class—the best place for someone as bright at Marisa. We're just gonna have to figure it out." She stopped, suddenly aware she was again overstepping. "I'm sorry," she said. "She's your daughter and it's not up to me. I'll support whatever you decide."

"Just give me a little time," he said. "My mind is going a million different directions and I don't know what's right." He looked directly at Sara. "We need to do what's best for our daughter, too."

Her eyes filled. *If only we had done that years ago*, she thought. She knew Carlos didn't mean anything by the comment, but it stung nevertheless. "I'm going to keep seeing her," she answered. "You let me know when you're ready, and I'll talk to Natalie. We spent months just texting. Maybe that's the way to start for you, too."

"Did you take a picture when you were together?" he asked, his eyes hopeful.

"No, I was afraid to ask," she confessed. "But you can find her on social media." She reached for her phone and opened Natalie's photos on Instagram. She warmed as she looked at her daughter's smiling face, then turned the screen to Carlos. "Here she is," she murmured.

His eyes widened as he reached for the phone. Tears gathered again as he scrolled through the pictures. "She looks like you," he breathed.

"And you," she added.

He looked up, his eyes shining. "She really is an angel."

Later that night, Sara was sitting at the kitchen table grading papers when Lauren walked in, threw her bag on the counter, and opened the refrigerator. "Please tell me we have wine or chocolate," she said in an irritated tone. "Preferably both."

"Rough day?" asked Sara.

"Unbelievable," Lauren answered as she reached into the freezer. "Aha! I knew we still had ice cream." She set the carton on the table, got a spoon from the drawer, and reached into the cabinet for a wine glass. "Wanna join me?"

Sara grinned. "Nah, my day was just fine. I'll stick with my hummus and celery." She pointed to the small plate next to her.

"Blech," said Lauren, miming a gag reflex. "I'll just go with the hard stuff." She poured a healthy glass of wine and sat down.

"What was so bad about today?" asked Sara, setting her papers aside to focus on her friend.

"I guess it wasn't really bad," admitted Lauren. "But so incredibly busy. This new client Susana scored is demanding and the work just keeps coming. First they wanted a rebrand, but now it's more than all the usual stuff. They're completely redoing their website, all their collateral, and renaming all their products. And it has to be done for a January premiere." She took a huge spoonful of mint chip ice cream and shoved it into her mouth. Closing her eyes, she groaned. "Ouch—too cold!"

Sara laughed and shook her head. "You never do anything halfway, do you?" She dipped her celery into the hummus and took a bite, laughing as Lauren scrunched up her eyes in pain. "So that sounds busy but it also sounds like fun. Isn't that why you went back? And isn't it great Suze put you on the new account?"

Lauren took a drink of her wine. "Yeah," she admitted. She looked up with a mischievous smile. "It's pretty freaking awesome, actually."

Sara looked askance at her best friend. "Okay, so I'm confused. Rough day or awesome day? What's got you all wound up?"

"The client. He's—well…." She trailed off and threw up her hands in an exasperated gesture.

Sara burst out laughing. "You fell for *a client?*"

"Omigod, Sara—he's gorgeous and single and smart and we just hit it off…." She looked chagrined. "It's so embarrassing." She took another bite of ice cream, this time smaller. "I'm pretty sure no one has noticed, but it's crazy hard to be around this guy and not want to kiss him until he can't breathe."

Sara shook her head fondly at her dearest friend. "Nothing like jumping to the chase," she said. "Do you know anything about him?" A sly look crossed her face. "Like, does he have Wolverine abs?"

Lauren barked a laugh, nearly gagging on her ice cream. "I would dearly love to find out," she said with a smirk.

The women laughed and then Lauren said, "Enough about my crazy life. How was your day? Did you see dumbass?"

Sara grimaced. "Yeah. At the worst possible time." At Lauren's questioning look, she added, "Carlos came by my classroom after school."

Lauren's shocked expression needed no words.

"Yeah," continued Sara. "He's been thinking about Natalie and wanted to talk. He pretty much had a meltdown." Her face fell, remembering. "Then Terrence walked in and saw us holding each other."

"Damn."

"Yeah, it was pretty awkward." Sara described the brief conversation in the hallway and her return to Carlos.

Lauren took another bite of ice cream and scooted her chair closer. "This is like some *telenovela*, my friend."

Sara laughed. Lauren's *abuela* watched the Spanish-language dramas constantly, and the two roommates used it as a running joke whenever they saw extreme drama anywhere.

Then Lauren's face grew serious. "But I do feel for Carlos. That's a helluva lot to process in a short amount of time."

Sara walked down the corridor to her classroom and could see Terrence waiting outside her door. As she approached, he stepped forward, a small bouquet in his hand. "I didn't think about a vase," he said, a wry grin on his face. "I hope they won't be dead by the end of the day."

"This isn't necessary—" she began.

"I didn't do it because it was necessary," he said softly. "I did it because they're beautiful and they made me think of you."

"Terrence—"

"I know, Sara. I know." He took a deep breath. "I need to slow down and regain your trust."

Sara looked at him, startled at the sincerity she saw on his face. For the briefest moment she remembered his arms around her, his lips on her breasts—

No. Stop it.

"Terrence," she began, her voice quiet. "I don't know what I need. I can't pretend I don't still have feelings for you but I am not ready to jump into anything. I'm still angry, to be honest."

He looked down, abashed. "You have every right to be. I just hope that there are enough good memories of us that you think of those, too."

"I do," she confessed. "But you're right—you didn't just hurt me. You broke the trust we'd built. What if that happens again? What if there's some other baggage you haven't shared with me that comes up and derails us? I'm not gonna go through that again."

He reached for her hand and this time she let him take it. "I'll do whatever it takes to prove to you that I'm not that guy. No matter what happens, I will never hurt you like that again." He looked deeply into her eyes. "I love you, Sara."

Her eyes widened and she stood rooted to the floor until the bell startled her. "Uh—I'll put these in a coffee mug," she stammered as she took the blooms. The burgundy and white blossoms were set off with small sprigs of pine, then tied with a silver bow. She looked away, then back at him. "They're beautiful. Thank you."

He seemed to relax at her thanks and held the door as she unlocked and opened it. "I'm glad you like them."

Sara found herself looking at the bouquet all day. They gave off a lovely scent, the pine reminding her that Christmas was only a couple of weeks away. When fourth period rolled around, Marisa caught her leaning over to breathe in their fragrance.

"Nice flowers, Miss Masterson. You never have stuff like that on your desk." The teen smirked. "Secret admirer?"

Sara felt a blush rising to her cheeks, but laughed it off. "Nah, just thought it would be nice to have a little holiday spirit." At Marisa's raised eyebrows, she added, "And I happen to like the smell of pine." She shooed the girl to her desk with a laugh.

Am I ready for this? she wondered. Her feelings for Terrence had been intense and serious only weeks before. She allowed herself the slimmest opening to imagine rekindling them. His remorse seemed serious but she was wary.

What do I want?

17

Sara's stomach was in knots all afternoon as she asked herself the same question over and over.

She was thankful Lauren worked late that evening, giving her the time to think alone. Memories of Terrence's kindness and tenderness warred with his thoughtless, almost cruel words. She thought of their long talks, their walks on the beach, their shared passion for teaching. She remembered the feel of his arms around her, the curve of her body nestling perfectly with his—and then the cold pain of his rejection.

What do I want?

Sara was by nature a loving, forgiving woman. Even after everything her mother had done to her, she harbored a desire for a relationship. Without making excuses for her parents' behavior, she thought she understood their choices. Her mother was a broken woman, always seeking—*needing*—the validation of her posh friends. Everything about Cecilia revolved around image management and a pregnant teenager didn't fit her country club profile.

Sara had forgiven Terrence but the question remained: *Can I trust him?* She'd shared her feelings about Natalie with Lauren, but it wasn't the same as having a partner who could understand and support her. If getting back together with Terrence meant sequestering her relationship with her daughter, she wouldn't do it.

But what if she didn't have to?

What do I really want?

She picked up her phone to text him.

Sara eased her car into the parking lot at Lala Latte, a cute new indie café Terrence suggested. She checked her lipstick in the mirror, grabbed her purse, and began to open her door. She was startled when someone from the outside pulled at it, then reached in a hand to help her out.

"Milady," said Terrence, smiling.

Sara looked up and, after a moment, took his hand. He held it as they walked to the front door. "I haven't been here yet but it keeps popping up in my Instagram feed," he said. "Looks good."

"Same here," said Sara. She gently pulled away from his grasp as they entered the café. Cheerful holiday decorations covered the whitewashed pine walls, and Christmas jazz music played in the background. Even with the silver festooned white flocked tree in the corner, the café exuded a typical sunshine state ambience. Along the middle of the café there was a long line of hanging chairs where a group of friends were swinging and chatting. At the back of the deep room were cushy seats and low tables, and Terrence gestured that direction.

"How's that?" he asked. "It's a little more private."

She nodded and they set their things down. "Why don't you sit and save this for us and I'll go order our drinks?" offered Terrence. "What would you like? Are you hungry?"

Sara was surprised to find she was starving. She thought back over her day and realized she hadn't eaten anything other than toast before leaving the house. Since deciding to meet with Terrence, her stomach had been in knots. "I'd love a mint tea and a scone or something like that," she admitted. "But I can go grab it—"

He was shaking his head even as she spoke. "I got it. I'll be right back."

She watched at him as he walked to the counter. After considering her decision for hours the previous night, she finally texted Terrence. *Let's talk*, she'd messaged. *How's after school tomorrow?*

He'd immediately responded with a heart on her message and *WONDERFUL!*

Terrence returned with their drinks. He set them down, then returned to the counter for their treats. "Cranberry-orange scone for the lady," he said, setting a plate down in front of her. "Pumpkin bread for the gentleman." He cocked his head at her. "No coffee this afternoon, huh?"

"Nah, it just doesn't sound good today." She sipped at her tea. "Oh, this is delicious! Thank you very much."

He sat down next to her and raised his mug. "Cheers?" he asked, a bit hesitantly.

She raised hers to clink with his. "Cheers," she said.

They enjoyed their treats for a few quiet moments and then Terrence set his coffee down. He turned in his chair to face her and began in a quiet voice. "Sara. I know you already accepted my apology, but I need to say it again. I'm so sorry. I can't begin to tell you how sorry I am. I was a complete and total jerk—I wasn't thinking of anyone but myself." He ran a hand through his hair and looked away. "It's no excuse, I know, but I had a bad experience a few years ago and I guess I wasn't over it." He looked back at her, pain in his eyes. "I took it out on you."

Sara sat without speaking, waiting for him to continue.

"I was engaged once," he began. "About five years ago. Her name is Stephanie. We met at the gym—just kinda bonded over working out and sitting at the juice bar afterwards. She was fun and beautiful, and we started dating." He looked away and blew out a sharp breath. "Anyway, after about a year, I thought I was in love. She was so different from me—she was an only child. Her dad had split when she was young, and her mom was still bitter decades later.

"I asked her to marry me and she wasn't all that thrilled about the idea. She wanted to just 'keep things the same'—" Terrence made air quotes as he spoke. "But I've always known I wanted to be married and have a family…a family like mine." He was quiet, looking down at his hands.

"So what happened?" prompted Sara gently.

"She finally agreed but the magic was kinda gone. And then she seemed stressed about telling her mom. We visited her one time—she lives in North Carolina. Stephanie told her over the phone and her mom's only comment was, 'Whatever you do, don't take his last name. Next thing you know he'll expect you to start cranking out kids.'"

Sara's eyes widened. "Ouch."

"Yeah. It was just a harbinger of the end before it ever started," he said. He glanced up. "Well, that wasn't pretentious at all."

"What?"

"Using the word 'harbinger' when I'm spilling my guts."

Sara smiled wryly. "I'm so sorry."

Terrence shook his head. "No, no—it's okay. It was for the best. I was stupid and I didn't pay attention to the red flags. I fell for her looks and the fantasy of what I wanted, not what was real." He reached for Sara's hand. "After she told me about the conversation with her mom, she made it very clear that she wasn't interested in having kids." He frowned. "That's a non-negotiable for me—"

"And you assumed I felt the same way because of the adoption?"

Terrence grimaced. "I guess. I didn't even think—I just reacted like a complete idiot. I didn't ask questions, I didn't stop to wonder about why I was so upset.

"I wasn't the man I should have been—the man I *want* to be."

Sara sat quietly as he spoke. She opened her mouth to respond, but Terrence interjected.

"I love you, Sara. I want to make things right. I want us back to where we were—hell, I want us to be more than we were." He took her hand and this time she didn't pull away. He lifted it to his lips, kissing her fingers gently. His voice grew more confident. "I can't imagine my life without you."

She had a sudden recollection of their first date. Terrence had interrupted her and then caught himself and apologized.

She'd been surprised at his self-awareness and humility even then. *He's the same man*, she told herself. *Everyone makes mistakes.*

And then she decided.

She reached up with her fingers to touch his cheek. His eyes bored into hers as she spoke, her voice soft but sure. "I feel the same way." She thought about her next words, knowing they could end this tenuous connection. "But first, I want to tell you about my daughter."

"You don't owe me any explanation," he broke in.

"You're right," she said simply. "I don't. But if we are going to make a go of this, we need to be completely honest with each other."

He reached for her hand. "Okay. Tell me."

Sara began quietly, describing the past months since Natalie contacted her. Her voice grew stronger as she spoke, finishing with the face to face meeting.

Terrence was quiet as he listened, his eyes never leaving her face. At last, he reached for her and she leaned into his embrace. "I'm really happy for you."

I believe you, she thought, but then pulled away and looked into his eyes. "There's something else I should tell you."

He brushed a stray hair from her cheek and smiled. "What else, love?"

"Carlos Segovia is her father."

Terrence stiffened and looked away. She watched as he struggled to manage his emotions. This was the moment, she knew, that would determine their future.

"So that's what yesterday was about?" he asked softly.

"It was. We hadn't seen each other in twenty-three years before our parent-teacher conference the other day. I told him about Natalie and it was just too much, given everything he's been through this year."

He took a deep breath and asked, "Do you see yourself with him again?"

Sara stared at him, understanding dawning. "Oh, no— nothing like that. We loved each other when we were *children*, Terrence. We share a daughter, yes. Will we be involved in each other's lives again? It looks that way. But us? A couple? No."

His relief was palpable and she saw his shoulders and face relax.

I was a child when I fell in love the first time.

Sara reached up to stroke his cheek. "I could never be with Carlos again because it turns out I've fallen in love with someone else."

When he leaned forward to kiss her, she knew she'd made the right decision.

Sara was asleep on the sofa when Lauren entered the living room. "OK, *perezosa*, wake up! I need to talk." She flopped down next to Sara's feet. "Why are you asleep out here?"

Sara rubbed her eyes and groaned. "What time is it?"

"Only 11:00," replied her friend as she tossed her legs across Sara's. "You're usually at the table grading papers this time of night."

Sara struggled to sit up, kicking at Lauren's legs. "Get off me, goofball." She looked intently at her friend. "So what's got you so amped?"

"We decided to start dating. We officially asked MPG to take me off the account and we're gonna start seeing each other." Lauren rolled her neck and shoulders in an exaggerated show of relief.

Sara laughed and patted her friend's leg. "That's great! So what's Mister Former Client's name? What's his story? And how did Susana react?" Now that she was fully awake, she was keen to hear the details.

Lauren grabbed the end of the throw blanket Sara had covering her. "It's chilly—gimme some of this." They managed to share the blanket across the couch and Lauren continued. "His name is Jayson Rivera. He's VP of marketing at Thompson Toys. It's a family-owned business, been around for a hundred years and it's their first time ever using an agency. He's 52, never been married, gorgeous, smart, funny—did I mention he's gorgeous?" The women laughed. "And Susana gave me that 'Right now, I'm not your boss, I'm your big sister' lecture about 'Are you sure and do you really want to give up this career opportunity' blahblahblah but then approved me moving off the account." She pulled on her end of the blanket and Sara yanked back. "So now I'm back on the business-to-business side of the house and off the consumer account team."

Sara looked fondly at her friend. Lauren hadn't dated anyone seriously in years—she always put her career first. "I'm really happy for you." She leaned back on the cushion and continued. "He's 52? That's like Azalea and Susana's age."

Lauren lifted an eyebrow. "So? All that means is he isn't immature." She pulled on the blanket. "Quit being a blanket hog."

"Now who's immature?"

Lauren grinned. "Whatever. So how about you? Anything exciting happen today? Any more Carlos drama?"

"I went out with Terrence after school."

Sara's best friend stared at her in horror. "No! Seriously? What happened?"

Lauren was fiercely loyal to her and it would take a lot for her to warm back up to Terrence. The fact that he'd hurt Sara so badly was a death knell in her friend's universe.

"I spent a long time last night thinking about everything and I decided to give him another chance." She smiled at Lauren's scowl. "He apologized, again. He was sincere and gentle and really vulnerable about his past." Her face softened as she remembered his words. "He loves me, Lauren." She looked squarely at her dearest friend. "I told him about Natalie and about Carlos."

Lauren's voice was tight. "And?"

"He was shocked at first but then he was really great. Supportive and happy for me." She waited, sensing her friend was trying keep from blurting out her first—and probably angry—reaction.

Lauren sat back, her eyebrows knit together in thought. After opening and closing her mouth several times, she finally asked, "You know I'd do anything for you, right?"

"I do."

"So you know that I will do my very best to get over how he treated you. I promise not to be rude or bitchy when I see him, okay?" Sara nodded, waiting for what would come next.

"But if he hurts you again, I will throat punch him and throw his body in the swamp where the alligators can have him."

The friends burst out laughing.

18

The next morning, Sara struggled to get out of bed, hitting the snooze button on her phone twice before she managed to fully wake. She took a quick shower and got ready in a hurry, pausing only to respond to Terrence's text message.

Good morning, love. I hope you slept well. Looking forward to seeing you today.

Good morning! I overslept so I'm rushing. See you soon

Without enough time to dry her long hair, she braided it and let it hang over one shoulder. "Good enough," she muttered at her reflection. She knew the students didn't care how she looked and she was fairly certain Terrence would be happy as long as she showed up at school.

As she opened her car door to leave, her phone rang. She held it to her ear as she started the car, allowing it to connect to the speakers before answering. "Hi, Natalie!"

"Hi, Sara—is now okay to talk? I wasn't sure what your mornings are like."

"Yep, I'm driving to school, so I have about 15 minutes free. Everything all right?"

"Ugh…sort of. I have a meeting with my advisor to talk about my thesis today and I'm not super focused. I keep thinking about my birthfather."

"I'm so sorry. Is there anything I can do?'

"You mean like listening to me blab while you're driving to work? Nah, it's okay. I'll figure it out." She paused, then asked, "So did he say anything about meeting me?"

Sara hesitated. She didn't want to discourage her daughter, but it had only been two days since she'd seen Carlos. "Not yet, but I'm sure he will. He just needs more time."

"I understand. It's a big deal for all of us." Natalie's voice betrayed her disappointment. "Well, wish me luck with the advisor and let's talk soon."

Sara stifled a yawn. "I'm sure you'll be fabulous, Natalie. I'd love to hear all about your project. Let me know when you want to get together again." She pondered her next statement as she drove. "I do have someone I'd like you to meet."

"Ooh, that sounds mysterious," said Natalie, her voice brightening. "Is this your roommate? Or someone else?"

"I definitely want you to meet Lauren," said Sara. "She's dying to meet you. But I've been seeing a guy…."

"'Seeing a guy?'" Natalie chuckled. "I don't think you introduce your long-lost daughter to just 'a guy.'"

Sara grinned. "Okay, he's more than a guy. But saying 'boyfriend' sounds kinda ridiculous at my age." She tilted her head, gazing out the window. *What do I call him?* she wondered.

"Well, whatever you call him, I'd love to meet him. How'd you meet?"

Sara spent the next few minutes answering her daughter's questions and then pulled into the parking lot at her school.

"So what's his name?'

Sara looked out her window just in time to see him stepping out of his car.

"It's Terrence."

The two teachers walked into the school and waved goodbye in the hall between their classes. Sara insisted their relationship remain private, not wanting to deal with nosy teenagers or colleagues. Terrence had agreed and only winked at her as they parted.

The day went by quickly and Sara found she was very ready to get home. As she packed her things, Terrence walked into her room. He made a show of looking around before he approached her for a hug.

"Just wanted to be certain no one was around before I got too close," he said, his voice playful. "How was your day?"

"Good," she answered, stifling a yawn. "I'm tired, though. This week felt like three weeks' with everything going on. I think everything just finally caught up to me. Two more days—I'm ready for vacation."

Terrence stepped back and held her hands. "I wanted to ask you about that. What are your plans for Christmas?"

"I'm going to Lauren's parents' house in Miami," she began. "I'm part of the Ochoa family after all these years." He gazed long at her and she grew uncomfortable. "What?"

"I know it's a lot to ask, but would you consider coming back to Ft. Lauderdale with me? My family would love to see you again." He squeezed her hands. "And I really want to spend the holidays with you."

The thought of another holiday with the Billings family warmed her heart. While she'd practically been adopted by Lauren's family and loved spending time with all of them, there was something different, something special about Terrence's family.

Something that pulled at her heart.

"I'd like that," she answered simply. "But I need to talk to Lauren. She's expecting me to drive down with her—"

"Well, we could all drive down together and she could just drop us off in Ft. Lauderdale. It's a quick drive to Miami from there." He laughed. "Might be fun."

Sara's stomach tightened at the thought of Lauren spending three hours in a car with Terrence. There were plenty of swamps along the Florida coastline where her fiery friend could drop him if he said the slightest thing that antagonized her.

"We'll see. I'll just talk to her," hedged Sara. "Thank you for the invitation—I had such a nice time at Thanksgiving."

"Everyone loves you," he asserted. "They'll be thrilled if you come."

Sara smiled, then covered another yawn with the back of her hand. "Sorry!" she apologized. "Couldn't get myself up this morning and I've been just beat all day."

He slid his arms around and and whispered, "I guess that means you wouldn't be interested in having dinner with me tonight?"

She tilted her head back to receive his kiss. "I didn't say that."

Sara and Terrence went for an early dinner at The Oyster Pub. She had math tests to grade but figured she could do them later that evening. She liked to give students their results the day after a test—the advanced students especially awaited grades and she didn't want to disappoint them.

They gorged on the restaurant's famous chargrilled oysters, ignoring the dozens of televisions showing every conceivable sport. They tacitly agreed to pick up their relationship where they had left off before the Thanksgiving debacle and chatted amiably, avoiding anything heavy. Instead, Sara peppered Terrence with questions about his family's holiday traditions.

"So how do you do presents?" she asked. "At Lauren's house, it's different every year." She frowned. "And at my house it was just one ridiculously expensive gift and then dinner at some swanky restaurant so my mother didn't have to cook."

Terrence looked sadly at her. "I'm really sorry," he began.

"Don't be. I've had lots of great Christmases with Lauren's family." She chuckled. "And I have a couple of nice Louis Vuitton bags from my parents. Pretty sure my dad's assistant ordered them for me."

He grimaced. "On that note, we're careful with what we spend on each other. There aren't any official limits, but nobody goes crazy. We buy for everyone and my parents still fill our stockings." He looked embarrassed as he concluded, "It's kinda dumb, but we all love it, even my brothers-in-law."

Sara grinned. "I think that's adorable!"

"Well, they'll do it for you, too," he warned. "We need to take your stocking with us."

She smiled. "As luck would have it, I just bought one. Lauren and I have never decorated the house before, but we were thinking maybe Natalie would visit so we got a tree and everything."

"I haven't decorated at all," he admitted. "But I would love to bring an angel to my apartment...."

Terrence slowly kissed her as they undressed, his fingers twining into her hair and gently caressing her shoulders. He seemed tentative, she thought, as if he were unsure of her reactions. *We're done with the past*, she told herself. *It's over.*

She pulled him fiercely to her, pulling his shirt up and over his head with barely a moment between kisses. "Stop being so careful," she whispered. "Either we're together or we're not.

"And I want you. Now."

He stared intently at her, then nodded. They stumbled to his bed where she pulled the covers down as he hurried to put on a condom. Without a word, she pushed him down and straddled his hips, sliding hard onto him as he moaned and reached for her. His hands stroked her breasts as she moved deliberately, clasping him tightly. Her skin grew warm and she flung her long braid over her shoulder, reaching back to grasp his thighs. Her breath quickened and her back arched as he moved his hands to her hips.

"Sara—" he gasped.

She was unaware of his climax, she was so focused on her own. Her body felt as if it were full of magic, of shooting stars and electricity. Her own cry of pleasure surprised her and she quivered, then lay on his chest, beads of sweat between her breasts.

They were quiet for a long time, and then Terrence spoke. "That was incredible. You've never been that...I don't know—"

She smiled against his skin. "I've never felt like that before," she whispered.

He wrapped his arms around her. "Don't leave. Please stay."

She yawned, then kissed his chest. "I can't. I don't have anything with me and I sure can't show up at school in the same clothes tomorrow. Can you imagine what the kids would say?"

They lay still for a few moments more, and then Sara yawned again. "I have to get up or I'm gonna fall asleep." She sat up, rubbing her eyes. She looked tenderly at Terrence, his face so dear to her. Something had changed with their lovemaking, she knew. She had felt free in a way she'd never experienced. She felt sexy and beautiful—and her body had reacted passionately.

She stood and dressed and kissed Terrence. "Don't get up," she said, pushing his shoulder back to the pillows. "I'll see you in the morning."

His curls lay damp on his forehead and he looked at her in wonder. "I love you."

"I love you, too."

Sara did her best to concentrate on her classes the next day but found herself daydreaming over and over about the night before. Terrence had stopped by her room before classes started and it was all she could do not to rip his clothes off. *What's going on with me?* she wondered. At the thought of him, her breasts swelled and her stomach tightened, and she could hardly wait until after school. They hadn't made plans, but she was certain they would see each other again.

Despite her excitement, she was tired from the late night. After she got home, she'd dutifully graded the math tests for her first four classes and hadn't gotten to bed until after one o'clock. By the time her fourth period class began, she was ready for a nap. Marisa and another student were working a problem on the board when Sara turned her head and covered her mouth to yawn.

"I'm sorry, Miss Masterson," said the teen with a sly grin. "Are we boring you?" She turned back to the board and quickly sketched a cartoon bed. Its occupant's eyes were closed, and she wrote ZZZZZ over the drawing.

Sara laughed. Was there anything this girl wasn't good at? Math, basketball, and now cartooning? "Very funny," she said, motioning to the board. "Quit stalling and finish the problem before John does."

"Too late!" exclaimed John. He circled the answer with a flourish. "Beat you—finally." Sara stood and took the markers from her students. "Well done, John," she said. "That's the right answer and you did a great job showing your work." Marisa scowled, but dipped her head in acknowledgment. No one in class ever beat her solving problems at the board.

"Good job," she said. As Marisa walked back to her desk, Sara heard her mutter, "Don't get used to it."

When the bell rang, Marisa hung back as the other students rushed out for lunch. Sara opened her laptop to enter grades for the fifth and sixth period tests she'd neglected the night before and hoped the teen didn't plan to stay.

"Everything okay, Marisa?"

The girl scowled as she zipped up her backpack. "You know I would have beat him if I didn't draw that dumb cartoon," she complained.

Sara laughed. "You know I can't comment on other students," she said primly.

Marisa rolled her eyes. "Whatever."

Sara looked down at her laptop, willing the girl to leave so she could finish her work. At last, Marisa spoke.

"No lunch today?" she asked, dawdling as she walked past Sara's desk.

"I have something in my bag. I just need to finish grading these tests from yesterday."

"Ah, okay. Well, have a good day, Miss Masterson. See you later."

Sara smiled at the girl as she shouldered her backpack and left. She felt a pang of guilt that she hadn't invited Marisa to stay for one of their talks. *I hope she's all right.*

She finished grading the last of the math tests and pushed back her chair. Terrence had been disappointed that she couldn't have lunch with him but he understood. It was nice to have a partner who didn't complain when she had a deadline and she wondered how other couples balanced their workloads. Susana and Enrique were both executives in their respective firms—she laughed at the thought of their schedules. One day of rushed eighth grade math tests likely didn't come close to their high powered careers.

She entered the final grade into her spreadsheet and closed her laptop. As she leaned back in her chair, she glanced up at

Hypatia's poster on the wall. *Was it always a struggle?* she asked. *Or did you have wonderful days like this, too?* She sat back, a smile on her face.

It was a wonderful day.

19

The remaining two classes went smoothly, and Sara was preparing to leave when Marisa surprised her by returning.

"Sorry to bother you, but do you have just a minute?" The girl looked uncomfortable but continued. "I have a question and I can't ask my dad."

Sara looked at her student. *So there is something wrong.* She set her bag down and motioned to the front row of seats. "Of course—let's sit. What's up?"

Just then, Terrence walked in and announced, "Okay, my queen—" His eyes widened as he saw Marisa, who hurriedly hid a smile.

"You can just call me 'Marisa,'" said the teen, losing the fight to keep the grin off her face.

Sara stood gaping at their student, then blew out a slow breath. "Mr. Billings, I'm working with Marisa right now, so I'll have to talk with you later." Her starched tone of voice didn't fool anyone.

"You guys are pathetic," commented Marisa. She looked back and forth between the teachers and giggled. "Don't worry—I'm not gonna tell anyone. Your secret is safe with me," she whispered conspiratorially. She sat back, appraising the two. "So *you* gave her the flowers. That's lit. You guys are a super cute couple."

Terrence laughed, seeming at ease with the situation. *How does he do that?* wondered Sara. She was still flustered, but he appeared unfazed.

"Well, then," he said, "I'll leave you to it…*Miss Masterson.*" He winked, bowed, and left the room.

"So…" began Marisa.

"Nope," responded Sara. "Not gonna discuss it." She resumed her teacher air. "So what did you want to talk about?"

Marisa grinned, the knowing smile on her face far too old for her thirteen years. Then she frowned. "It's kinda lame," she confessed, "but I can't talk to my dad about it." She made a face and threw up her hands. "What do I do about cramps? My period sucks and I have really bad cramps."

Sara relaxed. "Oh, the joys of being a girl, right? I've had really bad cramps my whole life. And my periods have always been heavy and unpredictable, which is super fun. I do have a few things that work for me." She motioned at the soda in Marisa's hand. "First thing is no caffeine. Drink lots of water. Also, you can take an ibuprofen—that helps me pretty quickly. And when mine are really bad, I just lie down with a heating pad." She shrugged. "My roommate swears by working out, but that never seems to help me." She leaned forward. "I know it's awkward, but I still think you should talk to your dad. He loves you and he'd hate that you're trying to figure this on your own."

Marisa scowled. "You can't really be serious," she said, arcing her soda can predictably into the wastebasket. "Anyway, I'm not on my own. I have you, right?" Her coy smile made Sara laugh. "And since you keep my secrets, I guess I'll keep yours." She left the classroom, still giggling.

Sara hoped Marisa was serious about keeping her relationship with Terrence private and was glad the girl had felt comfortable enough to ask personal questions. Sara had learned about menstruation from her friends' older sisters. Her mother never talked about anything other than Sara's grades, her weight, and her clothes.

Poor Carlos. She smiled, imagining him at the grocery store picking out tampons. She couldn't imagine her father ever having done it. Their housekeeper did all the shopping.

She finished packing her bag and then it hit her: *When is the last time I had a period?*

Sara rushed out of her classroom, nearly running into Terrence as he exited his own room.

Whoa!" he exclaimed. "What's the hurry?"

Not now, she thought. *I can't have this conversation now.*

"I was up until one this morning grading papers," she hedged. "I'm gonna go home and get some rest so I can be back tomorrow. I don't want to miss the last day before vacation."

He glanced around, but the hallway was empty. He pulled her in for a tight embrace, then kissed her forehead. "Can I do anything for you?" He held her at arms' length, his eyes twinkling. "Or should we go back to pretending?"

Sara groaned. "I really hope Marisa can keep a secret."

He cocked his head, then pulled her close again. "Would it be so bad for people to know?" he asked, his voice quiet against her hair.

She tensed, eager to leave. "Let's talk about that over the break, okay? I just want to get home."

He released her, his face unsure. "Even after last night? Are you having second thoughts?"

I'm having one single thought.

"No," she said, then kissed his cheek. "Not at all. I'm sorry—I just don't feel good." She smiled to defuse the situation. "I mean, I don't feel 'well,' Mr. English Teacher."

Terrence laughed. "All right, my love. Get home but please let me know if you need anything. You know I'll be there in no time—whenever you call."

They walked to the parking lot and embraced once again before she got into her car.

Thank God he drives in the opposite direction, she thought. *Please don't follow me to the drug store.*

As she pulled out of the parking lot, she texted Lauren: *Meet me at home, please. I need you.*

Sara and Lauren sat next to each other on the bed, staring at the plus sign on the stick. Neither moved, neither spoke. At last, Lauren put her arm around her friend and squeezed. "Whatever you decide, I'm here for you."

Sara was dumbfounded. She'd been overly tired this week, but chalked it up to the emotional roller coaster of meeting Natalie, talking to Carlos, and rekindling her romance with Terrence. *It all makes sense now,* she thought. Last night was the first night she and Terrence made love since their argument after Thanksgiving, but before that....

Before that, we were falling in love.

Over the weeks together, there were too many times to count as they eagerly explored each other's bodies and found a home in each other's hearts.

"I love him," she told Lauren, her voice quiet. *Would it be enough?*

"I know…I know." Her friend hugged her fiercely. "What do you need from me?" she asked. "Anything. You know that."

Sara sat back, her thoughts awhirl. *What do I need?* she wondered. The first time she got pregnant, she made the mistake of telling her mother. *That was a disaster,* she thought. Cecilia Masterson had berated her 16-year-old daughter, calling her a whore and worse before hauling her to the family doctor and, almost immediately, to the adoption agency.

She looked at Lauren, tears pooling in her eyes at the memory. "I lost Natalie for twenty-three years," she said softly. Sitting back, her voice grew stronger. "I'm not losing this baby." She wiped the tears away with the backs of her hands. "And I know I love Terrence. I don't know what he'll say, but I'm keeping this baby."

Lauren took her friend's hands and smiled. "I admit, I couldn't stand the guy after Thanksgiving, but I'm willing to give him the benefit of the doubt. It sounds like he's come to his senses and he does love you." She squeezed Sara's hands. "I guess we'll see if he's a man or just a boy, huh?"

Sara nodded. "He really wants children," she told her friend, hope kindling in her heart. But then reality hit. "It's not the best time—we've only just gotten back together." She closed her eyes and the tears slid down her cheeks.

"Is there ever a best time?" Lauren gently probed.

Sara leaned back and looked away, her eyes unfocused. "Probably not." She returned her gaze and her voice was more sure. "I'm thirty-nine years old, Lauren. I'm in love with a wonderful man who tells me he can't imagine life without me." She glanced back at the stick. "I'm scared to death, but I'm also just a tiny bit excited."

Lauren hugged her again and Sara knew in her heart that her friend would be there for her no matter what.

Oh, Terrence—be the man I know you can be.

Good morning, love read the text. *I went to sleep thinking of you and I woke up thinking of you. I hope you're feeling better.*

Sara looked at her phone and sighed. Despite her exhaustion, she hadn't slept well, going over and over the conversation she needed to have with him.

Good morning! I feel a bit better, just a little tired. And I woke up thinking about you, too.

She climbed out of bed and made it quickly, plumping the pink pillows out of habit. She looked at the spot where she'd awakened alone and wondered, *What must it be like to wake up next to someone knowing you've planned this together?* She wished the conversation were over and they could—*what?*

Begin our life together.

After a shower, she found that she actually did feel better. She wasn't as exhausted, anyway. Her stomach couldn't seem to decide if it were going to growl or flip over, so she decided on a small glass of ginger ale and a piece of toast. *Is this morning sickness or am I just nervous?*

Lauren walked into the kitchen as she finished the last bite. "Morning," her friend said, a hesitant lilt to her greeting. "How are you?"

"I'm okay," answered Sara. "Didn't sleep great." She held up the crumb-covered napkin. "Got down a piece of toast."

"It's gonna be okay," Lauren answered, reaching out to pat her shoulder. Then her voice grew thick with indignation. "I hate that you have to wonder how he'll react. He'd better not be a *cabrón* about this. He's damn lucky to have you in his life. I'm seriously gonna kick his ass if he blows this."

Sara sighed. She loved her friend but right now needed encouragement.

Lauren frowned. "I'm sorry—that was a shitty thing to say." She sat down at the table. "Let me start over: The truth is, he's a good guy. Of course he'll be surprised, but he loves you. This isn't what either of you planned, but it may turn out to be the most wonderful thing you could ever have hoped for."

As she wiped at her eyes, Sara realized how much she needed to hear those words.

Before she could get too emotional, Lauren added, "And the kid is super lucky because I'm the best auntie on the planet."

Sara laughed as Lauren flounced out of the kitchen and out the front door. Her friend, however, wasn't done.

"And the swamp is waiting if he doesn't act right," she called.

20

Sara stopped at the grocery store for cookies and candy canes on the way to school. No matter how she felt, she wanted to make the last day before vacation fun for the kids.

She was thankful her classes sped by, the students eager to finish the day and get home for their two-week holiday break. They laughed and chatted through the math puzzles she posed to them. Without the stress of being graded, the teens enjoyed the competition.

When fourth period began, Marisa entered the classroom and casually tossed a sealed envelope onto the pile of cards and packages on Sara's desk, then turned to find her seat. Sara divided up the class into teams and gave them challenging problems to solve, offering the treats as prizes. The advanced students enjoyed the math puzzles even more than the previous three classes, and the hour passed quickly. When it was over, the classmates left, many with candy canes sticking out of their mouths, wishing her a happy holiday.

Marisa held back but didn't pull out her lunch bag. Instead, she waited for the last student to depart and then came to the front of the class. Her face was somber, her eyes intent.

Sara looked at the teen and asked, "Marisa? Is everything all right?"

"I don't know. My dad gave me that note to give you and he acted all weird. What's it about?"

Sara glanced at the envelope. "I'm sure he's just checking in to see how things are going with you. He probably asked all your teachers."

"Nope." Marisa looked questioningly at Sara. "Just you."

Sara moved around to sit at her desk. It was time to change the subject. "How are your cramps today? Any better?"

Marisa rolled her eyes. "I get it. You're not gonna read the note in front of of me." She sat and opened her backpack to pull out her lunch. "I'm better. I took some ibuprofen this morning before I left and—" with a flourish she pulled a bottle of water out of her backpack. "I'm not drinking any soda today." She started in on her sandwich, seeming content to just sit with her teacher while she ate.

Sara smiled, glad to have something else to think about instead of the note from Carlos and her looming conversation with Terrence. "I'm glad to hear it." She nibbled on a salad while she sorted through papers on her desk.

At last Marisa asked, "So what are you guys doing for the break?"

Sara grinned at the teen's casual attempt to pull information about her and Terrence. "We're visiting Mr. Billings' family. How about you?"

"We're gonna hang out with my dad's parents. But I want to go see my mom's family." She frowned. "They're my family, too, even if he doesn't feel like they're his anymore."

"Maybe that's not it," suggested Sara. "It's probably just hard to be around people who remind him of your mom."

"You mean like me?"

Sara closed her eyes for a moment. "I'm sorry, Marisa. That's not what I meant. You know he loves you with all his heart."

"Well, if he loves me so much, then maybe he should do what I want to do once in a while." The teen balled up her lunch bag and arced it perfectly into the trashcan.

Sara smiled. Marisa could be so mature at times and yet she was still just a thirteen-year-old girl who could be petulant when she didn't get her way. "Maybe just try asking again and let him know how important it is to you."

"I'll try." The bell rang and Marisa looked at the clock on the wall. She sighed and said, "Great. Gotta go to Mr. Billings' class now. This book we're reading is so boring." She grinned, a bit of the light returning to her eyes. "But it's fun to sit in there and imagine him reciting poetry to you or something lame like that."

They laughed, and Sara was glad of the reprieve.

Marisa stood and looked at her teacher for a long moment. Then she grabbed her bag and walked to the door. "Thanks, Miss Masterson. Merry Christmas."

It was the end of the day and the last class left, the students laughing and saying their goodbyes. Sara's desk was littered with cards and small packages, the typical detritus of a popular teacher's space just before a holiday. One sassy boy in her fifth period class had put a shiny red apple in front of her before taking his seat. "Retro gift," he announced with a jaunty grin at his buddies.

Now that she was alone, the exhaustion hit her. She moved around the classroom, picking up candy cane wrappers and straightening desks. *I am so ready for a break*, she thought with a weary sigh. As she gathered the assorted cards into her bag, she noticed the envelope Marisa had tossed onto her desk and tore open the envelope to find a simple thank you card festooned with snowflakes.

Sara,

Thank you for everything. Merry Christmas

Carlos and Marisa

PS Check your email

Sara sat back and closed her eyes. All she wanted was to crawl into bed and sleep for two weeks. She glanced back at the card and then opened her laptop. Carlos' email had arrived earlier that day but she hadn't seen it. The subject line was simple: *Next Steps*.

Sara,

It's hard to know where to start, so I'll just dive in. I'm embarrassed by the other day but also grateful for your understanding. All the things I've buried for 23 years came up to kick me in the teeth and I wasn't prepared.

After you moved away, I was a mess. My family was there for me, but it was hard. Baseball was the only thing that kept me sane. I just poured myself into it and it paid off. I got a full ride to University of Florida and I really thought I'd end up in the pros but I got hurt my junior year and that was the end of that. I'm not complaining—it was just another dream that didn't come true.

I met Lisa my senior year and everything turned around. I graduated, we got married, and a couple of years later we decided to start a family. But that was another dream that failed. She had two miscarriages and we thought maybe kids weren't part of our future. Lisa knew about you and the baby, so she took it hard, blaming herself. When she got pregnant with Marisa, we were terrified we'd lose another child.

But then Marisa came and she was perfect. Everything was wonderful for 13 years. We were happy, Sara. I put the past behind me and just loved my wife, my daughter, and my life. So when Lisa died this summer, I fell apart. I didn't know how to be a dad without her and I know I haven't been there for Marisa the way I should have.

Anyway, sorry for this long letter. I just want you to know I've thought a lot about you and Natalie but my priority has to be Marisa. I plan to tell her everything over the break but I'm worried about trying to answer all her questions. I think—and I say this without a ton of confidence—that it would be good for her to meet her sister in person.

Sister. Even writing that word is hard.

I'm worried I'll mess this up, that I won't react the way Marisa needs me to. Or that Natalie needs me to, for that matter. I know it's a lot to ask, but would you be willing to go with us? Maybe all four of us can get together? Might be best to wait until after Christmas.

I'm sorry to put this on you, Sara. I can't imagine what you went through all those years ago. At least I had my family and I know yours wasn't great. I want to meet one daughter and I want to take care of the other. Will you help me?

Merry Christmas and thank you,
Carlos

Sara sat back and stared out at her classroom, her eyes unfocused. Despite her nervousness, she knew she would agree to Carlos' request—that they would meet Natalie over the holiday break and their little—*What? Family?*—would come together.

Her family. Her growing family.

She thought of the new life, snug in her body. Would it be another girl? One more daughter in the puzzle that had come to define her life?

Her classroom door opened and Terrence entered, his smile wide. "We are free!" he exclaimed. "Two weeks—and I am going to enjoy every minute of it." Sara stood and he swept her into his arms.

Just say it, she thought. But no. It wasn't the time or place for such a weighty revelation.

"I'm excited, too," she said instead. "But can we start with dinner and a walk on the beach this evening? I'd like to talk."

"Hmm," he answered. "That sounds mysterious." He kissed her and squeezed her tight to his chest. "Can we go now?

Sara nodded. She was ready.

Sara took another bite of lentil soup, her favorite item on the menu. They'd been to Dancing Avocado a few times since their first date and they both enjoyed the food and the quirky ambiance. Coming right after school meant an early dinner and no wait at the restaurant and she was surprised and happy to find she was hungry.

"So tell me more about the Christmas plans," she prompted.

"We drive down to Ft. Lauderdale on Sunday and spend a few days. Talia and Darren can't get there until Christmas Eve, so that gives us two days without the kids running around. Savannah and DJ will come by, but it'll be nice to have my parents to ourselves."

"It sounds lovely," she answered. "Are you sure you don't just want that special time alone? I could drive down on Christmas Eve—"

He was shaking his head before she finished. "No, Sara. I want you there. I'd like time alone with you, too. I wanna take you to some of my favorite places, show you around my home town." He grinned. "I know Daytona Beach is beautiful, especially during the holidays, but I'd really like to show you around Ft. Lauderdale." He cocked his head, questioning. "I want to share more about me with you. Is that weird?"

Sara lifted his hand to her lips and kissed it lightly. She was touched at the sweetness of his request, his desire to share his early life with her. The mixture of strong masculinity with his tender side always moved her. *This is why I love you,* she thought.

"It's not weird at all," she replied. "It's really sweet and I would love to go with you. But I do have to be here after Christmas." She sipped her water, then continued. "Carlos plans to tell Marisa everything and he's hoping they can meet Natalie. We're going to get together after Christmas."

"Oh, wow," he answered. He let out a long breath. "Are you okay with that?" Now it was his turn to kiss her hand. "How can I be there for you?"

She smiled, relieved. "I wish I knew. It's so new—for all of us."

"You know I'll do whatever you need, love. I'm here for you, no matter what."

Oh, Terrence. Please let that be true.

The couple left Sara's car at the restaurant and drove to their favorite beach spot. The sun was setting and Terrence asked, "You sure you still want to walk on the beach? It's getting dark."

She nodded. "I do. It's still warm—I just want to talk to you."

He frowned as he parked the car. He walked around to open her door and took her hand. "Sara, is everything okay?"

She nodded, hoping she was right.

21

They walked hand in hand down the beach, staying on the dry sand since neither was wearing sandals or beach clothes. Terrence was quiet, but Sara could sense his tension. At last, she squeezed his hand and began.

"Let me start by saying I love you," she said simply.

Terrence stopped walking and faced her. "Are you breaking up with me?" he asked, his eyes wide with concern.

"Oh, no—no, no, no," she said, grasping both his hands. She looked into his eyes, willing herself to say everything she needed to say. *That I love you. That I want us to be together.*

That we've created a new life.

He pulled her close, fiercely pressing her to his chest. "What is it? Please, Sara…just tell me."

Her cheek lay against the warmth of him and she could hear the pounding of his heart. *I just want to stay here*, she thought. *Just like this.*

But then she straightened and pulled away. She looked into his eyes, those beautiful brown eyes she'd fallen in love with, and spoke the words she knew would change their lives.

"I'm pregnant."

Every muscle in her body tensed as she waited for his response. Her chest tightened and breathing felt nearly impossible. The moment lasted forever as she watched the emotions flitter across his face. First shock, then—

"Oh, my God…Sara!" He pulled her hard, lifting her and spinning her around, carelessly staggering closer to the water. "A baby! We're having a baby?"

The rising surf lapped at his feet and splashed up at her ankles. "Terrence! Your shoes!" she laughed.

He staggered out of the water and they toppled onto the beach. Laughing, he reached for her and pulled her to him. They lay on the sand for a moment, her head on his chest and his arms around her. "I can't believe this. A baby," he whispered. A smile and wonder was evident in his voice and Sara's heart swelled.

This is everything I hoped for. Everything I was afraid to hope for.

Then he sat up and reached out to smooth her hair, his eyes glistening. "So this is why you've been so tired," he said. "Are you feeling okay now?"

"I'm great right now," she said, sitting to face him. "But I was definitely worried. We only just got back together and we weren't even together all that long before the breakup. It's kind of a whirlwind."

Terrence nodded, his face serious. "I know this isn't how we'd have planned things. But I love you, Sara." He took her hand and threaded his fingers between hers. "We aren't sixteen-year-old kids and we know what we want, don't we?" His eyes were pleading. "I know I want you. And I want our child."

Sara's heart felt like it would burst. She reached for him and kissed him lightly, her lips lingering on his as she whispered, "Yes, my love. Yes."

They wandered on the beach for another hour, sometimes in silence, sometimes tripping over each other's words in their hurry to share their thoughts. By the time they got back to Terrence's car, the moon had risen and the sky was flecked with stars. They stood leaning against the door, looking up out at the surf. Then Terrence glanced into the small backseat and chuckled.

"What?" asked Sara.

"I think we're gonna need a new ride."

"Oh, absolutely," Sara responded, her tone serious. "I think you are definitely a minivan dad." They burst out laughing and she felt a lightness she hadn't felt in years.

Everything is going to be all right.

Terrence dropped her off at her car but lingered at the door. "I don't want to say goodbye," he said, his face dejected. "It doesn't seem right to be leaving each other right now."

"It's just for the evening, love," she replied. Eager to get a start on their holiday, they decided to leave the next afternoon instead of waiting for Sunday. "We'll go home and get packed and we'll be together for days." She grinned. "You'll probably be sick of me in a week."

His face darkened. "Not a chance, milady. You're stuck with me." He reached in the window to stroke her cheek. "You are so beautiful. And you're gonna be an amazing mother." He shook his head in wonder. "I can't wait to see my parents' face when we tell them."

Sara's eyes widened. "What are they going to think?" She had no intention of telling her own parents, at least not yet. *How do loving parents react in this situation?* she wondered.

Terrence laughed. "You've seen them with Talia and Darren's kids," he reminded her. "They're fantastic grandparents. And they adore you." He leaned in to kiss her and she felt a dampness on his cheek.

"Are you crying?"

He rested his cheek against hers. "Only happy tears, my love. I'm just so happy."

"And so we're going to Ft. Lauderdale tomorrow," finished Sara. "I'll be back the day after Christmas so Natalie can meet Carlos and Marisa." She laughed. "My life is a bit crazy right now, but I kinda think I love it."

She and Lauren sat on the sofa, feet curled up beneath them and the throw blanket across their laps. She felt a warm sense of contentment as she talked with her best friend. Knowing that Terrence was happy—*no*, she corrected herself, *He was overjoyed*—gave her confidence and allowed her to feel the excitement she'd been holding at bay. Now she felt free to delight in her impending motherhood.

Lauren looked thoughtful. "My family is going to be really upset that you aren't there for Christmas," she warned, her tone somber.

Sara frowned. "But you said I should—"

Lauren's burst of laughter broke through Sara's sudden concern. "Ay, *mamacita*—you are so easy to tease. They'll be thrilled you're with your *novio*. They're just gonna want all the details and you have to send me pictures while you're down there."

Sara shook her head and smacked Lauren with a throw pillow. "You're such a brat," she scolded.

"That's *Tia* Brat to you. I'm an auntie now."

Sara was sitting on the sofa texting with Natalie the next morning when Terrence arrived.

Gotta run, honey, she wrote. *Time to head for Ft. Lauderdale, but I'll see you after Christmas. Can't wait!*

I'm super nervous and excited, Natalie wrote back. *Thank you so much for setting this up! I hope you have a wonderful Christmas.*

You, too! xo

Lauren opened the door and stood in front of Terrence, blocking his entry. Sara could see his puzzled look as he glanced over her friend's head. "Hey, Lauren," he said, his friendly tone belying the discomfort Sara could see written all over his face. "May I come in?"

"That depends," she said, an ominous tone to her voice.

He glanced again at Sara, his eyes worried. "On what?"

Sara started to rise when Lauren burst out laughing. "Oh, never mind," she said between breaths. "I can't keep up the charade." She stepped aside and glanced back and forth between them. "I wanted to keep you guessing and miserable for at least a minute." Then she turned back to Terrence, dropping her voice to a faux-fatherly timbre. "So, young man. What are your intentions toward my daughter?"

Sara barked out a laugh, relieved to see her friend being silly and warm toward Terrence. *Much better than leaving him for the gators*, she thought with a smile. "Just ignore her," she said, moving Lauren aside with a playful push.

But Terrence had gotten into the flow of the joke and took off his baseball cap, pressing it to his chest. "Sir," he intoned, "My intentions are honorable. I will do whatever you require."

"Indeed," mused Lauren, stroking a nonexistent beard. "Well, young man, you will have to pass three tests."

Sara stood back, smiling. "That's enough, you two—" she began, but Lauren broke in, still in character, her voice somber and manly.

"The first is the least of the trials, yet will test your mettle to the fullest. In the village next to ours, there is an ogre who has been killing livestock—"

The three of them burst out laughing and Lauren buried her head in Sara's shoulder. "I can't keep it up. But man, what I would have given to have a picture of your faces when I first started!" She looked at Terrence and reached for a hug. "C'mere, goofball. Looks like we're family now." The two embraced and Terrence winked at Sara over her friend's head.

It's gonna be okay, thought Sara as she gazed at the two people she loved most in the world. *It's all gonna be just fine.*

Terrence and Lauren loaded the car, dismissing Sara's attempts to carry anything. "I'm just pregnant, not made of glass," she complained.

"Quit whining," responded Lauren. "You'll be shlepping diaper bags in a few months. Take advantage of being pampered for a bit."

Terrence just kept grinning, staying out of the argument between the friends, but winking at Lauren as they closed the trunk.

At last, they were ready. Sara and Lauren embraced and wished each other a merry Christmas. "Please thank your mom for me and tell her I'm so sorry to miss out on the tamales," said Sara.

"Tamales?" asked Terrence. "You're giving up tamales to come to Ft. Lauderdale?"

"Right? Who gives up tamales for anything?" Lauren laughed, then reached for him and hugged him tightly. "Take care of that little mama," she said, her tone serious. "There's an entire family of Miami Cubans who will hunt you down if you hurt her again."

Terrence nodded. "Don't worry, Lauren. I know what an idiot I was and what I almost destroyed." He looked at Sara, his countenance solemn. "You have my word—I will take care of her."

Lauren slight smile turned into a laugh. "All right—I'll bring you home some tamales!"

Sara and Terrence were still laughing as they pulled away.

The miles flew by as the couple talked and talked. Sara found her worries evaporating as Terrence reassured her of his parents' support.

"I think it's a girl," said Terrence after a brief lull.

"What makes you say that?"

"I don't know. It just feels right."

"Do you have a preference?" she asked.

Terrence glanced at her, his eyebrows knit together. "No! I just want a healthy baby." He laughed. "Maybe we'll have twins—one of each."

Sara's eyes widened. "Is that even possible? Do you have twins in your family?" The thought struck a chord of panic in her. *One is plenty.*

Terrence kissed her hand. "No worries, little mama. No twins in my family. One baby at a time is enough, I think."

"Are you and Lauren gonna call me little mama for the rest of this pregnancy?"

"Maybe." He laughed again. "And speaking of calling *you* a name, what shall we call this one?"

Sara thought for a moment. "Maybe something literary? Since we both love to read, it might be fun to name her after a character we like?" She paused. "Just nothing weird."

"Oh, darn," he said, his face serious. "I was hoping for Galadriel."

"That's perfect," she answered, her tone matching his. "That means if it's a boy, it has to be Celeborn."

The two burst out laughing. "Okay, maybe no Lord of the Rings characters," said Terrence when he'd recovered. "How about Ariadne?"

"Hmm," mused Sara. "That's actually kinda cool." Then she frowned. "But will she have to explain it to kids all her life? I don't know if Greek mythology is a great place to start looking."

"How about family names? Did you have any family you would want to name a baby after?"

Sara looked askance at her lover. "Are you kidding? We've talked about my family."

Terrence glanced sideways at her with an apologetic look. "Sorry. I wasn't thinking."

"Let's go back to books," she said. "Or maybe authors? I love the Brontë sisters. Maybe Charlotte?"

The two continued to chatter, the hours passing quickly. By the time they arrived in Ft. Lauderdale, they were no nearer to picking baby names, but Sara felt a closeness to Terrence that buoyed her and carried her away. *This is everything I've ever wanted*, she thought. Still a bit nervous, she looked forward to sharing their news with Donovan and Alicia.

22

As they pulled up to the Billings family home, Sara thought back to her first trip there. The family had welcomed her and she'd loved every minute of her time with them. Raucous, loud, and endlessly active, Terrence's family had swept her into their orbit and she hadn't wanted to pull away. Yet after he hurt her so deeply on the way home, she never dreamed she'd return.

We're all family now, she realized. She prayed they would feel the same.

Terrence opened her door and led her up to the porch. "I'll grab the bags in a minute," he said. "Let's get you inside."

Sara snorted. "I'm only ten weeks pregnant, Terrence," she said. "I can help with the bags!"

He leaned down to kiss her cheek, then swatted her behind. "Nope. My mom would kill me if she saw you walking up with a suitcase."

She laughed. "Ah, so you're just trying to stay out of trouble, not taking care of me?"

He grinned. "You've met Alicia Billings, right?"

The door opened and there stood his parents. Donovan held out his arms. "Sara!" he cried. "Get over here and hug this old man."

She moved quickly past Terrence and embraced his father. "It's good to see you, Donovan," she said. "Thank you for having me."

"Are you kidding me?" asked his wife. Alicia looked at her fondly. "We're thrilled you decided to spend Christmas with us. Give me some sugar!" She threw her arms around Sara and kissed her cheek, then looked beyond her to Terrence, who stood patiently waiting. "You, too, young man," she said. "Get over here and kiss your mother."

Terrence obliged as Sara moved into the house after Donovan. "Give me your keys, Son," he said. "I'll grab your bags while you visit." Terrence tossed the keys to his father and followed Alicia and Sara into the kitchen where they sat at the table.

"What can I get you?" asked Alicia. "Dinner won't be ready for another half hour, but I have some crackers and cheese and some sodas."

"Just some water for me, please," replied Sara.

"Same here, Mom."

Alicia set two ice cold glasses of water on the table and sat down, her eyes shining. "I am so happy you're here," she said, reaching for their hands. "It's happy mama time."

Donovan walked in and set the suitcases down, then sat with the three of them. "How was the drive? At least you had nice weather."

"It was fine—we just talked our heads off and the time flew by. We were eager to get down here and see you both." Terrence smiled at Sara, then cleared his throat. "And we're about to turn happy mama time into something else," he said, looking pointedly at his mother.

Alicia cocked her head, puzzled. "What do you mean?"

Donovan reached for his son's arm. "Son?"

Terrence answered. "How about happy grandmama time?" He smiled broadly at Alicia and Donovan's puzzled faces, but Sara sat very still, uncertain of their reaction. "We're having a baby!"

The older couple shared a knowing glance and then Donovan pounded Terrence on the back while Alicia rose to wrap Sara in a warm hug.

I didn't know how much I needed this, thought Sara. She melted into the woman's embrace, her concerns evaporating with the love she felt.

If only I'd ever gotten this from my mom.

Donovan took his turn and kissed Sara's cheek as he hugged her. She glanced up to see Terrence beaming at them. Her longing for family, her grief over losing Carlos and Natalie—everything catalyzed in a single moment with the love and acceptance she felt. Her hand strayed to her still flat belly and she knew.

New life. A new beginning.

They sat back down and Donovan took Alicia's hand. He spoke quietly to the couple. "You don't need me to say this is a big step for you," he said. "But we believe in you both. Your mother and I saw something special about this relationship over Thanksgiving." He patted Terrence's shoulder. "We were very glad to hear you'd made amends, Son."

Terrence grimaced. "I'm just thankful she didn't give up on me."

After dinner, Sara cleared the dishes from the table, shooing Terrence away. "I'm fine," she said. "Go spend some time with your father." She smiled at Alicia. "I want to chat with your mom anyway."

The two women moved about the kitchen, cleaning the table and filling the dishwasher. They were done quickly and Alicia thanked Sara for her help. "So, how about a slice of pie and a cup of tea? I know I have some decaf peppermint in the pantry. Sit, sit—I'll get everything."

"That sounds scrumptious," replied Sara as she sat back down. She sighed heavily, the now familiar exhaustion catching up to her.

"I remember those sighs," laughed the older woman. "How far along are you?"

"Only ten weeks," she answered. "Just far enough to almost be done with the morning sickness." She smiled as Alicia handed her a mug, redolent with peppermint. "Mmm…this smells divine."

"I didn't have a lick of sickness with Talia but I threw up every day for three months with Savannah." Alicia chuckled at the memory. "I knew she'd be a handful even before she was born." She sat down and sipped her tea, then looked at Sara with a serious expression. "So how are you two, honey? I have to tell you, I nearly killed that boy when he told us what happened at Thanksgiving. I wanted to call you and apologize myself! No child I raised should ever behave so horribly—especially not Terrence. But I knew it was none of my business and all I could do was give him a piece of my mind and then pray for you both."

Sara's heart swelled at the older woman's words. "I won't pretend it didn't wreck me for a bit," she confessed. "After you and I talked and after things seemed to be so good between him and me, I just felt like it was time to tell him my story."

Alicia sighed. "I owe you an apology for that mistake," she said. When Sara objected, Terrence's mother held up a hand. "No, I do. I never once imagined my son would react that way and I was dead wrong. You made a decision based on what I thought and it caused you both a lot of pain." She frowned and shook her head. "I'm sorry, Sara."

Sara nodded. "Thank you, Alicia. I don't think he ever imagined acting that way either. I guess we all have baggage that catches us by surprise."

Alicia looked down at her hands for a long moment. "I couldn't stand that girl," she said at last, her voice uncharacteristically rough. "I tried to be nice but I couldn't imagine her with my son. Terrence got angry with me one time because she complained that I didn't like her." She pursed her lips. "She was right."

Sara tried unsuccessfully to hide a smile. It was nice to see a little crack in the perfect niceness that was Alicia Billings. "Well, if there's anything you don't like about me, I hope you'll tell me."

Alicia glanced up, a surprised look on her face. "Darlin', I knew from the first day you were here that you were perfect for Terrence. He just had to figure it out for himself."

Sara smiled and then took a bite of the blackberry pie. She closed her eyes in bliss. "Oh, Alicia—this is fabulous." She dabbed her lips with a napkin and continued. "Well, I think he's figured it out. He's done everything he can to apologize and make things right. I was really scared to tell him about the baby, but he was ecstatic." She smiled, remembering their time on the beach.

Alicia looked at her, her face solemn. "And you? How do you feel about it?" She leaned forward and said, "I don't mean to pry and please tell me if I'm getting too personal. But this is a big change for you and I imagine it's brought up some feelings from the first time?" She shook her head. "I'm sorry—this is none of my business. Just ignore this old grandmother!"

Sara gazed at Terrence's mother—their baby's grandmother— and smiled. "I don't mind, honestly. I don't know why but you make me feel safe sharing my heart." She grew sorrowful, then spoke softly. "I haven't told my mother about the baby. I'm sure she won't react well and I just don't want to deal with it." Tears pricked her eyelids and she looked away.

Alicia reached for her hand and squeezed. "I'm so sorry, honey. I didn't mean to make you cry."

Sara smiled wanly, her heart heavy. "You didn't. It's an old hurt that never really goes away. And you're right—I'm remembering a lot about the last time and it's painful." She sipped her tea, willing herself to smile. "But having you and Donovan be so happy outweighs those memories." She sat up and took another bite of pie, ready to change the subject. "This really is the best pie I've ever eaten," she said.

Alicia took the hint and talked more generally about car seats and diaper services, regaling Sara with stories of Terrence as a baby. The two chatted until they finished their dessert and rejoined the men. As they sat in front of the fireplace, Sara couldn't contain her yawns and Alicia shooed the couple off to bed.

Sara snuggled closer to Terrence, her back tight to him, his hand draped across her hip. He gently rubbed her abdomen and kissed her shoulder. She felt a peace she hadn't known in—*Well, forever,* she thought. She'd never felt this way.

She was surprised to feel him shaking as he buried his head between her shoulder blades. As she rolled to face him, she realized he was crying. He wrapped his arms around her and she pulled him to her breast, cradling his head, soothing him with a murmured "Sshhh…it's all right…I'm here." Silent sobs wracked his body, and Sara held him close.

When at last he stilled, she asked, "What is it, love?"

He raised his eyes to her and whispered, "I love you so much. I can't believe I almost lost you. I…I was such an idiot—"

She shushed him again, stroking his hair. She kissed his forehead and whispered, "We're good, my love. All is well."

She was nearly overcome with emotion—her chest felt too tight and she clasped him to her.

All is well.

The next morning they awakened still curled around each other, Terrence's cheek against her shoulder. They'd slept soundly and Sara felt a warm sense of oneness with her lover.

"You awake?" he whispered, nuzzling her neck.

"Yes," she answered, pressing her hips into his.

Terrence pulled her even closer. "You better stop that or we'll never get out of bed," he warned with a laugh.

She smiled and rolled to face him, reaching up to stroke his cheek. She felt his body all along hers—his longing was evident. Part of her yearned to feel him inside her; another recoiled at the idea of making love in his parents' house. Before she could make up her mind, Terrence turned his face and kissed her palm.

"I need you, Sara," he said simply.

She nodded, and they fumbled under the covers, hands sliding over each other as they slipped out of their nightclothes. She stroked him gently as he kissed her throat, her collarbone, her breasts. Pregnancy had made them extra sensitive, and her breath caught as his tongue flicked her nipples, his curls soft against her skin.

She rolled onto her back and he followed her, sliding into her as if they were one. At his soft moan she wrapped her legs tightly around him, arching her back in pleasure. Everything in her body felt alive and she lost herself in the slow and steady rhythm of their lovemaking.

It was tender and gentle and she found herself reaching a climax both physical and emotional. As her body shuddered, she was surprised to feel tears sliding into her hair. Terrence met her release only a moment later, his body tensing just as hers began to relax. He lay on her, his breath rough until he pushed himself up and saw her tears. "Sara—love. Did I hurt you? Are you all right?"

She smiled, her lips quivering. "I'm just so happy," she whispered. "I love you so much."

He closed his eyes, relief plain on his face. "I love you, too," he said, leaning down to kiss her. "You are everything to me, Sara." He rolled to his side and lay his hand on her belly. "You and our baby. You mean the world to me and I have never been so happy."

Sunny skies and a light breeze greeted them as they left after breakfast, promising to return for dinner with Donovan and Alicia. Sara grinned at Terrence's eagerness to show her around his hometown. *He's like a little boy,* she thought. It just added to the loving feelings that had nearly overwhelmed her that morning.

They started at Sunrise Middle School. "So here's where it all began, the home of the mighty Sunrise Falcons," intoned Terrence, before bursting into laughter. He took her hand as they drove through the parking lot. "I know it sounds crazy, but this is where I decided I wanted to be a teacher when I grew up. I'd always loved stories—I was a total nerd, hanging out in the library or sitting at lunch with a book. But I got the chance to be a peer tutor in seventh grade and it just lit something up in me."

Sara felt a thrum of nervousness from him. She was becoming attuned to his moods, his mannerisms, and his emotions. *He really wants to share this with me,* she thought. *He wants me to know him.* Deeply touched, she squeezed his hand, then raised it to her lips. "My mighty falcon," she murmured, smiling. She looked across the lawn to the school and nodded slowly. "I can picture you here," she said. "Isn't it amazing how some things have such power to mold our lives? Who would have known that you at thirteen would become you at thirty-six?" She kissed his hand again. "I'm grateful for the teacher who encouraged you to become a tutor. We'd never have met otherwise."

Terrence smiled as he pulled out of the parking lot. She noticed how his shoulders relaxed as he turned the steering wheel. *He was genuinely nervous,* she marveled. "Thank you for bringing me here. I love learning about you." He glanced at her, his eyes alight.

"Now let's go see the other place that molded me," he said with a grin. "Your little central Florida beaches can't compare."

Sara sighed contentedly and leaned back in her seat. Her voice took on a sonorous, gothic tone. "Lead on, mighty falcon. Lead on!"

He burst out laughing. "Not a bad Ebenezer Scrooge, milady. For a math geek, you're pretty good at this literature thing."

They exchanged a warm smile and drove east.

I love this man.

23

"So this," said Terrence as they pulled into a parking lot at the beach, "is where I learned to surf." The sand was white and soft, and the sun glinted off the waves. "I haven't done it since high school, but it was my favorite activity for a lot of years."

The couple got out of the car and walked to the beach hand in hand.

"It's weird, but I never learned," said Sara, slipping off her sandals to walk barefoot. "I guess growing up in Orlando kept me far enough from the beach that it wasn't something a lot of my friends did. And once I got to Tampa, I didn't really hang out with surfers." She gazed appreciatively at the ocean. "But it looks like a lot of fun."

"Maybe let's not get you started for a while," laughed Terrence.

She grinned. "Can you imagine me in a bikini with a big belly out on a longboard?"

He slid his arms around from behind her and held her close. "I can't wait to see you in a bikini with a big belly."

Sara sighed and snuggled against his embrace. She thought of how she would look and feel once the pregnancy progressed to that state—how different it would feel as an adult making the choices she and Terrence were making. She looked forward to the experience, especially with the man who was holding her.

"I had my first kiss on this beach," he murmured into her ear. "Tiffany Stevens, in the sixth grade."

Sara turned to face him, her arms sliding around his neck. "Oh, yeah? What was so special about Tiffany Stevens?" she teased.

"She didn't mind that I kept books in my bag and just read on the sand when I wasn't surfing," he smiled. "She didn't care I wore braces and was a super-nerd."

She threw her head back and laughed. "Super-nerd? Is that a technical term?"

He leaned down to kiss her. "Yeah. I think it's Latin for 'Don't get too stuck on Tiffany because an angel is gonna drop down from heaven when you're thirty-six.'"

Sara moved her arms to encircle his waist and pressed her cheek to his chest. "Good answer, Mr. Billings."

The air was brisk but the sky was crystal clear and she sensed he had a deeper reason for visiting this beach. They walked along the sand hand in hand for a few minutes before the wind picked up and Sara shivered. "Oh, babe—you're cold!" He frowned and shook his head. "I really wanted to sit here for a bit. I have a blanket in the car." Without another word, he left her and ran quickly to the car, then back to where she stood.

He wrapped the blanket around her shoulders, running his hands up and down her arms for warmth. "That better?"

She nodded and he motioned her closer to the surf. "Do you mind if we just sit here?"

Sara looked at him and realized he was nervous again. "Not at all," she answered. "It's beautiful." She pulled the blanket closer and smiled. "I'm nice and warm now."

They sat on the sand and Terrence put his arm around her. Sara lay her head on his shoulder, content to wait for him to speak. The waves lapping just feet away had a soothing effect and she felt as if she were being rocked to sleep. At last, he let her go and turned to face her.

"Thank you for this morning," he began. He gazed intently at her, taking her hands. "I felt closer to you than I ever have. You make me so happy, Sara."

She smiled. "It was special for me, too."

"I know we haven't been together for long, but I can't imagine my life without you," he continued. "We aren't kids—we know what we want, right?" His voice quavered a little and she wondered yet again why he seemed nervous.

"Yes," she answered simply. "I know I want you."

Terrence took a deep breath and brought her hands to his lips, kissing them softly. "Sara…my love….

"Will you marry me?

She wondered if her heart had stopped—time stood still. Only months before, she'd been a happily single woman. And now? Her life had turned upside down with a new job, a relationship she'd never imagined with the daughter she lost, a new baby on the way….

And a man I adore.

"Yes," she answered, her heart full. "A thousand times yes."

Terrence's smile was electric as he wrapped his arms around her, then kissed her over and over. The couple sat on the sand smiling and laughing, then kissing again.

After an hour on the beach, they were both chilled and ready to leave.

"You hungry?" asked Terrence.

"Not really. Your mom made such a big breakfast, I'm sure I won't be ready to eat until dinner. But if you're hungry, let's go grab something." She pulled the blanket closer. "I could use a nice cup of tea to warm up."

"There's a great little café a couple of blocks away," he answered. "I can grab a snack and you can get some tea or hot chocolate."

They walked back to the car and made their way to a small bistro. Terrence devoured a sweet roll and a cup of coffee while Sara sipped a peppermint hot cocoa. When they were finished, he said, "If you've warmed up, there's one more place I'd like to take you."

She looked at him and he seemed almost shy. "Where?"

"It's a surprise."

"Another surprise?" She laughed and took his hand as they stood to leave. "Lead on, my love."

The couple drove without speaking, Terrence's old school R&B playlist soft in the background. From time to time, he'd reach over to stroke her cheek or squeeze her hand. Sara leaned the seat back and closed her eyes. She was more content than she could ever remember.

At last, they pulled into a parking lot and he turned to look at her. "Welcome to the Riverwalk," he said softly. "This is sort of the heart of Ft. Lauderdale." He took both of her hands. "There's a really nice jewelry store here and I want to get you a proper engagement ring."

Sara's eyes widened. "Oh—" she began. She felt her heart pounding and a smile bloomed on her face.

He grinned, leaned forward to kiss her, and got out of the car. When he opened her door, she got out and embraced him. They stood quietly for a moment and then he said, "C'mon. Let's go look at diamonds!"

They walked along the Riverwalk and Sara was entranced by its beauty. Even in December, the lawn and the trees were green. It was decorated for Christmas, and families strolled along the walkway, children running and laughing. There were other couples, too, sipping hot drinks on benches or walking arm in arm. Sara felt a deep sense of belonging, of hope. It surprised her. *I never imagined feeling like this*, she marveled. She leaned into Terrence and he tightened his arm around her shoulder.

"You okay?" he asked, a worried expression on his face. "Do you need to sit down?"

She laughed and patted his chest. "I'm more than okay, love. I'm so happy I could burst." She looked around and joy filled her. "I love your town and I love you, my falcon." She reached up to kiss him softly. "I've never been this happy either," she whispered against his lips. She felt his smile as they kissed and he squeezed her tightly.

They approached Moreno's Jewelers and Terrence slowed. "This is it," he said. "Tons of jewelry stores in this city, but this is where my family always comes. Both of my sisters got their rings here and my dad bought my mom her twenty-fifth anniversary gift here, too. They've been in business for a hundred years—the family is wonderful and the service is fantastic. I'm sure you'll find something you like."

Sara laughed. "You could tie twine around my finger and I'd be happy."

He scowled. "No way is my wife wearing twine." He bowed. "Nothing but the best for milady."

They walked inside and were met by a striking young woman. "Terrence!" she greeted him warmly. "So this is the lucky lady. Welcome, Sara. I am Magdalena Moreno and I'm delighted to meet you."

Sara looked at her in surprise. "Hello. It's lovely to meet you." She looked at Terrence, who beamed at her, and then back at Magdalena. "So you knew—"

"Oh, yes," replied the woman. "We've been working with the Billings family for years." She smiled fondly at Terrence. "We've been waiting for someone to capture this guy's heart." She turned and waved a hand across the store. "Welcome to Moreno's. Let's get you two seated over here." She pointed at a couple of comfortable chairs. "Now tell me: What do you like? What have you been dreaming of? I know we can find something perfect for you."

Sara was enthralled. The store was small but finely appointed. The walls were the palest blue but everything else was white. The marble floor was polished to a high shine, and the glass cases glistened. *I've never even thought about what I would like.* Nervous, she answered, "I'm honestly not sure. What do you recommend?"

Magdalena's laugh rang out like bells. "Oh, Sara—that is for you to decide. But why don't you sit down and let me show you a few things. Surely something will sing to your heart."

The elegant woman ushered them to the tasteful but comfortable chairs. "May I?" she asked, reaching across the glass counter for Sara's hand after they sat down. Sara nodded, and Magdalena smiled, her light touch cool.

"You have beautiful hands," she said. "You could wear anything and it will look lovely." She sat back and looked at the couple. "Why don't we build something just for you? We'll start with the setting." At Terrence's nod, she pulled out a small velvet tray and began describing the various pieces. After a few minutes of "solitaire, halo, three stone, pave," Sara was overwhelmed.

"I'm not sure," she said, looking at Terrence, feeling unexpectedly unsettled. "I don't want anything flashy." She looked back at Magdalena. "Something simple is fine."

"We're not going for 'fine,' babe," he said, reaching for her hand. "I want you to find the perfect ring, something that's way beyond 'fine.'"

"Maybe we should move on to the center stone," suggested Magdalena. "Do you have a favorite shape?"

Sara shook her head. "Honestly, I've never thought about it."

Magdalena rose. "I'll be right back with some stones and you can see what speaks to you."

As the woman left, Sara squeezed Terrence's hand and whispered, "These look incredibly expensive. I don't need anything this ornate. I mean, we're middle school teachers, not movie stars."

A knowing smile crossed his face. "Sara. My love. I'm not going to bankrupt us buying you a ring. I've saved and I don't want you to think about what it costs." She started to speak but he interrupted her gently. "No—this is a once in a lifetime purchase and we're getting you something special. I promise you, I'm not irresponsible with money."

"I didn't mean that I thought you were," she responded. "It's just a little overwhelming."

Magdalena returned with another velvet tray, this time with single diamonds on it. She smiled and began. "Let's see what you think of these." She took finely pointed tweezers and lifted one stone. "This is a classic round diamond."

Terrence squeezed her hand and Sara nodded. "It's beautiful. I do like that." Magdalena went through the various cuts, describing how each might be set to fit Sara's yet to be discovered style.

"This is very popular, an emerald cut—"

"*No!*"

Sara's voice was hard. Her hands shook as she brought them to her mouth, surprised at her own vehemence. "Not that one," she whispered, her voice tremulous.

Magdalena's eyes flickered, but otherwise she showed no reaction. She lowered the diamond to the tray as Terrence put his arm around Sara's shaking shoulders.

"Would you give us a minute?" he asked.

"Of course. Take your time." The elegant woman collected the trays and stepped away.

Terrence folded Sara into his arms and stroked her hair. "It's okay," he whispered. "We don't have to do this today if you're not up to it."

Sara quieted in his arms, her shaking slowing. She was embarrassed by her outburst—Terrence and Magdalena had no way of knowing what she felt or why.

I will never wear the same diamond as my mother, she thought. She pictured Cecilia's garish stone atop a multiple diamond setting. She couldn't imagine what her father had paid for the thing, but it represented everything she hated about her mother. Flashy, self-absorbed, and attention-seeking, Cecilia Masterson was the polar opposite of her daughter.

"I'm okay," she said at last. "I'm so sorry. I—I didn't expect that."

"What is it?" he asked, a tender note to his voice.

"That's the stone in my mother's ring," she said.

Terrence frowned and pulled her in close. "You are not your mother, Sara. Nothing like her." He stepped back and looked directly into her eyes. "You are the kindest, sweetest, most loving woman I've ever known." He took her hands and they stood. "C'mon. Let's just look around for a bit." She nodded, fearing that if she spoke again she would cry. They strolled along the cases, looking at the various pieces. Suddenly, Sara stopped short.

One ring grabbed her attention. The small round center stone was the palest pink, surrounded by a petite diamond halo. The white gold band glinted with tiny diamonds.

It's perfect.

Terrence turned to see what had transfixed his bride. He looked down and saw the delicate ring and smiled. "Oh, babe… it's you. It's totally you." He looked across the store and met Magdalena's eyes and she joined them.

"I think my fiancée has found her ring," he said with a smile. Magdalena took the ring out of the case and reached for Sara's hand but Terrence forestalled her. "May I?" he asked, reaching for the band.

"Of course," she answered.

Terrence took Sara's hand and slid the ring onto her finger, looking deeply into her eyes. It fit perfectly and Sara felt a warmth fill her body. There seemed to be no one else in the room as she looked first at her hand and then at the man she loved.

"It's beautiful," she breathed. "I love it."

24

The holidays passed joyfully as everyone descended on the Billings family home. Terrence's sisters were thrilled, both at the engagement and the pregnancy, and Sara was showered with love and sisterly advice.

"So did you set a date yet?" asked Savannah on Christmas morning.

"Not yet," answered Sara, glancing at Terrence. "But I guess I'm old fashioned enough I'd like it to be before the baby arrives."

Terrence smiled at his fiancée. "The last day of school is the Friday before Memorial Day. How about the following weekend? The baby isn't due until the first week of July."

I'll be huge by then, thought Sara.

"Are you crazy?" scoffed Savannah. "She'll be huge by then! Why don't you do it during spring break?"

Talia had her phone out and was looking at the calendar. "Perfect," she declared. "You'll definitely be showing, but we can still fit you in a beautiful wedding gown in March." The two sisters huddled over the calendar until Terrence broke in.

"Um, I don't mean to interrupt you planning our lives, but maybe ask the bride and groom what they think?

The sisters stopped short and looked up, surprised. "You don't count," asserted Savannah. She turned to Sara and asked, "What do *you* think, little mama?"

Sara grinned at the nickname—*Is everyone going to call me that?* Terrence scowled at his siblings in mock disapproval, but Sara agreed with the girls. "I think that sounds great. Doesn't give us much time, but I don't think we need anything too complicated."

Alicia joined the young people, sitting beside Sara, a notebook in hand. "What do *you* want, honey?" She gestured at her daughters. "We'll do whatever you need—you're the boss." She looked pointedly at Savannah. "Right?"

Her youngest sighed dramatically. "Right, Mom. Sara's the boss." She snatched the notebook from her mother's hand. "But I do have some good ideas—"

Everyone laughed, but Sara sat quietly. *What do I want?* she wondered. *Something small and intimate.*

Something with my daughter.

She began slowly, piecing her thoughts together. "I don't want anything big," she began. "Just family and my closest friends. You haven't met Lauren yet, but we've been best friends for years and I'd like her to be my maid of honor." She looked at Terrence, who nodded. "And I'd like my daughter Natalie to walk me down the aisle, if she will."

The table was hushed until Alicia reached across to clasp her hand. "That sounds absolutely wonderful, honey."

Talia dabbed at her eyes and Savannah smiled. Terrence stood behind Sara's chair and leaned over to kiss the top of her head. "Wonderful," he repeated.

The family went outside for their annual football game and Sara went upstairs to lie down. She pulled out her phone and texted Natalie. *Merry Christmas, love!*

Natalie's response was immediate. *Merry Christmas, Sara! I hope you're having a great day.*

It's wonderful. How are you? How's your mom? I hope she's feeling well.

She's having a great day, answered Natalie. *We cooked together last night and this morning we made her favorite Christmas scones. What are you guys doing?*

Sara took a moment before responding. She didn't really want to share her news via text but didn't want to wait until she returned home. *Can I call you?* she wrote.

Her phone rang almost immediately and Natalie's face appeared on the screen. Smiling, Sara answered, "That was fast!"

"I figured it was important if you wanted to talk live," responded her daughter. "Is everything all right?"

"More than all right." Sara's breath quickened. "I have some news: Terrence and I are getting married!"

Natalie's squeal pierced Sara's ear. "Sara! That's so exciting!" She skipped a beat. "And when am I gonna meet this guy? No getting married without us meeting first!"

Her daughter's enthusiasm warmed her heart and Sara was surprised to find that she'd been tense. Her shoulders relaxed and she lay back on the bed. "Let's do that soon," she said. "I'd actually like you to walk me down the aisle, if you would."

Natalie was quiet for a brief moment before answering. "I'd be honored." And then she began her excited, rapid-fire questions. "Did you set a date? Did you get a ring? How'd he propose? Tell me everything!"

"Well, there's a bit of a story—"

"Ooh, sounds juicy," interrupted Natalie.

"He proposed on the beach on Sunday and we picked out a beautiful ring that afternoon." She looked down at the sparkling pink stone. "But there's more news."

"What?"

"We're—we're having a baby."

The silence was palpable and Sara held her breath. *Should I have told her in person?*

"Natalie? Are you okay?"

Her daughter's voice was thick with emotion. "So I'm gonna have another sibling." She let out a ragged breath while Sara held hers. "When is the baby due?"

"Not until July," she answered. *Please don't let me lose this girl just when I got her back.*

The wait seemed interminable until Natalie spoke. "I guess now I really need to meet Terrence—"

"Of course—" Sara began.

"—because we're gonna be a family."

Sara's tears cascaded down her cheeks and she clutched her phone.

Family.

The next morning, everyone gathered outside to send them off.

"I can't believe how fast that went by," said Sara as she and Terrence pulled away from the Billings family home. Donovan and Alicia stood arm in arm on the porch, waving their goodbyes.

"It was great, right?" asked Terrence.

"It was wonderful. Your family is incredible. I love them so much." She sat back and smiled, relishing the warmth and acceptance she'd experienced. "You're very fortunate."

"Well, they're your family, too, babe," he responded, squeezing her hand. "You're part of us now."

Thank God, she thought.

"Are you okay that we don't spend time with my family? It wouldn't be anything like this and I really don't want to expose you to just how horrid they can be—especially my mother."

Terrence glanced at his fiancée, concern written on his handsome features. "I don't care about me being exposed to them, babe. I don't want them hurting *you.* They've done enough damage already." He gripped the steering wheel, his jaw set. "If you never see them again, I'm fine with that."

She reached up and stroked his cheek and his muscles relaxed. "I love you, Terrence Billings, my mighty falcon," she murmured.

He turned his face slightly to kiss her palm. "And I love you, Sara Billings, my beautiful—" He stopped abruptly. "Wait—you don't have to change your name if you don't want to. My sisters hyphenated theirs, but you do whatever—"

Sara's grimace stopped him. "Believe me, I'm eager to get rid of my last name. I have friends who keep theirs and friends who hyphenate. But I have no attachment to mine at all." Then she smiled, breaking the tension. "And the thought of being one of the Billings clan is half the charm of marrying you," she teased.

Three and a half hours later, they arrived back in Daytona Beach.

"I hate dropping you off," muttered Terrence as they entered Sara's house. "Can't we just move you into my apartment now? We can figure out where we'll live after the baby comes, but this sucks."

Sara grinned as she set her purse on the bed. "Let's talk more about it this week," she said. "I don't want to just leave Lauren in the lurch—we share expenses here. She doesn't even know we're getting married in three months. She'd lose her mind if I move out now."

He pulled her in for a kiss. "Three long months," he groused. "Can't we just elope?"

She pulled back and searched his face. "Are you serious? I guess we could talk about it, but—"

He stopped her with another kiss. "I'm just kidding, my love. I know you want a wedding. So do I." He shrugged. "I'm just impatient."

Smiling, she reached up to tousle his hair. "Maybe you should put that energy into finding us a place to live," she teased. "I'll worry about wedding plans and you get us someplace big enough for a family."

"March? Are you kidding me?" Lauren's eyebrows shot up. "Do you realize how much we have to do in the next two months?" She shook her head in disapproval. "Dresses, venue, flowers, food, an officiant—good grief, Sara, how are we going to get all this done? And why are you grinning like that?"

Sara's smile widened. "It's really funny watching you spin over *my* wedding," she laughed and stretched out on Lauren's bed while her roommate paced. "Alicia and the girls will help. I think Savannah would pretty much do everything if we asked her."

"No way," snapped Lauren. "She may be your new sister-in-law, but I'm your best friend and no one is planning this without me."

Sara continued to grin as her friend fumed. Lauren grabbed a notebook from her desk and began writing. "Okay, first things first: we need a place." She looked up, wondering. "How many people are we talking?"

"Not many," answered Sara. "Us, Terrence and his family—so that's Donovan and Alicia, Talia and Darren and the kids, Savannah and DJ. His best friend Corey will probably come out from California. Then there's Azalea and Esteban and Susana and Enrique." She counted off the group on her fingers. "That's fifteen. And of course, Natalie. So sixteen."

"No Cecilia and Gregory?"

Sara grimaced. "Am I horrible for not wanting my parents at the wedding?"

"With your parents? Hell, no." Then Lauren cocked a smile. "Any chance I can bring a plus one?"

Sara's eyes widened. "Oh? Something you need to tell me?"

"I did tell you," started her friend. "Remember? The client?" She sat cross-legged on the end of the bed. "After Susana pulled me off the account, we've been seeing each other. It's been a month."

"A whole month? Why haven't I heard all the details?"

Lauren pulled a face. "Seriously? Like you've had time or brain space for anything except the baby and your man. I wasn't gonna dump this on you."

Sara frowned. "Don't do that. We've always said we'll be there for each other, no matter what. I want to hear all about him!"

Lauren smiled. "Okay, okay. He's really great. He's smart and ambitious and creative—"

"And hot?" laughed Sara.

"Yeah…and hot."

"Remind me his name?"

"Jayson, with a 'y.' Jayson Rivera."

"Ooh, a Latino," answered Sara. "Your *familia* must be very happy."

"They are," agreed her friend. "He's also Cubano and very close to his culture and his family. Luckily both families are in Miami. He came over for Christmas Eve and then I spent Christmas afternoon at his parents' house. He has six brothers and sisters, so it was a little wild with all their families." She squeezed Sara's hand. "So can I bring him to the wedding?"

"Of course! But we have to double date before then so Terrence and I can make sure he's good enough for you."

Lauren snorted. "Well, for what it's worth, I can pretty much guarantee he's good enough to never buy me a pink ring. I can't believe you talked Terrence into that."

Sara glanced down at her hand and smiled. *One more reason to love him*, she mused. *He understands me.*

Lauren interrupted her reverie. "So back to you and your crazy life. Is Terrence gonna go with you tomorrow? Do you want me to come?"

Sara shook her head. "No, I think it's gonna be enough for Natalie to meet Carlos and Marisa. I'd like to bring her over here to meet you and Terrence, maybe later this week?"

"Makes sense. But let me know if you change your mind and want some back up. You know I'll be there in a heartbeat." Lauren stretched, shoving Sara's legs to the side.

"Ouch!"

"You're the one who flopped on my bed," retorted Lauren, laughing. "Go lie on your own bed if you're gonna be a pregnant diva."

Sara sat up and smiled at her best friend. "Do you ever think about it? About maybe having a baby yourself?"

Lauren's eyebrows shot up as she gaped at her friend. "Have you lost your damn mind?"

25

The next morning, Sara awakened early to a text from Natalie.

Good morning! I'm nervous and excited for tonight. Any tips?

Sara sat up and rubbed her eyes. It was only 7:00 and she hadn't set her alarm, hoping to sleep in. She didn't know how late they'd be out that night—she remembered how she and Natalie had talked for hours when then met the first time. Would tonight be the same for Carlos and Marisa?

Before she could give in to feeling sorry for herself, she thought, *Poor thing. This is such a big deal for her. It's a big deal for all of us.*

She wrote back, *Just be your wonderful self. They will love you.*

Moments later, another text arrived, this time from Carlos.

You awake? Sorry for the early text—I'm just a little nervous. Any tips?

Sara sat up, now wide awake.

No worries, she responded. *I'm up. Already texting with Natalie. She's nervous, too. How's Marisa?*

I'm not sure. She's been kinda quiet.

Sara hesitated before responding. She wasn't sure about Marisa either.

Could we meet a little earlier? texted Natalie. *Maybe half an hour before they get there?*

Sara flipped back and forth between windows. *Of course,* she wrote to Natalie. *I'll see you at 5:30.*

Are you bringing Terrence?

I hadn't planned to, typed Sara. *I figured it was enough for the four of us to meet this time.*

I want to meet him soon, wrote Natalie.

Let's talk tonight. He's eager to meet you, too.

Carlos' message lit up her screen. *Marisa is everything to me. I'm looking forward to meeting Natalie but Marisa is my world.*

Sara sat back, looking at her phone, making sure she was answering in the correct window. *I know—and I'm sure she knows that. You're a great dad.*

Terrence's text came next and she laughed at the sudden juggling of messages. *Good morning, my love,* he wrote. *How are you feeling? Ready for tonight?*

I am, but Natalie and Carlos are so nervous they are already messaging me.

You sure you don't want me to come with you?

She pondered for a moment, then responded. *I really appreciate you offering, but I think it's better to keep it just to us tonight. You're still Marisa's teacher and she might feel awkward if you're there and she gets emotional. But Natalie brought up meeting you again. We need to schedule something soon.*

That would be great, he responded. *Whenever you're ready, I'm there. And if you change your mind and need me tonight, don't hesitate to call. I've got you.*

Sara heart swelled with love. *I know you do and I treasure that. Thank you xo*

Sara watched as Natalie crossed and uncrossed her legs. "Were you this nervous before you met me?" she asked.

Natalie stopped bouncing. "Oh, sorry…" she mumbled.

"Don't be. You're fine." She squeezed the young woman's hand reassuringly. "I can guarantee you they are every bit as nervous as you are."

"What if—" began Natalie.

"No what if's," interjected Sara. "This is a special night and it's gonna be just fine. I promise."

Natalie made a weak attempt at a smile. *Poor baby*, thought Sara. *I wish I could make this easier for her.* She started to speak, but then saw Carlos and Marisa enter the restaurant. "They're here," she said. "Don't worry."

Natalie's eyes widened and she simply said, "Oh."

"Just be yourself and they will love you." She stood and waved at father and daughter. She saw Carlos give Marisa a quick hug and he leaned down to speak in her ear. The teen took a deep breath and nodded as they approached.

Natalie stood and turned. Sara stood next to her and welcomed the newcomers to the table. "Carlos, Marisa—this is Natalie."

Marisa stood still but Carlos came closer. He gazed at Natalie, his hands starting, then stopping to reach out. "Natalie," he breathed. "Could I…would it be okay if I—"

Natalie nodded mutely and the two embraced. She buried her face in his shoulder while Carlos looked over her head at Sara. His eyes were swimming in tears as he held their daughter. At last, they parted and Carlos turned to motion Marisa forward. "Marisa, come meet your sister."

"Hey," said the teen. She stood very still with her hands in her pockets.

"Hey," responded Natalie, smiling. "I'm so glad to meet you, Marisa." Her face turned somber. "I was really sorry to hear about your mom."

Marisa's jaw tightened. "Yeah. Thanks."

The silence grew awkward and Sara interjected. "Are you guys hungry? The food here is really good." She motioned to the chairs and the four sat around the table, Natalie and Marisa across from each other. She looked carefully at each person. Carlos was dabbing at his eyes with a napkin while Natalie looked back and forth between father and daughter. Marisa sat stony, poring over the menu. Sara blew out a breath.

I'm the common denominator here, she realized. *They're all waiting for me.*

"Thanks for coming," she began. "Shall we order first and then we won't be interrupted?"

Marisa shrugged, her nonchalance obviously feigned. "Whatever."

"So what's good here?" asked Carlos, setting aside his menu and looking at Sara.

"Pretty much everything," she answered. "I've heard you can't go wrong with the mahi sandwich, though."

A perky young waiter approached the table. "Hi, everybody! How are we this evening? My name's Skylar and I'll be taking care of you tonight." He waved a hand at their glasses. "Anybody want something other than water? A cocktail, maybe?"

"Sprite," said Marisa, her tone sharp. Her father looked askance at her, but she didn't meet his eyes.

"Water is fine for me," replied Sara. "May I please have some lemon wedges?"

Natalie nodded. "Me, too."

"Corona, please," said Carlos.

"I'll be right back with your drinks," said Skylar, his smile bright.

"That's just great, SKYlar," murmured Marisa at his retreating figure.

Natalie turned to Sara with a quizzical look but her mother just shook her head slightly.

She's just nervous, thought Sara. *She'll get over it.*

She realized Marisa was staring at her hand. The teen looked up at her and asked, "Something you'd like to share, Miss Masterson?"

Sara fumbled with her napkin, then answered in a tone she hoped was casual, "Well, yes. I guess so. Mr. Billings and I got engaged."

"Aren't you just full of surprises," mumbled Marisa.

"Marisa, you don't have to be rude—" began Carlos.

"It's okay," interjected Sara. "We're all a little…uncomfortable right now." She smiled at Marisa. "All of us."

Carlos looked at her, clearly embarrassed by Marisa's behavior. "Congratulations, Sara. I'm really happy for you."

Sara smiled as Skylar returned with their drinks. She was thankful for the distraction, and the tension abated a little as they ordered their meals.

"Why pink?" asked Marisa. "Aren't you supposed to get a diamond?" The teen was almost surly and her father scowled.

She's just a kid, thought Sara. *She's nervous and probably a little scared.*

"Well, that's sort of traditional, yes. But I really like pink. And when I saw this ring, it just sort of jumped out of the case at me." Sara smiled. "Don't you like it?"

Natalie broke in. "I think it's beautiful. Really unique." She smiled at her sister. "Who wants to be like everyone else, right?"

Marisa shrugged. "I guess."

Before she could continue, Skylar arrived with their plates and the four began eating, the tension slowly dissipating.

"So Sara tells me you were a superstar baseball player," said Natalie between bites of her sandwich. "I'm not much of an athlete. I've been into painting and creative writing most of my life."

"I don't know about 'superstar,'" hedged Carlos. "I did go to college on a baseball scholarship—"

Marisa broke in, a defiant look on her face. "You must take after her." She pointed a french fry dripping with ketchup at Sara, then nodded toward her father. "*We're* definitely athletes."

"I think the painting talent is all her own," offered Sara. "I'm a math teacher, remember?"

Carlos looked stricken and Sara realized he was torn between assuaging his younger daughter's obvious jealousy and attempting to connect with his firstborn. She tried to imagine a way to ease the tension when Natalie leaned forward and spoke directly to her sister. "I also hear you're a brilliant math student—the smartest kid in all her classes."

Marisa colored and then shook her head. "I'm pretty good, I guess—"

"You're much better than 'pretty good,'" refuted Carlos, a relieved smile on his face. "Straight A's in math since kindergarten." He put an arm around his younger daughter and squeezed. "She's the brains of the family, that's for sure." He leaned down to kiss the top of her head and Marisa scowled. But Sara noticed the pride that flared in the teen's eyes. *Good move, Carlos*, she thought.

Carlos began talking about Marisa's exploits, both in the classroom and on the basketball court. His pride in his younger daughter was plain and she seemed to relax, at last entering the conversation. Father and two daughters chatted companionably as they ate their dinner and Sara sat back, content to observe. *It's a different kind of family*, she mused. *But it's going to be all right.*

Skylar came to offer them dessert and Marisa immediately answered. "We'll have the crème brûlée and the chocolate cake with ice cream," she said firmly. "With four spoons for us to share."

Carlos raised an eyebrow at Sara and then gave her a quick wink. *It's nice to have her engage*, thought Sara, thankful the teen finally seemed to settle into the conversation. She was surprised and grateful for Natalie's deft handling of her younger sister. *She's such a kind girl—she knew exactly how to reach Marisa.*

Sara reached for her water, but nearly dropped it as a strong cramp rippled through her abdomen. She gasped, but quickly regained her composure.

"Sara?" asked Natalie. "Are you OK?"

"I'm fine—I just almost dropped my glass. It's slippery." She took her napkin and wiped the condensation and noticed how her hand shook. "I'm gonna use the restroom—be right back." She took her purse and hastily rose from the table. "Save some for me!" she called to Marisa, hoping she appeared nonchalant. As she approached the restroom door, another cramp gripped her. *What is happening?*

Shaking, Sara entered a stall and hung up her purse. Sweat began to bead on her forehead as she pulled down her jeans. She sat on the toilet seat and saw the blood on her panties. *No*, she thought. *Please, God, no, no, no....* Her breath shuddered as she tried to clean herself up. There was more blood on the toilet paper and she struggled to keep from crying. She folded up more tissue and placed it in her panties, checking her jeans to be sure it hadn't leaked through. When she finished, she washed her hands and looked at her face in the mirror. Haunted eyes gazed back at her and her lips quivered.

Calm down. Just breathe.

Sara walked unsteadily back to the table. "I'm so sorry," she said, "but I need to go. I'm not feeling that well." All three of her companions started to stand, but she waved them off. "Carlos, could you please get this and I'll pay you back?"

"Don't be silly," he said. "I've got it—you get home." He looked at her with concern. "You don't look so good, Sara. Do you need me to drive you?"

"No, no…I'll be fine," she lied. "Lauren had a nasty stomach bug a couple of weeks ago—maybe she gave it to me." She blew Natalie a kiss. "I'll talk to you soon, honey." She waved to Marisa and walked as quickly as she dared to the car. Once inside, she felt the wetness seeping out of her with another surge of pain. She started the car, pulled out of the lot, and called Terrence.

He answered immediately. "Hey, babe! I didn't expect to hear from you so early. How'd it go?"

Sara choked back a sob. "I need you," she whispered.

"Sara?" Terrence's voice was alarmed. "What's wrong? What happened?"

She couldn't hold back her tears. "I'm bleeding. I'm bleeding a lot." She began to sob. "It really hurts and I'm scared and I'm so sorry—"

"Sara!" Terrence's voice was commanding and broke through her haze. "Where are you? I'm coming to get you right now. We need to get you to the hospital."

She looked around as she drove, but had a hard time reading the street signs through her tears. "I just left the restaurant. I'm not sure what street I'm on…."

"Pull into a parking lot wherever you can, my love." His voice was soothing. "Share your GPS location with me. I'll be there in just a few minutes."

Sara turned into an empty bank parking lot. She took a deep breath—*Calm down*, she thought. *Calm down*. She opened Terrence's contact on her phone and shared her location.

"Got it," he said. "Don't go anywhere and I'll be there in less than ten minutes." She heard him grabbing keys and closing a door. "It's gonna be okay, babe. Everything's gonna be okay."

No, it's not, she thought as the grief overtook her. *I'm losing our baby.*

Sara hung up the phone and shivered. It wasn't cold, but her skin felt clammy as she pulled her sweater closer around her. She could feel wetness seeping through her pants and she whimpered softly. She regretted hanging up with Terrence—the last thing she wanted was to be alone.

I want my mom.

The desperation of the thought hit her like a brick wall— it came unbidden, even against her own will. Nothing about her mother had ever brought her comfort in times of pain, yet something deep inside her, something subconscious and purely instinctual, craved motherly affection in this moment.

She lifted her phone and scrolled to her mother's name.

This isn't a good idea.

She had no reason to believe her mother would be any different, that she'd hear the pain in her daughter's voice and suddenly transform into a loving, nurturing parent, yet Sara couldn't stop herself. She tapped the number as yet another wave of pain engulfed her.

"Sara?" Her father's voice surprised her.

"Hi, Dad," she said, her voice thin. "I thought I called Mom's phone…."

"You did," he said brusquely. "She's taking a bath. Maybe call back later."

"Dad, please." Sara's voice was nearly a whisper. "Let me talk to her." She shivered again, her teeth chattering. "Please."

Her father was quiet and she knew he was debating whether to bother his wife in the tub. At last, she heard him open a door and say, "Cecilia, Sara's on the phone. She doesn't sound good."

"I'm in the bath, Gregory! Tell her to call back in an hour."

A sob escaped Sara's throat and she shouted hoarsely, "Dad! Please!"

"Cecilia," he said, a plaintive note to his voice.

"Oh, for God's sake, take the damn phone and get out of here!" her mother snapped. Sara heard sloshing and then the door closing.

"I'm sorry, Sara, she's just not able to take your call right now."

He sounds like a fucking answering machine.

Sara hung up the phone without another word, then stared at the screen. *Why did I do that?* she wondered. *Nothing ever changes.* She glanced up to see headlights coming toward her car and the phone slipped from her fingers as she tried to open her door.

He caught her before she slumped to the ground.

She'll never change, Sara thought, tears streaming down her cheeks as she curled into Terrence's arms. *She'll never, ever be a real mother.*

"Oh, my God—" whispered Terrence, his voice rough with anguish. "Sara—Sara—" She heard his voice as if it were miles away.

I just wanted my mom, she thought as the darkness overtook her.

26

"I thought I could trust you," said Terrence. "I thought you would keep our child safe."

Sara stared at him, her arms reaching for him, but he turned away. She tried to speak, but nothing came out. She couldn't cry—couldn't do anything. She was wracked with guilt and fear as she saw the love of her life turning his back on her.

Perhaps forever.

Again she opened her mouth to defend herself, but nothing came out. Terrence strode away without a backward glance, leaving her alone in her classroom. In agony, she looked around and saw row after row of empty chairs.

Except the back row, where Natalie sat.

Her daughter looked somberly at her, then shook her head in… what? Sorrow? Disapproval? Sara remained mute, however, unable to ask. Unable to cry.

At last, Natalie spoke. "Maybe you should get your tubes tied, Sara. Clearly you don't have what it takes to be a mother. You couldn't hang on to either one of us." Her voice was soft, her cruel words masked by an almost businesslike tone.

Sara tried to protest, but the accusation struck her with the force of a bomb exploding in her heart.

It's my fault. It's all my fault.

At last, the sobs burst from her and she slumped to the ground.

Sara woke from her nightmare to a nurse checking her IV line. Her hair was wet where the tears had run down her face and for a moment she wasn't sure where she was. Terrence was asleep on a chair nearby, his dark curls hanging over his eyes, his breathing slow.

"How are you this morning?" asked the nurse, her voice quiet and kind. "I'm sorry to wake you but I need to check your vitals." She looked down at her watch as she measured Sara's heart rate. "You can go back to sleep as soon as I'm done."

Sara closed her eyes, the tears beginning again. Her throat and lips were dry and her insides felt like she'd been hit by a bus. She longed for a glass of water, but hesitated to ask.

I don't deserve water. I don't deserve anything.

The hollow she felt was deeper than any pain she'd ever known and she fell back into a fitful sleep, littered with the accusing voices of those she'd failed.

Sara felt the light touch of a hand on her right cheek and a tighter clasp of her left hand. Through her exhaustion, it slowly dawned on her that there were two people next to her. She stirred and the hand holding hers gripped harder while the one stroking her cheek grasped the side of her face. She felt a scratchy beard and heard Terrence whisper raggedly, "Sara…." His weeping roused her enough to slowly open her eyes.

"Terrence?" Her voice cracked. She looked to her left and saw Lauren, her face drawn and tired. "Lauren? What are you doing here?"

"It's okay, honey," said her best friend, squeezing her hand. "You're in the hospital but you're all right now."

Terrence continued to hold her head to his chest, his sobs slowly subsiding. "I thought I was gonna lose you," he murmured into her hair. "I was so scared."

Sara closed her eyes and tried to wrest her mind from the throes of the nightmares. She wasn't in her classroom—she was in the hospital.

Because I lost our baby.

Tears slid down her cheeks as she remembered the pain at the restaurant and the blood....

"I'm sorry," she began.

"No!" Terrence's anguished response cut through her haze. "You didn't do anything wrong, my love." He crushed her to his chest, rocking her and murmuring words she couldn't understand.

Lauren touched Sara's arm and stood up. "I'll leave you two alone," she said softly. "I'll be in the waiting room. Not going anywhere."

Terrence slowly released her and Sara turned to look at him. His unshaven face was exhausted, with dark circles under his eyes. "What time is it?" she asked, her voice barely over a whisper.

He sat back and took her hand. "It's almost six o'clock," he said, looking at his watch.

"In the morning?" Sara was stunned. She'd left the restaurant no later than seven the previous night.

He nodded. "We've been here all night." He stroked her cheek. "You were hemorrhaging and then you blacked out. I didn't want to wait for an ambulance so I just drove like a maniac to the emergency room." His eyes filled again. "You weren't able to give consent, love. I explained what was happening and they did an emergency D and C." He pointed to the IV stand. "You'll probably be here for a few more hours but then we can go home."

She stared mutely at him, grief and guilt knotting themselves in her heart. "So it's really over," she whispered at last. "Our baby. It's over." Sara pulled away, wrapping her arms around herself. *We're over.*

Terrence gently tugged her arms apart and drew her to him. "Don't do that. Don't pull away. We'll get through this and we'll try again. It's gonna be all right."

Sara's eyes were hollow and her voice was small. "It will never be all right. I'm never going to be a good mother."

He looked at her, stricken. "What are you talking about? You're a wonderful mother. We had a miscarriage, Sara. It's tragic and awful but it's not your fault."

Sara closed her eyes, the exhaustion overtaking her despite her fear of the nightmares returning. She had needed her mother last night but Cecilia had not been there for her—she had simply refused to care.

My baby needed me last night, too, she thought. *And I failed her.* She didn't know why she felt certain the baby had been a girl—it just seemed right. As she slipped back into sleep, other mothers drifted through her hazy, troubled thoughts. Her friend Azalea was a wonderful mother. Her sons had turned out so well and Sara wondered idly how Tomás and Emily's little girl was doing. Surely she'd been born by now. She thought of Lauren's mother, always so welcoming, warmly including Sara in their family.

Her last thought before she succumbed to exhaustion and grief was of Alicia Billings. *I wish I could have been her daughter. I wish I could have been a mother like her.*

Unshed tears pooled against her lashes as she slept.

Sara woke to harsh whispers outside her door.

"Be reasonable, Terrence," she heard Lauren say. "We have a house—you have an apartment. We have one storey—you have stairs. I can work from home—you can't. It doesn't make sense to take her to your place."

"I just—" Terrence spluttered.

"I know," her friend responded quietly. "I know. Look, just pack a bag and come stay with us."

There were more words, but Sara couldn't make them out. She knew they were worried and wanted to take care of her but all she could think about was going home and burying her head under her covers.

I just want to be alone.

Terrence and Lauren walked in and Sara saw their deep concern. When Terrence realized she was awake, he rushed to her side, kneeling beside her bed and taking her hand. Lauren stood quietly behind him.

"You're awake," he said, his eyes intent on hers. "How do you feel?"

Sara looked back at him but couldn't seem to focus. "I want to go home," she said at last, her voice monotone.

"We will, love. As soon as you see the doctor." He reached for her hand but she drew it away. His hurt was palpable, but she couldn't muster enough emotion to care. She closed her eyes, willing them both to leave. *I just want to be alone.*

Terrence cleared his throat softly. "The doctor's here, love."

She looked up to see a woman standing beside Lauren.

"I'll go grab some coffee," said her friend, looking gravely at Sara. "You wanna come?" she asked Terrence.

"I'd rather stay," said Terrence, looking at Sara. Then he glanced back at the doctor. "I—I'm the father."

"What do *you* want, Sara?" asked the doctor.

Sara glanced at Terrence and was surprised by his anxious countenance. She sighed heavily and shrugged. "That's fine."

The doctor looked at the couple, then motioned for Terrence to move from the bedside. He gently rubbed Sara's arm, then stepped away so the physician could approach.

"I'm Dr. Davidson, Sara. I looked after you last night." She lifted Sara's chart and reviewed it, then looked at the nearly empty IV bag. "How are you feeling?"

Sara looked at the doctor and then at Terrence. Talking took an effort, but she said, "I'm really tired and pretty achy. My insides feel all beat up and my head hurts." She was mildly surprised to feel tears. "When can I go home?"

"Let's have a look at you and see, shall we?" Dr. Davidson raised the bed and had Sara lean forward. The ER doctor listened to her breathing and her heartbeat, and gently palpitated her abdomen. Sara groaned slightly and Terrence moved toward her protectively. The doctor looked at him and smiled. "It's all right," she said, her voice soothing. "She's going to be sore for a few days and she'll be weak from the loss of blood. But she's out of danger." She looked at Sara. "You're out of danger, but you need a lot of rest. I'll let you go home today, but you need to stay home from work for the rest of the week and no strenuous exercise."

Terrence interjected, "She'll stay in bed, I promise, Doctor."

The doctor's eyebrows raised as a slightly sarcastic look crossed her face. "Oh, will she?" She turned to Sara. *"Will you?"*

Terrence glowered at the doctor but said nothing.

"I'm a teacher, so I'm off all this week. I promise to just rest," said Sara.

The doctor smiled kindly. "Good. Now, do you have any questions for me?"

Sara glanced up at Terrence, sadness flitting across her face. She closed her eyes and shook her head. She had all the answers she needed.

"Why did this happen? And will it happen again?" She heard the hurt and fear in Terrence's voice. "Will we be able to have another child?"

"No one really knows why women miscarry," began the doctor. "Research shows that up to fifteen percent of all pregnancies end in miscarriage. And it doesn't mean anything for future pregnancies." She paused. "I take it you want a family."

Sara opened her eyes and looked at Terrence as he nodded.

"I don't see any reason why you can't successfully carry to term, Sara," she said. "This was an unfortunate circumstance—and yes, it was unusually severe. You hemorrhaged in a way that most women don't experience. I think your obstetrician will want to monitor you closely with any future pregnancy, but I don't think you have anything to worry about. I certainly didn't see anything that would cause me concern during your D and C."

Sara looked up at Terrence. "Thank God," he whispered.

"When can I get this out?" Sara asked, nodding toward the IV stand. "And when can I go home?"

Dr. Davidson stood and smiled at the young couple. "I'll send the nurse in shortly. She'll take out the IV and you can get dressed and sign some papers. They'll bring a wheelchair—"

"A wheelchair?"

The emergency room physician nodded. "It's hospital policy. They'll come and wheel you to the car." She looked at Terrence. "While she's signing out, you can go get the car and bring it to the entrance to pick her up." At his crestfallen look, she sighed. "She'll be just fine for fifteen minutes, young man."

The doctor turned to Sara, her face kind. "Take care of yourself and be sure to call your doctor for a follow up. And remember, it's not unusual to have some feelings of grief after a miscarriage. You may find you're crying a lot, or can't sleep, or sleep too much—it's different for everyone. But if you feel like it's no better after a couple of weeks, don't try to manage it yourself. Postpartum depression is a real thing, and you shouldn't neglect your emotional health just because you're physically healed."

Postpartum depression? Don't you need to have a baby to get that?

"But I didn't have a baby," she said softly.

Dr. Davidson took her hand. "Sara, you lost a pregnancy. Be kind to yourself. If you need help, don't try to manage things yourself."

I don't deserve kindness.

The doctor smiled and left, and Sara felt a twinge of remorse at Terrence's stricken look. "Go get Lauren—she can get the car and you can wait here with me."

He clasped her hand and this time she didn't pull away. "Thank you," he said hoarsely. "It's gonna take a few days for me to let you out of my sight, I think."

"You heard the doctor. There's nothing to worry about."

He bent to kiss her fingertips. "I know, I know. I guess I'm still shaken up at seeing you like that." He closed his eyes and whispered, "I was terrified, Sara."

I don't deserve you.

She closed her eyes and didn't answer.

The nurse arrived to remove her IV. "Time to unhook you, Sara," she said, a cheerful smile on her face.

The couple parted and Terrence stood. "I'll go get Lauren," he said, wiping again at his eyes. "I love you, Sara."

Why?

She couldn't respond and, after a moment, he left the room.

As they drove home, Sara leaned her head against the car window, eyes closed. She didn't want to talk and was thankful Terrence seemed to understand. She could feel his gaze on her from time to time, but she couldn't muster the energy to look back at him.

I just want to be alone.

When they pulled in to the driveway, she opened her eyes and sighed. The thought of walking to the door overwhelmed her. Terrence got out and came around to open her door, reaching in to help her out of the car. She was so exhausted she let him, leaning against his shoulder as they walked slowly to the front door.

Lauren opened it as they approached, her smile disappearing when she saw how weak Sara was. "I've got your bed all ready for you," she said. "C'mon, let's get you down before you fall."

Sara noticed the fearful look her friend gave Terrence. "I'm fine," she said, her voice thready and weak. "Could you get me some water?"

She stumbled over the doorstep and Terrence scooped her up as if she were a child. "Are you all right? Do we need to go back to the hospital?" She shook her head, too tired to speak. He carried her into her room and laid her gently on the bed. The comforter was turned down and the pillows arranged for her to lean back, and she sighed with relief.

When Lauren returned with a glass of water, Sara took it with a trembling hand.

Terrence and Lauren exchanged worried glances and Terrence gently took the glass from Sara's hand. "Here, love. Let me help you."

Sara felt a flash of annoyance at the two of them. She wasn't broken. She could put herself to bed and drink a glass of water without help. But the feeling passed almost immediately and she couldn't keep the tears from rolling down her cheeks. *How can you be so kind to me?* she wondered.

Lauren handed Terrence a tissue and he gently blotted the tears from Sara's face. He held the glass for her to sip and then set it on the nightstand. "Do you think you could sleep?" he asked.

I could sleep forever.

She nodded and he pulled the covers over her. "Are the pillows okay or do you want—"

"They're fine," she spat, regretting her tone as soon as the words were out. Flatly she continued, "They're fine. I'm—I'm just tired."

Terrence laid his palm against her cheek and leaned down to kiss her forehead. "I'll check on you in a bit, but I'll be in the living room if you need anything."

I need to be alone.

27

Sara stood and held out the wine bottle. "Want the rest?

"Nah, I'm good," answered Lauren. "I'm gonna go to bed, too." She stood and hugged Sara. "I'm really, really happy for you."

Sara smiled at her friend, then looked down to see blood running down her legs, pooling on the floor....

She woke with a start, her heart hammering in her chest, her gasping sobs bringing Terrence running into the room.

"Sara? Sara? What is it, love? Are you hurting?"

She clutched at him, desperate to speak, but her grief gave her no space for words. He climbed onto the bed and held her tight to his chest. "Shh…shh…it's all right, my love. I'm here. It's all right."

Terrence rocked her and tried to console her, but Sara began to shut down, the heartache consuming everything.

At last she fell quiet, her sleep mercifully dreamless.

In the middle of the night she awoke. She was groggy and sore, and her head was pounding. Terrence was curled up next to her, snoring softly. She looked at his face, so handsome as he slept and she felt her heart might shatter. Only two days before, she'd been giddily happy. Engaged to this beautiful kind man, she was pregnant with their child. She'd introduced Natalie to Carlos and Marisa. Her life was everything she'd ever hoped for and she was part of a real family.

But not now.

A darkness seemed to envelope her as she considered her life. Sara knew who she was. She was a fraud. How could she be a good mother when she couldn't even protect her baby in her womb? Terrence may love her now, but how long would it be before he realized how broken she really was?

The next morning, Terrence kissed her and got up, stretching and arching his back. He hadn't changed his clothes since he rescued her in the parking lot, and his t-shirt was rumpled, his jeans in a pile on the floor. He pulled them on and told her, "I need to go to my place for some clothes and stuff but I'll be back as quick as I can. Lauren's here if you need anything."

Sara looked away, then spoke slowly and quietly. "You don't need to come back."

He stared at her, his face puzzled. "What?"

She looked back at him, her face dull. One part of her yearned to feel, yet the darkness sapped the life from her. The part of her that still cared for Terrence nearly broke. But if she ever loved him, she knew what she needed to do. "I said, you don't need to come back." She struggled to sit up, holding out her hand to stop him from helping her. "Isn't it obvious? This isn't right, Terrence." She took a deep breath. "You deserve so much more."

"Sara, you don't mean that—you can't mean that." He sat back down on the bed and tried to take her hand. "I know you're hurting and so am I, but, baby—my love—" He shuddered as he struggled to keep from crying as she pulled away.

"This is my fault," she said simply. "I'm not the woman your family would want you to have." She closed her eyes and let the bleakness overtake her. "Please go."

After a long moment, she heard him leave, closing the door quietly. She could hear voices outside her room, but couldn't make sense of them. At last, she heard the front door close as well.

It doesn't matter, she thought. *It's over.*

Scowling, Lauren burst into her room. "What the hell did you just do?" she asked, incredulous. "Look, I get that you're sad and I'm trying very hard to be understanding but seriously, Sara. What the hell?"

"Leave me alone, Lauren," she whispered. "I can't do this now."

Lauren stood agape, staring at her friend. "Sara, what's going on?" Her voice lost its harshness. "What happened? Don't you see how much that man loves you?"

Sara gazed at the door where he'd left. "He only thinks he does," she said slowly. "He loves the person he thinks I am."

I'm broken.

Lauren started to sit on the bed, but Sara shook her head. "Please let me sleep," she said, her voice a whisper. "Please just leave me alone."

Sara couldn't tell what day it was. She heard angry voices in the living room but couldn't make out what they said. She was having a hard time even caring. When she heard the front door slam, she barely registered a flicker of emotion.

Lauren walked into her bedroom without knocking. Sara knew she'd been in there before, but it was all a blur. Her friend's face was a mixture of anger and confusion and she stood for several heartbeats before she spoke.

"I'm not sure what to say to you," she began. "You've laid here for five days, Sara. You won't eat. You haven't showered. You haven't talked to me—or Terrence. You ignore messages on your phone. Did you know Natalie's been trying to reach you? I finally plugged your phone in this morning because it's been dead for two days. She's probably frantic by now."

Natalie.

Oh, God. My daughter.

Sara's lips began to tremble. She looked at Lauren with glassy eyes.

"I know I'm being a lousy friend, but this is fucked up, Sara. I get that you're hurting, but you're hurting everyone who loves you—"

"I know!" shouted Sara, her voice hoarse with disuse. She pushed herself up and her head swam with dizziness. "I know…" she repeated, her voice solemn. "I'm a horrible mother and a horrible friend and a horrible fiancée and no one—*no one* should love me."

Lauren stood, her face perplexed. "What are you talking about?" She sat down hard on the bed. "Sara, do you hear what you're saying? *You had a miscarriage.* That's it. Just like thousands of women every single day." She shook her head. "I don't understand," she pleaded. "Help me understand."

Sara looked up, the grief crippling her, driving out every shred of emotion beyond her loss. Her desire to curl up and give in to the anguish warred with her longing for relief. She saw Lauren's pain through a fog of self-condemnation and couldn't bear it.

"Sara," whispered Lauren, this time in a voice plaintive with worry,. "*Help me understand.*"

At last, Sara broke. The grief overcame her while Lauren's love split her heart in two. Her tears became guttural, wrenching sobs. She struggled to catch her breath and she gripped the comforter, wringing it in her hands.

Lauren stared at her friend and then wrapped her in a fierce hug. Sara groaned in wordless agony against Lauren's shoulder, her grief a feral monster erupting from her soul.

At last, her sobs subsided and she slumped in Lauren's arms, completely wrung out. "I don't want to be a bad mother, too," she whispered. "I hate her…I hate her."

Lauren pulled a little away. "Who are you talking about?"

Sara looked up at her with reddened eyes, her face blotchy from her anguished crying. "My mother."

Lauren looked confused. "You worry you can't be a good mother because you have a bitch for a mother?"

Sara nodded.

Lauren took a deep breath and laid Sara back against her pillows. "My sweet, sweet friend." Her voice was tende. "You are nothing like your mother. Nothing."

Sara gazed at her, heartsick and weary.

Then Lauren's face lightened. "Because I love you, I'm not gonna laugh at you," she said gently. "But that has to be the most ridiculous thing I have ever heard."

Sara began to speak, but Lauren cut her off. "Seriously. Your mom is a *bitch*. There's nothing good about that woman. She's arrogant, selfish, conceited, and just plain mean. How you came from her is an absolute mystery."

"But I'm *so broken*, Lauren," answered Sara. "I gave away my first baby. And then I lost the second one. I'll never be a mother. Terrence wants a family—how can I be his wife?"

Lauren's face hardened. "Not gonna lie, Sara. You're starting to piss me off." She sucked in a breath and held it, then began again. "I'm sorry. You don't need me jumping down your throat. Just remember: You had your first baby taken away from you. You didn't have anything to do with that. And you got her back! You know Natalie is starting to love you. And this miscarriage doesn't say one thing about you as a person. It happens all the time. All. The. Time."

Sara sat very still. She spoke in whispers, but her despair was evident. "You know I wasn't sure about connecting with Natalie in the beginning. I worried it would open up old wounds and upend my life." She wiped her eyes with the back of her hand. "That's not loving. It's exactly what my mother would have done."

"Bullshit," said Lauren, dismissing her argument. "Your mother would've looked up Natalie's résumé first to see if there was any advantage to them meeting. Loving her would never have crossed her mind." She took Sara's hand. "And can we talk about Terrence? If you could see the agony you have put that poor man through, you'd never say that about him. He told me today that even if he knew you guys would never have another child, he can't imagine his life without you. He comes over every day, hoping you've changed your mind. He adores you."

The tightness in her chest loosened the barest amount. Was it possible? Was Lauren right? "He feels that way now. But what about the future?" she asked.

Lauren grimaced. "The future isn't guaranteed for anyone," she said firmly. "But I'd say you have all the ingredients for a great life, Sara. You have a good man, a good career." She chuckled. "And the best friend in the history of best friends. Honestly, there are only three bad things about you."

Sara's brows furrowed. *So here it is*, she thought. *The truth.* "Tell me," she whispered.

Lauren's voice was emotionless. "You like pink, you're a vegan, and you're obsessed with that ancient numbers guy."

Ancient numbers guy?

"You mean Fibonacci?"

"That's the one. It's embarrassing." Lauren burst out laughing, the mood broken. "Seriously, Sara. You have a great life. You've *chosen* to become the woman you are and everyone loves you for it." Her friend squeezed her hand. "Sara, you need to talk to somebody. This isn't you—it's not just run of the mill sadness. You need someone who knows how to help you. Terrence and I love you, but that's not enough. Will you please think about it?"

Sara looked away. *Do I need a counselor?* she wondered. Therapy was not a Masterson thing. She'd heard her mother make disparaging remarks about women she knew who "threw away money on shrinks," as she put it. But she didn't need her mother's opinion. She thought back to the emergency room doctor's admonition to take care of herself. She knew she was at a crossroads—the darkness fluttered at the edges of her consciousness, just waiting to overwhelm her. She knew that she needed to make a choice—would she accept the story that she was a lost cause? Or would she choose to pursue life and love?

Sara pondered her friend's words. Could she be the woman she longed to be?

She felt a glimmer of hope. *I can choose.*

An hour later, Sara braided her damp hair and slipped into clean pajamas. Lauren had changed the sheets on her bed while she showered and she lay thankfully onto the fresh linens. Just showering had been enough to tire her, but it was only that—she was tired, not exhausted. For the first time in days, she felt clean. Renewed.

Lauren came in with a tray. "Think you could eat something?"

Sara realized she was hungry and nodded. "Yes, please." She looked at the glass of something fizzy and the slice of toast. "Ginger ale?"

"Yup—I thought you should probably go easy since you haven't eaten in a while."

"Thank you, Lauren. Thank you for everything. I'm so sorry. I didn't mean to scare you."

Lauren sat on the corner of the bed. "You don't have to apologize—I should. I can't even begin to imagine how you're feeling. I'm sorry for snapping at you. I *was* scared and I know I overreacted."

"No—I needed that. I needed to hear the truth." She sipped the soda and sighed. "I felt like I was in this fog that I just couldn't get out of. Like I couldn't think straight except for one thing: that I was an awful person and everyone was better off without me." At Lauren's horrified look, she hastened to add, "I don't mean I was suicidal. Just that no one should want to love me or be in my life."

"That's depression," said Lauren slowly. "Like real, serious depression. Not just feeling down."

"The doctor warned me about postpartum depression. I feel it still kinda hovering," admitted Sara. "It's like this unstoppable monster—like it's swirling around just waiting to steal my soul. And I'm scared to fall asleep because I've had these horrible dreams. But I can feel just a little bit of sunshine—like I can find a way to come out of it if I'm willing to do the work." She looked away, then back at Lauren. "You're right. I need to see someone."

"And Terrence?" asked Lauren. "What about him?"

Sara's face fell. "I need to talk to him. Hopefully, he'll understand."

Lauren smiled. "I'm pretty sure that's the least of your worries. If you call, he'll be here in minutes."

"And I need to talk to Natalie," added Sara. "I can't believe I put her through that worry."

Lauren stood. "Finish your breakfast and make your calls. I have a feeling today is going to be a hard but good day." She blew Sara a kiss, then left the room.

Sara finished her toast and set the tray on the ground beside her bed. After a long moment, she picked up her phone and called the man she loved.

28

"I'll be there in fifteen minutes," said Terrence. "Don't go anywhere, okay?" He tried to joke, but Sara could hear the relief in his voice.

While she waited for him to arrive, she texted Natalie.

Hi Natalie—I'm so sorry for making you worry. I've been kind of a mess these last few days and I hope you'll forgive me.

She paused, then added: *I had a miscarriage.*

Her phone began to ring seconds after she sent the message.

"Sara! Are you all right? I'm so sorry." Sara could hear the sorrow in her daughter's voice.

"I'm okay. I ended up in the emergency room because I was hemorrhaging. The doctor says I'm fine now."

"It started at dinner? At the restaurant?"

Sara closed her eyes, remembering. She'd nearly dropped her glass at the table when the cramping began. "Yeah. I'm sorry for scaring everyone."

"Don't be silly. Everyone was just concerned."

Sara changed the subject, unwilling to think more about that night. "So how did the rest of the evening go?"

She could hear the smile in Natalie's voice. "It was really great. Carlos is so nice and super funny. And Marisa finally warmed up a little. We talked for another hour after you left." She paused, then continued in a quiet tone, "Thank you, Sara. Thank you for bringing us all together like that. I don't know what the future holds, but I feel like pieces of my life have fallen into place and it's—I don't know.… I don't really have words for it."

"I'm so glad, honey. I really am."

"So are you honestly okay? Do you need anything? Can I help?"

Sara smiled at her daughter's offer. "I'm fine. Lauren's here and hovering every few minutes and Terrence is on his way over."

"I'm glad you have them. I can't wait to meet them! When you feel better, can we all get together?"

Sara smiled. "Absolutely! I'd love to have you come over for dinner—maybe next week?

"I'd love it." Sara heard Natalie speaking away from the phone. "Okay, gotta run. My mom and I are going grocery shopping. Not sure what she's gonna do when I move out, but I'm glad I'm here to help for now."

"Have a great day and thank you for checking on me."

Natalie's voice was somber. "Please take care of yourself." Sara barely heard her daughter's next words. "I just found you."

Sara felt a tendril of happiness and strove to grasp and hold it. "I will, I promise."

She awoke to a light touch on her cheek. *Did I fall asleep that quickly?* she wondered. She thought she'd only just hung up with Natalie.

"Hey there, sleepyhead," said Terrence, his voice soft. "How are you feeling?"

She leaned into his hand and closed her eyes. Emotions rekindled—relief at his touch, regret at their parting. "I'm fine now," she whispered. She looked up at him, tears threatening to spill. "I'm so sorry, Terrence. I'm so, so sorry."

"Angel," he said, pulling her into his arms, "it's all right. It's over—everything is going to be all right."

Sara leaned into his embrace, then pulled away. "Can I please talk about it?"

Terrence nodded, his face solemn. "Of course. But may I lie next to you while you talk? I really need to be close to you."

She scooted over and held the covers open for him to slide in. He put his arm around her shoulders and she lay her head on his chest. He twined his fingers around her long braid and she lay still for a long moment.

And then she told him everything.

Terrence was quiet for a long while after she finished. She lay still, letting him process and waiting for his response.

At last, he hugged her and rolled to his side to face her. He traced her jawline with a finger, then brushed it lightly across her lips. "I couldn't love you more," he said softly. "I'm sorry you ever had to wonder."

"I didn't actually wonder about you," she said. "I wondered about me…whether I could be worthy of you."

"Sara—my love. I know you're not perfect. No one is. But you're the most important person in my life and I am not going anywhere. For better or for worse, right? We're going through this together, no matter what happens. If we have a dozen kids or none at all, I'm here for you. If you have another one of these awful dreams, I'll be here to hold you while you cry." He brushed away a lone tear on her cheek. "We all have demons, Sara. But with love, we can slay them together."

Together. My mighty falcon.

The three of them sat at the table that evening for dinner. Lauren and Terrence convinced Sara to eat some fish with her vegetables, arguing that she needed some healthy protein to keep her from anemia. Sara was surprised at how hungry she was, although she ate sparingly to be safe. She laughed at the way they babied her, finally able to accept it without remorse.

"So when do we get to meet this guy?" Terrence asked. "Must be pretty special if you're willing to give up his account just to date him."

"Omigod, he's great," gushed Lauren. "I know you guys are gonna love him."

The three chatted amiably until Sara began to droop. Terrence noticed immediately and interrupted Lauren's story.

"Babe? Let's get you back to bed."

Sara nodded. "I'm sorry—I'm just running out of steam."

"Don't be sorry," said Lauren.

"It's gonna be a few days until you get your strength back," agreed Terrence. "You lost a lot of blood."

She rose and started to take her plate to the counter. Lauren waved her off. "Leave it! I'll clean up. Just get some rest."

After brushing her teeth and slipping on pajamas, she climbed into bed. "I'm so sleepy," she yawned. "I wonder how long I'm going to feel this way."

Terrence slid in beside her, propping up a pillow behind him. "Go to sleep, love. I'm just gonna read." He glanced at his watch and chuckled. "A bit early for me. I don't normally go to bed at seven o'clock."

Sara closed her eyes and fell asleep in minutes.

"Why don't you get your tubes tied?" asked her mother. "You've nearly ruined your life twice." She held up a jeweled mirror and reapplied her lipstick, then looked back at Sara. "Better yet, why not a hysterectomy? Make it impossible to reproduce. Then you can finally make something of your life."

Sara stared at her mother. Her stomach knotted as she considered her answer.

"Are you just going to sit there staring at me? You know I'm right." Her mother's voice was smooth, oily. Poisonous.

At last, Sara spoke.

"Why did you ever have a baby? Why did you have me?"

Her mother's perfect eyebrows rose in disdain. "Do you really think it would have looked good for us to be childless in the eighties? Having a child was de rigueur, Sara. How else could one hire the proper nannies, find the right schools, and fit in with the other wives?"

Sara's mouth dropped open. "You had me to fit in?" She was stunned.

"Grow up, Sara. Your father's business required a certain lifestyle and having a child was part of that tableau. Nothing more. It's time you stopped trying to make this more than it has ever been."

Sara stared at the woman who'd birthed her. The cord that bound them, weak as it was, finally snapped. She thought of Natalie and the bond they were forging and a sense of wholeness filled her, replacing the longing that had shadowed her entire life.

"You're right, Cecilia," she said at last, her voice firm. "It's time."

"Sara? It's okay, love. It's just a dream." Terrence soothed her.

She leaned back to see his concerned expression. "I'm okay," she whispered. She reached up to kiss him, amazed at the contentment she felt as the darkness began to withdraw.

The next few days were peaceful as Sara continued to heal, both physically and emotionally. She had no more nightmares, and spent her nights in her fiancé's warm embrace.

On Saturday morning, she, Terrence, and Lauren were sitting at the dining room table having breakfast when she got a text from Natalie.

Good morning! Just checking on you. Hope you're feeling better.

Sara smiled. "It's Natalie," she said, then answered quickly. *I'm much better. Thank you so much for checking!*

"So when are we gonna meet her?" asked Terrence. He and Lauren were devouring donuts and Sara laughed as she dabbed at a fleck of powdered sugar on his lip.

"I guess any time," she answered.

Lauren spread her hands and looked around. "What are we waiting for? Why can't she come over this weekend?"

Terrence nodded his agreement. "That is, if you're up to it," he added.

Sara looked at them and smiled. "I think that would be lovely," she said. "Let me ask."

I know it's last minute, but would you like to come over for dinner this evening? You could meet Terrence and Lauren.

She realized how much she wanted Natalie to agree and felt a little flutter of apprehension as she waited for her text.

A minute passed before her daughter responded. *I would love to! What time is good and what can I bring?*

Sara lay back against her pillows reading. Her eyes were tired, and she set the book down to rest them just as Terrence walked in the bedroom.

"How are you feeling?" he asked. "We've got the house all straightened up and it looks really nice." He kissed her cheek, then said, "Oh, I almost forgot. I hope it's okay, but I talked to my parents. They were ready to jump in the car and drive up here to take care of you but I told them we're fine. They sent their love and said to tell you if you need anything at all to call. My mom actually ordered dinner for us tonight since she's not here to cook for you." He grinned. "Lauren tells me she's not much of a cook and I'm not much better."

She smiled, her eyes fluttering with tiredness. "That's so sweet," she murmured.

"Get some sleep, love. You have a couple of hours before Natalie gets here." Sara gazed at him. "I love your parents. Please thank them for me." She squeezed his hand. "Do you realize how lucky you are to have them?"

"Well, if I'm lucky then you are, too. We're all family now."

Two hours later, Sara finished her preparations with a quick swipe of lip gloss. She looked in the mirror and wrinkled her nose. She knew she looked tired, but at least it wasn't the wan, exhausted look from earlier in the week. It would have to do.

Lauren knocked on the open bedroom door and came in. "You look pretty," she said. "You feeling okay?"

Sara nodded. "I am. It's not like we're going on a hike. All I have to do is sit there and let you guys get to know each other." She glanced out the door toward the living room. "Where's Terrence?"

Lauren laughed. "That guy. He's a nervous wreck. When you got in the shower he went to the grocery store to get some fresh flowers for the table—said he wanted something special for Natalie's first visit. He's been gone for 45 minutes so I'm not sure if he got lost or what."

Just then, Terrence entered the house. Both women looked out to see him carrying an armload of flowers. He peeked around the bouquets with an embarrassed grin. "I couldn't decide and I wasn't sure what her favorite color is, so I just bought a bunch of different ones."

Sara's heart swelled with love, but Lauren burst out laughing. "Let's hope we have enough vases for them all."

Lauren and Terrence worked together and set the fresh arrangements around the house. After they finished the last bunch, Sara leaned over to kiss Terrence. "This is very sweet. Thank you."

He grinned and shrugged. "I guess if I'm gonna be sort of a stepdad, I want to make a good impression."

Stepdad. She hadn't even thought about what Terrence would be to Natalie—she'd been so consumed first with sharing her secret and then introducing him to her daughter.

"She doesn't even call me Mom," she cautioned. "I don't know if she'll see you that way." She hugged him. "Please don't be disappointed if she doesn't warm up to you immediately."

Terrence smiled and kissed her cheek. "Not at all, my love. I just want to do everything I can to make her feel comfortable. It's not about me."

The doorbell rang and Lauren answered the door. Sara and Terrence walked into the living room to hear Lauren's squeal of welcome.

"I'd know you anywhere. You look just like your mother!"

Sara groaned and looked at Terrence. "Not the way I'd hoped to start the evening," she whispered.

But then she heard Natalie's clear laugh.

"Well, thank you for the compliment. Does that mean I can come in?"

Lauren stepped aside to let the girl enter as Sara approached. "I'm so glad you could make it," she said.

Natalie stopped and gazed at her mother, concern written on her face. Sara spoke quickly, "I know, I know. I don't look so great, but I'm really okay."

The younger woman stepped forward and hugged Sara. They stood in the middle of the room in silence for a long moment before Natalie pulled away. She blinked away tears and then glanced back at Lauren. "So you must be Lauren," she said brightly, clearly attempting to lighten the mood.

Lauren nodded, then closed the front door. Sara took Terrence's hand and he stepped forward. "And this is Terrence. Terrence, this is my daughter, Natalie."

Natalie put her hand out and the two shook hands. "It's nice to meet you, Natalie," said Terrence. "Sara has told me so much about you."

"Great to meet you, too."

This is awkward, thought Sara. She held out a hand and offered to take Natalie's purse and jacket. The young woman handed them to her but Terrence took them. "I'll just put them in the bedroom," he said.

Natalie looked around the room. Lauren hadn't taken down any decorations and the Christmas tree twinkled brightly. "Your home is lovely."

She's nervous, too.

As Terrence returned, the doorbell rang again. "That must be the food," he said, and went to the door.

Sara motioned Natalie to the dining room. "Let's go sit and these two can get dinner on the table." She glanced back at Terrence and Lauren. *It'll be okay,* she mouthed.

As Terrence dished up the food, she gaped at the portions. "Are you planning to feed me for the entire week from that plate? How about a little piece of fish and a spoonful of broccoli to start?"

Lauren grabbed the plate from him and swapped her empty one. "I'll eat these," she said. "*And* a bowl of the clam chowder with the bread. She's never gonna let you feed her like that."

Sara groaned. "You know I hate you, right? You have the metabolism of one of my middle school boys." Natalie laughed at the roommates' banter and suddenly the mood seemed lighter.

Lauren took the lead and peppered Natalie with questions about her schooling and plans for the future. Terrence occasionally interjected comments while Sara sat back and listened. She was tired but delighted to have the three people she loved most sitting around a table together.

At last, the conversation turned to her. Natalie turned to Sara and asked, "So, honestly…how do you feel? I can't tell you how sorry I am."

Sara's eyes filled with unexpected tears and Natalie rushed to apologize. "I didn't mean to make you cry—"

"No, no…it's okay," she said. "It hurts and I'm terribly sad. But I can't imagine how it would feel if I weren't surrounded by all of you." She looked around the table. Her beloved fiancé. Her beautiful daughter. Her dearest friend. "I'm very glad you're here." She smiled at Natalie and added, "And I decided I'm going to see a counselor. This has hit me very hard and I think I could use some help processing everything."

"I started seeing a counselor when my mom got diagnosed," said Natalie quietly. "It was the best thing I could have done."

Sara felt a surge of pride. *If Natalie is getting help, I can, too,* she thought. *I can, too.*

She smiled and nodded. They were all ready to change the subject, she thought. "So you mentioned the watercolors class you're taking. Tell us more."

"Well, I think I'm going to combine my writing and my painting into a children's book for my spring project. I have some ideas but I was thinking you might have some insight into what works best for kindergartners." She looked expectantly at her mother.

From the corner of her eye, Sara could see Terrence's grin. "I would love to help," she said.

Then Lauren broke in. "Okay, okay. You two hug it out while I get the ice cream."

29

On Monday, Sara and Terrence sat in the principal's office before school.

Jenna sat back and smiled. "I didn't see this coming," she said, "but I confess I'm pretty happy about it."

Sara and Terrence looked at each other and then back at the principal. "So are there any district rules we need to worry about?" asked Sara. It was the one concern they had about announcing their engagement.

"No, you're fine," replied Jenna. "If one of you was a principal and the other a teacher, that's a different story. We can't have married couples in manager/subordinate roles. But since you're both teachers, there's no issue." She grinned at the couple. "I'm thrilled for you. Have you set a date?"

"We were thinking this weekend, with a two week honeymoon after that," said Terrence, his face a mask of sincerity.

Jenna's mouth dropped open and Sara rolled her eyes. "It will be this July," said the bride-to-be. "We aren't going to miss either the end or the beginning of a school year." She shook her head fondly at her laughing fiancé. "Just ignore him—he loves to tease."

The bell rang and the three stood. "Well, back to it," said Terrence. "It'll be nice to see the kids after the break and not have to pretend we aren't crazy in love with each other."

The principal looked askance at them and Sara hastened to add, "He's just joking again, Jenna—relax. No inappropriate behavior here."

Terrence laughed again and the couple left the office, heading to their respective classrooms.

"You know you're a brat, right?' said Sara as they parted in front of the language arts door.

"I know," he answered. "I also know I *am* crazy in love with you and I'm just happy you're well enough to be back in school." He glanced around and saw students beginning to enter the hallway. "Just pretend I'm kissing you," he whispered. "Have a great morning and I'll see you at lunch."

Sara smiled and walked to her classroom. The week resting at home had done her good and she was glad to be back to work. It was nice having Terrence home with her, she thought. Waking up every day with him and now driving to work together was a good way to start her morning—she was eager for them to find their own home and start their new life together.

And this week she would start to see a therapist. Sara knew the depression wasn't gone, just hovering and ready to pounce if she wasn't mindful of her emotional health. The years of yearning and confusion over her mother's behavior had crashed into the grief of losing her baby. That wasn't something that would heal in a week and she found that she was at last ready to face her pain.

First things first, she chided herself. She opened her backpack and began setting up her desk as the students entered. Everyone seemed resigned to coming back to class after the long break but she was determined to get them re-engaged.

The first three classes went by without incident, the students slowly getting back into the swing of the school day. By the time the bell rang for the fourth period class, though, Sara began to tire. She was thankful it was the advanced class and she intended to break them into teams and let them battle over some new, thorny word problems. This class was full of competitive students and it would give her the chance to sit at her desk and watch them without having to walk around the room.

She greeted the students as they filed in and, as usual, Marisa was one of the last to enter. "Hi, Miss Masterson," said the teen, flashing a happy smile. "Glad to see you again." Marisa pointedly looked at Sara's hand and winked.

The class ended with both teams claiming victory. "You both finished at exactly three minutes and twelve seconds," Sara announced. "It was a tie." But neither team was willing to concede—they were each convinced they'd won.

"Okay," she said. "We'll do this again tomorrow and the winners will get five extra credit points each." The bell rang and the students left, many advising her to expect a devastating win from them the next day. Sara laughed at their energy and marveled at how seriously they took the competition. She began straightening her desk and sighed deeply. She was worn out and looking forward to having lunch with her fiancé.

"So…tell me all about it," said Marisa. The teen brought her lunch up to the front of the class and sat down in front of Sara's desk. "Was it super romantic? How did he propose?" She took a bite of her sandwich. "And seriously—why *pink*?"

Sara groaned inwardly. All she wanted was to sit with Terrence and enjoy a quick and private lunch break. She looked at Natalie's younger sister and sighed. "First of all…gross. Don't talk with your mouth full."

Marisa rolled her eyes. "You're my sister's mom, not mine, but okay." She wiped her mouth. "Go on."

"Yes, it was super romantic," she began, just as Terrence walked in the door.

"Ready for lunch?" he asked, then stopped when he saw Marisa.

"Miss Masterson was just telling me how romantic you were when you proposed," grinned the teen. "After she scolded me for talking with my mouth full."

He frowned and answered, "It was the most romantic thing you could possibly imagine, but you know Miss Masterson was sick last week and I think she should rest a bit." He raised his eyebrows at Marisa. "Don't you agree?"

"Fine," she answered, making a show of stuffing her sandwich into her mouth and grabbing her backpack. She swallowed dramatically and said, "I still want to hear details. And I want to talk about my sister—she's actually pretty cool."

Sara smiled as Marisa left the room. "See you tomorrow," she called.

Terrence came around Sara's desk to embrace her. He looked at her, concern etched on his handsome features. "You look beat. Do you need to go home?"

She sighed and leaned into his embrace. She was tired and wished she could leave. "I'm okay. Just a little worn out." She looked up at him and leaned up to kiss his chin. "It's great to be back, but I'm not gonna lie—it's gonna take a minute to get my strength back.."

"We don't have a lot of time, but shall we go to the lounge and eat? You must be hungry."

She nodded and pulled slowly away. "What I really want is a nap," she admitted, "but I know I need food." She gestured to the door. "Lead on, my falcon."

Only moments after the students left her last class of the day, Terrence walked in her door. "C'mon, love. Let's get you home," he said. She nodded, too tired to argue. She was thankful she had no papers to grade, her typical evening activity. They walked to the car and Sara felt the exhaustion take hold.

"I don't understand why I'm so tired," she said. "I didn't do anything all day."

Terrence stared at her as he opened her car door. "You're kidding, right? You *hemorrhaged* only a week ago. Babe, give yourself a break."

She was asleep before they got home.

The next day was better and Sara made it to fourth period without feeling utterly spent. The students walked in, chattering about the rivalry between the two teams. Each was determined to gain the five extra credit points, and Sara grinned at their exuberance.

The hour flew by as the teams battled back and forth. At last, the bell rang and students groaned, unwilling to give up on the difficult last problem. *What kid wants to miss lunch to stay in math class?* marveled Sara, then remember that years ago she was that very kid. "Okay, okay—get out of here," she told them. "John's team won this time but I'm sure there will be more opportunities over the rest of the semester." The middle schoolers packed their backpacks and headed for the door, the winners high-fiving each other while the losing team grimaced and grumbled.

Marisa slowed as she approached Sara's desk. "Thanks for a fun class, Miss Masterson." She bit her lip and waited until the last student left. "So, I have a kinda weird question." Sara waited as the girl seemed to collect her thoughts. "If you're my sister's mom, what are you to me?" The cocky teen had disappeared and Sara saw instead the young girl who lost her mother. "Are you like an aunt or something?"

Sara walked around her desk to face the girl. She knew her next words could make a significant difference in Marisa's life and she chose them carefully. "Your dad and I wondered if it would be weird for you to be in my class once you knew about us—and about Natalie." Marisa started to interject, but Sara stopped her. "Just a second. I happen to think you're mature enough to handle it, and I think maybe we can have one kind of relationship in class and a different one outside."

Marisa looked puzzled. "Like what?"

"Well, I imagine the four of us, or I guess five when Mr. Billings is around, will do things together. We're a different sort of family, but a family nevertheless. What if you called me Sara when we're outside school?"

The girl's face lit up and she threw her arms around her teacher, embracing her tightly. When she released her, the playful look had returned. "And can I call him Terrence?'

Sara burst out laughing and shooed the teen away. "Go eat your lunch, you silly girl."

Marisa giggled and walked out the door. "See you later… Sara," she whispered.

"So I told Marisa she can call me Sara outside of school when we're doing family stuff with her and Natalie and now she wants to call you Terrence."

He laughed as he drove them home. "That kid is hilarious."

"Oh, and Natalie texted this morning and said you are a truly lucky man."

"Believe me, I think about that every single day."

Sara looked at him, her heart full. *He really does love me.* She smiled, then answered in a soft voice, "I'm always going to grieve but I promise I won't always be this sad."

His brows furrowed and he shook his head. "Babe, we're both sad—there's nothing wrong with that. You take as much time as you need. If I'm rushing you, just tell me. All I want is for you to be happy."

She ran her fingers lightly on his arm. "It's strange to feel sad and so happy at the same time."

He nodded and Sara knew he understood. The past months had been like years, she thought. She'd begun the summer excited for her new job, content with her life.

And now? Everything had changed. She had a scar on her heart but also a new life with Terrence. She'd meet her new counselor tomorrow and was determined to reconcile her past with Carlos and overcome the anguish her mother had caused.

Life can be hard but also joyful, she concluded. *I'm going to treasure it all.*

30

Two weeks later....

Sara and Lauren drove to Orlando and met Natalie outside the chic bridal store. They walked in to an open and airy foyer and there was soft music playing in the background. The air smelled of gardenias and the women stood transfixed in the lobby. A young woman stood at the desk with an expectant smile.

"Good morning!" she said brightly. "Right on time. Which of you is Sara?"

Natalie and Lauren both turned and pointed and they all laughed. "That's me," said the bride.

"Welcome to Gossamer Bridal! Emma is your consultant and she'll be right—oh, here she is!" An elegant woman in a dove gray dress with matching heels approached the trio. Her hair was swept up in a French twist and Sara admired her understated makeup and jewelry. The woman looked like a professional model.

"Good morning, Sara. And these must be your attendants?"

Sara introduced the women. "Yes, this is Lauren, my maid of honor, and this is Natalie, my daughter. She's walking me down the aisle." She looked toward the door. "My mother-in-law and my two sisters-in-law should be here shortly." The Billings family had arrived in Orlando the day before and were staying in a nearby hotel. Terrence and his father were going out for a "guys' day," as Donovan put it. They all planned to meet for lunch in the afternoon.

The front door opened and Savannah, Talia, and Alicia entered. "I'm so sorry we're late, honey," said Alicia. "These two are a nightmare sharing a bathroom."

Savannah glared at her sister. "You only live an hour away—I still don't know why you needed to come stay with us in the hotel."

Talia cocked an eyebrow. "And miss the chance to get away from the kids for one night?"

Sara smiled as she hugged her mother-in-law. "No worries. We just got here." She turned to the bridal consultant. "This is Alicia, Talia, and Savannah. Emma's going to help us find this last minute perfect gown."

"I have no doubt we will find something you love," the consultant said with confidence. "Gossamer Bridal is known throughout Florida for the best off the rack dresses. We've helped brides who are getting married in a week! You've given us nearly six months to work with." She beckoned the group. "Come with me and let's talk about what you're looking for. Shannon," she looked at the young woman at the desk, "would you please bring these ladies some champagne?" She smiled at the group. "It's never too early in the day for bridal party champagne."

Alicia whispered to Sara as they followed Emma. "I'm so sorry for the reason, but I'm thankful you two can wait until July."

"Even with the extra months, getting a dress won't be easy," answered Sara. "I really hope this place is as good as they claim." She hugged the older woman. "Thank you for coming, Alicia. This means the world to me."

The women were ushered into a room with comfortable but elegant sofas. As they sat, Shannon arrived with a tray of delicate champagne flutes. Emma sat in a chair facing Sara and crossed her long legs. She asked, "So, Sara—when you dream about your wedding, what do you see yourself wearing?"

"I really don't know," confessed the bride. She looked down, then up shyly. "I have a big chest and wide hips—I don't know what style is best."

Emma smiled knowingly. "Not to worry. We'll find something that makes you feel like you're the most beautiful you. And do you have a preference for color?"

"I'm the worst bride ever," laughed Sara. "What are my choices?"

"Most brides opt for either white or ivory," said the consultant. "But we do have a few other options."

Lauren broke in with a grin. "You can even wear pink if you want," she declared. "As long as I'm not wearing it, I don't care and I promise not to make fun of you."

"Wait, what color *are* we wearing?" asked Savannah. "I was hoping for pink!" Talia nodded and Natalie just grinned.

Lauren scowled. "We aren't five years old. Can't we wear something more mature?"

Emma smoothly interjected. "Perhaps we can set aside the bridesmaids' dress question for now. Let's get back to the bride." The girls looked chagrined and the consultant returned her attention to Sara. "Let's start with the basics. I'll pull a variety of styles for you to try on and we can see what makes you feel the best." She sat back in her chair. "Now, before I start selecting gowns, what is the budget you'd like to stay with? We have gowns up to $20,000 and I don't want to bring anything you fall in love with but then find it's out of your price range."

"I have a maximum of $3,000," replied Sara. "Can we find something in that range?" On her teacher's salary, it was all she could manage without wiping out her savings. *I can do some tutoring this summer to build it back up*, she reasoned.

The elegant woman smiled. "Of course we can. But keep in mind we *are* looking at sample gowns. And they'll all be from last season."

Lauren smirked. "Oh, that simply won't do," she muttered in her best British accent and Savannah stifled a laugh.

Emma glanced at them but continued unperturbed. "Before we start, I want to be sure to set your expectations, Sara. The chance of finding your dream dress that fits you perfectly is just about zero. Depending on how much needs to be altered, that can run up to another $1,000 or so."

Lauren raised a hand. "That's on me." Emma raised a perfectly groomed eyebrow and Sara's maid of honor explained. "Find a dress that fits her budget and I'm covering the alterations."

Sara thought back to their drive from Daytona Beach to Orlando that morning. The roommates had talked happily nearly the entire hour but when Lauren mentioned that her gift to Sara would be to pay for the alterations she'd surely need, the bride protested. "That's too much. No way."

Lauren persisted. "Let me do this, Sara. I want you to have the most perfect gown on your special day." She glanced at her friend in the passenger seat, then back at the road. "It's important to me."

Sara sat back in wonder. *How did I ever end up with such a good friend?* She knew Lauren was generous, but this? She asked, "What's so important?"

Her friend was quiet for a moment and then Sara saw Lauren's jaw tighten. "Your mother should be the one doing this," she blurted. "She should be spending some of her millions on her daughter, making sure you have the most beautiful dress and the most perfect wedding."

Sara was stunned at her friend's vehemence. Lauren was furious.

"I'm not your mother and I don't have that kind of money, but dammit if you aren't gonna get what you want today."

Sara smiled at the memory and returned her attention to the consultant. "That's a very generous gift," Emma said. "All right, let's get you into a fitting room and I'll start pulling some gowns." She waved a beautifully manicured hand at the bridesmaids. "Get comfortable and enjoy your champagne."

"Alicia?" asked Sara. "Would you come in with me?"

Alicia's smile lit the room. "I would love to, honey."

The two women went into the fitting room and Sara undressed. Emma joined them in minutes, bringing three gowns. "Let's start with these," she said. "It will give me an idea of what you like and what suits your body."

Sara smiled shyly. "I'm kinda nervous," she confessed to her mother-in-law. "Terrence has only seen me in casual clothes—we've never actually gotten dressed up for anything." She laughed. "I want him to look at me and not be able to breathe."

Alicia burst out laughing. "Oh, please—don't you see the way he looks at you? I think he spends his entire life trying to breathe around you."

The consultant helped Sara pull on the first gown, using clips to hold it fast. A strapless white ballgown with a sweetheart neckline, it accentuated her ample bosom and hips. The bodice was white satin decorated with seed pearls and the skirt was layers and layers of tulle. Sara gasped at her reflection.

"You look beautiful," murmured Alicia. "Let's go see what the girls think."

They walked out to the viewing area and Emma helped Sara up to the raised platform. She fanned out the skirt and they looked at the bridesmaids.

"Geez, Sara—I would kill for your boobs," gushed Savannah. "You *have* to get something with that neckline."

Talia shook her head at her younger sister. "You need something more fitted on your hips. You have those great curves, Sara. Don't hide them under a big skirt like that."

Sara looked at Lauren who was shaking her head and frowning. "Nope. *Way* too Disney princess."

Natalie agreed. "You look gorgeous, Sara, but I don't think that's the one."

Sara and Alicia returned to the dressing room where Emma helped her out of the miles of fabric and into a mermaid gown. It also was a size too large, but with the clips, it skimmed her body. The bodice was appliquéd with flowers that continued over her hips. The skirt held close to her, falling into a pool of soft fabric below her knees.

"Oh my," said Alicia, her eyes wide.

They walked back into the viewing area and as Sara stepped onto the platform, she was startled by Lauren's hoot of laughter. "No, no, no!" exclaimed her maid of honor.

Talia looked askance at her. "What are you talking about? She looks incredible!"

"She looks like freaking Jessica Rabbit," chortled Lauren. "Don't blame me—I was drawn this way!" she said breathily, mimicking the cartoon. "I mean, c'mon…yes, you've got the body for that, but damn…this is a wedding, not a centerfold."

"It *is* a bit much," agreed Savannah.

Sara looked at her daughter who shook her head. "Again, you look gorgeous. But it's not the one."

The women returned to the dressing room and spent the next hour trying on gowns. Each time, her bridesmaids assured her she was beautiful—but the dress wasn't "the one." Sara began to feel deflated; she knew she hadn't seen the right dress and wondered if it even existed on the sample rack. "I still don't know what I'm looking for," she confessed.

"You'll know it when you see it," answered Alicia.

"Don't get discouraged. That's why these appointments are for two hours," said the consultant. "We're getting closer, I promise." She held up another gown. "I know this is nothing like what you've looked at so far, but let's give it a try." Sara shrugged, trying to create some enthusiasm for yet another gown. She stepped into the new dress and allowed Emma to clip her into it. The off-the-shoulder bodice was covered in ecru lace that cascaded down the length of the skirt. It was fitted and the train pooled elegantly on the floor. Sara and Alicia looked at each other questioningly and Emma smiled.

"I like this," said Sara, hesitating. "Maybe?"

They walked out and the women all ooh'd and ah'd as she stepped up to the platform. The consultant spread the long train and everyone began talking at once.

"I absolutely love the lace," began Talia.

"It shows off all your curves without being 'Bam! I'm sexy,'" added Savannah.

"Maybe," mused Lauren, cocking her head and stepping forward to look more closely at the fabric.

"Sara—" called Natalie from across the room.

"You could totally do a beautiful tiara with this," said Savannah, walking up to the platform.

"Sara—"

"This train is divine," said Talia, walking behind the bride. "Sara?"

Lauren stood with her arms crossed. "It's the closest one yet. I'm still not 100% sure."

Sara grinned. "I feel like a horse at a livestock sale."

"MOM!"

Startled, everyone stopped talking and looked across the room. Sara's daughter stood with a gown draped over her arm.

Sara thought she might topple off the platform.

She called me Mom. She called me Mom!

"I found it," said Natalie proudly. "I found your dress."

Natalie strode across the room as Sara stepped down from the pedestal. The two locked eyes and smiled. Sara's eyes swam with tears and she couldn't find words.

"Why don't you two go together," offered Alicia, her voice soft. "I'll wait out here with the girls."

At Natalie's slight frown, Sara shook her head. "No, we can all fit." She looked at Emma. "We'll be fine by ourselves."

The consultant's perfect brows drew together but she remained pleasant. "Sara, I think—"

"It's fine, Emma. We'll be fine." Her heart swelling, Sara turned and walked toward the dressing room, her daughter and mother-in-law following closely behind. They entered the dressing room and the older woman helped her out of the lace gown while the younger woman stood by.

Natalie unzipped the new dress and held it open for Sara to step in. The white silk slid across her skin with a whisper as she slipped on the narrow straps. Delicate pink rosebuds with fern green leaves dotted the bodice, cascading across her hips. Natalie stood behind her and zipped the dress.

Sara glanced at her daughter's reflection in the mirror. The girl's astonished look met her own.

No clips.

It fit perfectly.

"Oh, Sa—" Natalie stopped abruptly. "*Mom,*" she breathed. "You are so beautiful."

Three generations of women looked in the mirror and smiled.

As the three walked back to the viewing area, they overheard the girls chatting.

"Just forget about the tiara, Savannah. She's way more Daytona Beach girl than Fort Lauderdale princess." Sara and Alicia glanced at each other and shared a quiet laugh. Talia was scolding her sister and Lauren was nodding in approval.

"She'll never go for it," agreed the maid of honor.

"Well, if I can't talk her into a tiara, at least I can get her to pick a good color for us. Why do you hate pink so much?" Savannah glared at Lauren.

At the sight of Sara, the three women stopped talking, their eyes wide. The bride stood silent on the platform as Natalie straightened the small train behind her, then walked around to join the others.

"Forget a tiara," murmured Savannah. "Forget a veil. You just need a wreath of flowers and your hair down like that."

"You look like a goddess, Sara," said Talia.

Sara looked at each of them—admiration shone every face. Natalie simply smiled, her eyes twinkling.

It was the one.

"Sara," interjected Emma, glancing at her notebook. "I'm sorry, but this is exactly what I tried to prevent by selecting the gowns myself." She looked at Natalie with kindness. "This gown is seven thousand, one hundred—far outside your budget. It's last season, but it's Italian silk and the embroidery is hand sewn." At Sara's downcast look she added, "I'm sorry."

The room was hushed as Sara lifted her chin and forced a smile. Natalie looked devastated as she took her mother's arm. Sara took a deep breath and stepped off the platform to return to the dressing room.

And then she heard her mother-in-law's voice.

"We'll take it."

Sara stopped and turned to stare at Alicia. The woman smiled widely, looking first at Sara and then Emma.

"We'll take it," she repeated. She winked at Talia and Savannah. "Donovan and I paid for our daughters' wedding gowns and we'll pay for yours, too, honey." Sara, Natalie, and Lauren stood mute, stunned at the gesture.

"It's way cheaper than Savannah's was," said Talia, nudging her sister. "Wasn't yours like ten thousand?"

"Twelve," she corrected.

"Spoiled much?" muttered Lauren.

Savannah laughed gaily and hugged Lauren. "I am, actually. Baby of the family and all that."

What is going on here? thought Sara, her thoughts spinning. *Who are these people and how are they in my life?*

Natalie rushed to Alicia and threw her arms around her. "Thank you, thank you," she repeated. The older woman returned the hug, looking over the girl's shoulder to smile at Sara.

"Oh, c'mon," said Savannah, jumping up from the sofa. "Group hug." She laughed at Lauren as she grabbed the maid of honor's arm. "Even you, Miss I Hate Pink."

The six women stumbled together, arms wrapped around each other's shoulders and waists. Natalie clasped Sara's arm and whispered into her ear.

"Love you, Mom."

An hour later, they arrived at the restaurant, Sara still in shock.

"Okay, I've texted them," said Alicia as she slid into the booth. "Your father got hungry and apparently they decided they couldn't wait for us to get lunch. We'll catch up with them later." She smiled, an impish look on her face. "Who needs the men today anyway? This is all about the ladies."

The six of them continued chatting, at last coming back around to the topic of the attendants' dresses. They barely paid attention when the waitress brought their food, they were so engrossed in the debate.

"I know it's not all about us," continued Savannah after the waitress set down the last plate. "But hear me out: Sara's dress is perfect. Our dresses could be pink like the rosebuds and Lauren's could be green like the leaves." She smiled, and dusted her hands in a show of gloating and accomplishment. "See? Done."

Lauren looked contemplative as she took a big bite of her burger. She wiped her mouth and said, "Okay, I can do green. You guys do pink." She looked across the table at Sara who was picking at a salad. "Happy?"

The bride smiled warmly at her best friend. "I'm very happy. My dress is gorgeous and you guys will all look amazing." She took in all the women at the table. "And I think as long as they're the same color, you should pick your own dress styles. They don't have to be all matchy-matchy. I want you to wear whatever you like best."

Savannah's eyebrows shot up. "Really?" She looked at Talia. "I'm totally going for Disney princess. You probably want the Jessica Rabbit version."

Talia laughed. "I wish. I don't have the chest for it."

Lauren snickered around a mouthful of fries. "Yeah, nobody has Sara's cleavage."

Sara looked at her daughter. "What about you, honey? What style do you like?"

Natalie sipped her iced tea, then pursed her lips in thought. "I think I want something strapless and simple," she answered. "Something elegant and artistic."

Sara's heart warmed. She'd never been this content. Leaning her head on her daughter's shoulder, she said, "Just like you."

Her phone buzzed and she looked at the screen. "Looks like they can't stay away," she laughed as she texted back. "The guys are coming after all." She looked up at Alicia. "Apparently they have room for dessert."

Ten minutes later, father and son arrived and the waitstaff added chairs to the table. Sara watched as Donovan leaned over and kissed his wife's head before sitting next to her. He had a questioning look on his face and Alicia nodded. He smiled and hugged her. "Good," he said quietly. "That's good."

Sara was still in awe over their generous gift. She looked across the table at Donovan, put her hand on her heart, and mouthed, "Thank you."

He grinned and winked, then asked the table, "So did you ladies order dessert yet?"

The group decided on three desserts with plates for everyone to share. While they waited for their treats to arrive, Terrence and

Sara excused themselves from the table. They headed for the lobby and stood apart from the host desk.

"So? You found something?" Terrence asked.

"I did," she answered, her smile warm. "Actually, Natalie found it after I'd tried on about a dozen dresses." She took his hands. "Terrence…your parents paid for my gown."

He smiled and embraced her. "I thought they might. I overheard them talking about it this morning at the hotel when I went to get my dad." He hugged her again, then pulled back to look at her. "They really do love you, Sara. They just want everything to be perfect for us and it was something they could easily do."

Unexpected tears pricked her eyes.

He reached up and gently wiped a tear at the corner of her eye. "Why the tears, love?"

Her voice was a whisper as she tried to contain her emotions. "Terrence, Natalie called me 'Mom' today. She's the one who found my dress."

His eyes widened and he took her into his arms, squeezing her tightly.

They walked hand in hand back to the table. "Better hurry up if you want any of this, big brother," said Savannah. "You have competition with this one." She flicked a hand toward Lauren. "She might even beat Dad."

"We've all decided to hate Lauren," announced Talia. "I, for one, cannot wait until she's had two kids and loses that perfect body."

Sara and Lauren burst out laughing. "Uh, yeah…about that," started Sara.

"No way, no how," asserted Lauren. "This *mujer* is child-free and happy to remain so…forever."

The couple sat and Terrence reached for the chocolate brownie. "I just want one bite, Lauren. Don't stab me with your fork." Everyone at the table chuckled and the friendly banter continued until Sara sighed heavily.

"Love? Are you all right?" Terrence's face went from laughter to concern in a split second.

"I'm fine," she said, squeezing his hand. "I'm actually fine." She looked around the table at the people she loved. "Look at my beautiful life, Terrence. I have my best friend. I got my daughter back. I have a new mother and father and sisters.

"And I have you." Tears glinted on her lashes. "After everything we've been through, *my heart is full*." She turned her face up to his and kissed him. "We're a family."

ACKNOWLEDGEMENTS

After I wrote *Bread Pudding in. Barcelona*, I wondered if I had anything left to say. I certainly wasn't burning to start another book, but I had friends who fell in love with these four women and they clamored for each of them to get her own story. Once I got my brain around the idea, the stories just poured out. I'm deeply grateful for the nudge to put Sara, Susana, and Lauren in the spotlight.

Like Sara, I had a baby when I was a teenager but, unlike Sara, I had a wonderful mother. No, she wasn't keen on me dropping out of college to have a child, but there was no prouder or more doting grandmother than Carole Sue Florence Villanueva. Sadly, she died from cancer in 2011, but she sort of lives on in Alicia—kind, generous, and full of love for her growing family.

As always, I'm grateful for my wonderful editor, Michelle Meade. Her love for these characters gives her incredible insight into their psyches, and she brings out the best in them (and me!) through her insight and encouragement. I know I'm a better writer every time she gets her hands on my manuscript.

Once again, the inimitable Samantha Sanderson-Marshall created a magnificent cover, perfectly capturing the beauty of the Florida coast where this story takes place. I'll never forget bursting into tears when she showed me the incredible work of art she created. You'll see more of her work in the next two years as Susana and Lauren get their stories. I can't wait to see what she does with them!

To every one of "My Lovelies" who follow me on social media: Thank you for all the likes and hearts, for coming to see me at book signings, and for cheering on these women as they traverse life's challenges. Together we are all finding that genuine happiness comes, no matter our age or how many times we've been around the block, when we are willing to take big risks for friendship and love.

I'm indebted to five absolutely brilliant, entrepreneurial women here in central Florida. Thank you to Jenny at Get Lit

Boutique, Stephanie at Novel Tea Book Shop, Jane at The New Romantics, Alison at Gypsy's Book Nook, and Anne at Needful Books & Things. You've taken a chance on me and my work—I treasure you! I'm pretty sure my favorite words in the world are, "I'm out of stock—any chance I can get a few more copies for the store?" You're the best!

Lastly, my deepest thanks to my husband Ted. If it weren't for Azalea, I would never have met you or taken a chance on love. Your encouragement and belief have sustained me through three *Blooming* books—now onto the fourth! Your steadfast love is teaching me what it means when you say, "Go live your dream."

I'm living it.

Enjoy this preview of

A Thistle in the Cevennes

Book Three
BLOOMING
The Series

Coming soon!

Susana admired the bamboo arch festooned with pink and white flowers. The soft breeze ruffled the tulle wrapped around the wooden beams—and the groom's hair. She was glad the wedding was late in the afternoon, the breeze just cool enough to keep the usually oppressive Florida heat at bay. Beyond the arch, the sun began its descent and the clouds glowed with soft pinks and blues, making everything just slightly hazy and romantic. Her design team called this "the golden hour," their favorite time of the day to shoot outdoor videos. The Fort Lauderdale beach was still full of people, many within a hundred yards of the soon-to-begin ceremony. Some, she noticed, had cameras out. *Who takes pictures of someone else's wedding?* she wondered. "Tourists," she muttered.

The music started and the wedding began. Susana looked down the aisle as the first pair of attendants approached. Savannah, Terrence's youngest sister, clearly enjoyed the spotlight. She wore a pink chiffon strapless gown with a sweetheart neckline and snug bodice over a huge skirt. Her groomsman partner smiled down at his wife as he escorted her toward the flower-festooned arch, the waves gently lapping in the background. Susana nudged her best friend and whispered, "A bit Disney princess, dontcha think?"

Azalea covered her laugh with a hand and the two looked back toward the next bridesmaid. Talia, the middle of the Billings clan, was likewise dressed in pink. Her gown was a one-shoulder satin column with a tasteful slit—elegant and simple. The bridesmaid seemed to glide across the sand, and she glanced at the groomsman next to her with a loving smile. "That's her husband, right?" whispered Azalea and Susana nodded.

The two pair of bridesmaids and groomsmen veered apart as they reached the arch, moving into their respective places.

She looked back to see Lauren. The maid of honor was wearing a leaf green halter sheath, its satin skimming her tall, lithe frame. Her dark hair was swept to the side in glamorous Hollywood waves, her makeup perfectly applied. As she approached Susana and Azalea's row, she glanced over and winked at the women.

"How does she do it?" Susana whispered to Azalea. "She's always so chic. And you know she probably had a triple cheeseburger right before sliding into that dress."

Enrique nudged her. "Shhh," her husband said softly, trying not to laugh.

As Lauren took her position, everyone stood for the bride and her daughter. Susana took a moment to glance at Terrence before Sara and Natalie got close. He stood, mouth agape, next to the pastor and to his best man. Susana giggled as she noticed his friend nudge Terrence with an elbow and the groom's mouth abruptly shut. Yet he never took his eyes off his bride.

Sara and Natalie walked slowly down the aisle, Natalie's eyes glowing with pride as she looked at her mother. They were hand in hand, their love for each other palpable. Natalie also wore pink: a simple, off the shoulder tea-length dress, her dark hair caught up in a messy chignon at the base of her neck. She carried a smaller version of her mother's bouquet—pink tiger lilies for her, white for Sara, with cascading greenery and jasmine.

"They look so much alike," Susana whispered to Azalea. "They could be sisters."

Sara was incandescent, her sun-kissed hair grazing her shoulder blades and threaded artfully with babies' breath. Her gown, a simple white silk dotted with embroidered pink roses, set off her curves and her tan. Susana looked again at Terrence. He was mesmerized. She was certain he was completely oblivious to anyone or anything around him. He only had eyes for his bride.

She felt Kique's hand in hers and glanced down at the tissue he'd placed in her palm. She looked questioningly at him, then shook her head. "You've met me before, right?" she whispered, then grinned. "You're the one who needs the tissue."

Her husband shrugged and pulled her close to his side, his lips pressing her cheek before murmuring, "A guy can dream, *mi cardito.*"

My little thistle.

After the ceremony, Susana stood with Enrique, Azalea, and Esteban. The wedding had been simple and beautiful, and the reception was a modest affair, with drinks and appetizers at a pub walking distance from the beach. She was thinking about another glass of champagne when the bride and groom approached them.

Sara had become like a younger sister to the older women and Susana's heart warmed to see her so happy. When she and Azalea learned about Sara's teen pregnancy and the heartbreaking way her parents had torn the baby from her, they were appalled. But when Sara told them the good news that her daughter had found her all these years later, they'd been thrilled. They met Natalie only weeks before the wedding and fell in love with her, occasionally including her in their ladies' night events—typically sangria and guacamole on Azalea's patio. Esteban and Enrique would go out and leave the women to talk and laugh and share their lives.

As much as we can, now that Azalea and Esteban live half the year in Spain, thought Susana. She wondered if she'd ever get used to her best friend's new life.

She shook off the unwelcome thought and hugged Sara. "You look absolutely radiant, my friend," she said. She glanced at Terrence. "You do know how lucky you are, right?"

Terrence beamed. "I am the luckiest man in the world," he said, hugging his new wife tight to his side.

"And we're very lucky to have you guys," Sara added. "We can't thank you enough for the gifts. You're so generous."

Azalea and Esteban were leaving directly from Fort Lauderdale the next day to return to Spain for the autumn and winter. They knew the young couple—on their paltry teachers' salaries—could not likely afford an expensive honeymoon, so their gift to them was two weeks at Azalea's beach house. Terrence and Sara had been overjoyed—and even more so when Susana and Enrique added the Ritz-Carlton honeymoon suite for their wedding night.

"We planned to just drive back home after the reception," Sara had confessed. "We figured we could have more of a staycation before school starts in a couple of weeks." Susana and Enrique had insisted they stay in Fort Lauderdale for their wedding night. They could drive back north the next day, and the couple was delighted.

As the four chatted, Lauren approached with a distinguished looking young man. "You remember Susana, my boss?"

The handsome man reached out a well-manicured hand. "Of course," he said with a pleasant smile, shaking her hand firmly. "It's nice to see you again."

Jayson Rivera was the vice president of marketing for Thompson Toys, a client of Miles Porter Gelbarr, the marketing agency where both Susana and Lauren worked. Susana had pulled Lauren off the account several weeks earlier when it became clear she and Jayson were interested in each other. It appeared they were now in a serious enough relationship that Lauren brought him to her best friend's wedding.

Lauren was introducing Jayson to Enrique, Azalea, and Esteban when Terrence broke in. "I don't think you've met my brother Corey," he said, his arm around the broad shoulders of his best man. He clapped Corey's back and added, "We're not blood brothers, but we've known each other since we were kids. Went to high school and college together."

Corey shook hands all around. He was taller and wider than Terrence, with a surfer's shaggy blonde hair and a mischievous grin. "I couldn't miss this, although I'm not sure how this Neanderthal ended up with such a fabulous wife." Sara grinned up at him as Terrence glared. "Anyway, very nice to meet all of you." He looked back at Terrence and asked, "Where can a guy get a beer around here?"

Sara patted her new husband's arm. "Go on—get the man a beer." He kissed her soundly and the two friends headed off for the bar. Sara looked back at her friends. "They haven't seen each other in two years," she said. "Corey moved to California after college—

he's a high school English teacher in the Bay Area." She looked fondly at the men laughing at the bar. "I think he'd probably like to move back here, but he got divorced and they have an eight-year old daughter. He would never leave her."

Susana heard the note of sadness in her friend's voice. Sara had suffered a miscarriage earlier in the year and still struggled with the loss. She reached for Sara just as Lauren did, with Azalea a beat behind. The men looked knowingly at each other and stepped away as the four friends pulled each other close, their foreheads touching, their arms around each other's waists.

Need to know what happens next?

Sign up at cindyvillanueva.com or follow on
social media to receive preorder info for

A Thistle in the Cevennes

Coming in 2026!